THE AGGRAVATION

CYRIL KERSH was born in London in 1925 and was educated at Westcliff High School in Essex. After leaving school, he worked variously for a newsagent, a wool merchant, and an illegal toy manufacturer, resisting his family's attempts to make him settle down in his uncle's bakery business. Kersh served in the Royal Navy from 1943 to 1947 and on demobilization pursued a career in journalism. He worked at various publications, including a stint as a feature writer for the *Evening Standard* and for three years edited *Men Only*.

In 1963, Kersh joined the Mirror Group, where he would remain the rest of his career. He was features editor of the *Sunday Mirror* and editor of the magazine *Reveille*, eventually retiring in 1986 after being promoted to managing editor of the *Sunday Mirror*.

Kersh was well known in the journalists' bars of Fleet Street, which he would frequent wearing a bow tie and recounting humorous anecdotes. His keen sense of humour is on display in five novels published during the 1970s, of which *The Aggravations of Minnie Ashe* (1970) is the best known. Cyril Kersh died in 1993.

SÉAMAS DUFFY lives in Glasgow. He has published *Sherlock Holmes in Paris* (Black Coat Press, 2013), and has recently completed the forthcoming *Sherlock Holmes and the Four Corners of Hell*. He has written reviews on the novels of Gerald Kersh and Norman Collins for the London Fictions website and contributed an article on Sir Arthur Conan Doyle to *The Baker Street Journal*. He is currently working on a historical crime novel, *The Tenants of Cinnamon Street*, set in 1811.

THE AGGRAVATIONS
OF MINNIE ASHE

CYRIL KERSH

With a new introduction by
SÉAMAS DUFFY

VALANCOURT BOOKS

The Aggravations of Minnie Ashe by Cyril Kersh
First published London: Michael Joseph, 1970
Reprinted from the 1971 Pan Books edition
First Valancourt Books edition 2014

Copyright © 1970 by Cyril Kersh
Introduction © 2014 by Séamas Duffy

Published by Valancourt Books, Richmond, Virginia
Publisher & Editor: JAMES D. JENKINS
20th Century Series Editor: SIMON STERN, University of Toronto
http://www.valancourtbooks.com

ISBN 978-1-939140-91-3 (*trade paperback*)
Also available as an electronic book.

All Valancourt Books publications are printed on acid free paper
that meets all ANSI standards for archival quality paper.

Set in Dante MT 11/13.5

INTRODUCTION

WITHIN the last decade there has been a remarkable, and welcome, resurgent interest in forgotten writers of London fiction, authors whose books have for too long been out of print. This rediscovery has led, happily, to the republication of some lost literary treasures. Cyril Kersh (1925-1993) is one such author whose texts are presently undergoing critical re-evaluation. Kersh came from a long line of Jewish writers and poets – Israel Zangwill, Emanuel Litvinoff, Avram Stencl, Alexander Baron, Bernard Kops, and more recently, Rachel Lichtenstein and Naomi Alderman, to name but a few – who have written about the London *diaspora* with compassion, nostalgia, humour and, occasionally, irreverence. Socially, the Kershes seem to have been a fairly middling sort of family, who migrated from Teddington to Southend-on-Sea where Cyril was born. Most of his novels are set in west London, with occasional forays elsewhere, although *The Diabolical Liberties of Uncle Max* (1973) is set largely in a Kosher Guest House in the Southend suburb of Westcliff-on-Sea, a spot favoured by the more socially, as well as geographically, mobile members of London's East End Jewish community.

Kersh is probably more commonly remembered for his various roles in Fleet Street, and his tabloid reminiscences and revelations are gathered together in *A Few Gross Words: The Street of Shame and My Part In It* (1990), to use Private Eye's famous self-description. In the field of fiction writing, Cyril was perhaps overshadowed by his brother, Gerald, whose novel *Night and the City* managed not only to reach the silver screen (twice), but has also retained cult status amongst *film noir* aficionados; nevertheless, Cyril had a run of successful novels in the 1970s, the best of which is, arguably, *The Aggravations of Minnie Ashe*, followed closely by the equally funny and heart-rending sequel, *Minnie Ashe at War* (1979).

After a spell in the Royal Navy, Kersh spent most of his working life in publishing, mainly with the Mirror Group (though he claimed that his employment record included 'one day' at the *Daily Express*), and his name crops up in a remarkable variety of intriguing circumstances. At *Reveille* in 1976 he became editor of the first electronically produced newspaper in Britain. A year later, during the now infamous *Gay News* blasphemy case, *The Spectator* described him as 'hovering on the wings uncertain of his precise role' as editor of a down market weekly which undoubtedly set out entirely to titillate. Cyril Kersh was often able to exploit the funny side of these situations. At the *Mirror*, he was an observer of investigations into paranormal phenomena: after one experiment in Electronic Voice Perception, the editor-in-chief refused to publish the controversial results; however Cyril later turned the episode to comic effect with the character, and exploits, of Mr Rataplan in *The Soho Summer of Mr Green* (1974). As editor, he was behind a well-publicised expenses purge visited upon *Mirror* journalists and reporters who were as a result forced to 'forgo their second round of Havana cigars and port'. Creative expenses claims by journalists were the stuff of legend, and the apocryphal story was told of a *Mirror* reporter who had to have his car towed out of a bog in the west of Ireland having taken a wrong turning. A local farmer had helped to rescue the journalist's car using his tractor and a rope, and received the customary bung for his efforts. The claim subsequently arrived on the editor's desk endorsed: 'Money for old rope, £10'! In *A Few Gross Words* he certainly does not paint the world of journalism in a rosy light, nor is there any attempt to conceal the general lack of ethical standards of the period.

Most of Cyril Kersh's novels deal with similar themes: the protective, suffocating, fug of family life; eccentric Jewish characters; the world of publishing; and that *leitmotif* of the Kersh canon, the failed small-time entrepreneur. Obviously modelled on a member of the Kersh genealogy, this character is brought to life, by both Gerald and Cyril, through a succession of fictional 'business geniuses' – Solly Schwartz, Sam Yudenow, Uncle Mendel, Arnold Green and Max Flegel. Kersh also had some success with *The Shepherd's Bush Connection* (1975), a sparkling parody of a gangster novel, replete with 'That scene's cold. And the take wasn't good enough' type dialogue, and a cunning denouement held back almost until the very last page.

The Aggravations of Minnie Ashe is partly autobiographical and, in appraising reviews of previous editions, the most common adjective one comes across is 'hilarious'. The novel is set between Minnie's home, Daffodil Square, in 'the bleak wasteland between Swiss Cottage and Kilburn' and Zanzibar Terrace in Stepney, 'a cobbled row of damp disintegration . . . just north of London Dock'. Zanzibar Terrace is the citadel of Minnie's ageing mother, Cissie Abrams, whom no one can equal when it comes to cursing so nicely in Yiddish. The period is post-Munich and the threat of war is all-pervading – for Chamberlain's empty posturing and blind appeasement has fooled no one in the Jewish community. The mood of the novel varies from poignant to picaresque, from stoically fatalistic to the absurd, but is leavened throughout with a very Yiddish blend of gallows humour, and has something funny to say on almost every page.

It is also peopled by a cast of irresistible eccentrics: take Iron Foot Yossell, pedlar, prophet, and claimed descendant of the *Baal Shem Tov*, who foretells our narrator's future in the world of publishing (well, as a railway bookstall assistant). Yossell Teitelbaum is not only a false prophet but a fatuous one whose uproarious pronouncements ('anti-Semitism . . . I said it would be bad for the Jews, and was I wrong?') do not fool even the foolish old women who pay him to read their fortunes. Then there is Uncle Mendel (the 'business genius'!) whose schemes in watchstraps, cracked wineglasses, and Hebrew/Croat dictionaries end inexorably in financial disaster; Uncle Ben, shell shocked in the green fields of France during the great war, picks tulips off the wallpaper when he's not pushing Mendel's barrow around or evening up the score with Cable Street fascists ('try saying "Madagascar for the Jews" with no teeth!'); the *Rebbetzin* Rachel Tsimmus endures, or perhaps enjoys, a rubber fetish, and Mrs Kemensky has a secret past as a Bolshevik. We hear of the Fogels caught stealing silver spoons and fish forks at the wedding of the year, and observe with *Schadenfreude* the demise of Angus McKenzie, kilted Blackshirt and general purpose bigot.

First among equals in this human menagerie is the magnificent Minnie Ashe herself, bearing her matriarchal chalice amongst a throng of foes: idle landlords, thieving butchers, anti-Semitic council officials, and treacherous neighbours. Religious and superstitious in equal parts, self-pitying in her widowhood, and generous to a fault, she is the high priestess of a coven of similar mammas and childless widows who sit in the Square's public garden gossiping, reminiscing over their grandparents' days in the *shtetls* of Poland and Russia, and lapsing into Yiddish when they get sentimental or, more commonly, when they don't want the children to know the subject they are discussing, which is usually sex. At a time when the Viennese Jews are forced to scrub pavements on the Sabbath, when Hitler (*'scheisspot!'*) has annexed the Sudetenland, and Mosleyites are goose-stepping around the Square, the worst insult in the lexicon remains *'dirty Cossack!'*

Whether it is Cissie recalling from her youth the lighting of the Sabbath candles to symbolize *zachor* and *shamor*, or Uncle Mendel explaining that smashing wineglasses at a wedding commemorates the destruction of the Temple in Jerusalem, the effect is a lingering fascination with the mysterious sensuality of Hebrew ritual, mixed up with the mild shock of casual blasphemies: an Al Jolson record wrapped in an old prayer shawl; derision at the over zealous Charlie Westbourne's sudden Pharisaic conversion to Judaism (who wants 'a religious maniac' in the family?!).

Picture a warm afternoon in the autumn of 1938; the children are at school and the men at work. The women are sitting in the garden after a game of *klaberjacz*, trying to interpret the meaning of Esther Cooperman's dreams; Sophie Tucker is singing 'My Yiddishe Momme' on the gramophone; the Russian tea and seed cake is being handed around; Mosley, the landlord, the council, and the cheating fishmonger are being cursed alike. Welcome to Daffodil Square!

SÉAMAS DUFFY
Glasgow

December 17, 2013

THE AGGRAVATIONS OF MINNIE ASHE

To the memory of
GERALD KERSH

One

DAFFODIL SQUARE lies in the bleak wasteland between Swiss Cottage and Kilburn. It is not really a square; more a blunt-apexed triangle of crumbling Victoriana; the tall, balconied, claustrophobic houses peeling and pockmarked; rabbit warrens of flats and bed-sitting rooms. Once the centre of the square had been railed and paved, with grass and flowers around the huge elm tree. But I knew it only as a patch of dusty weeds and household detritus: for me a splendid place for games and make-believe, for my mother yet further proof (not that any was needed) that life was a vast and cunning plot aimed at the humiliation and ultimate destruction of herself and her family.

Through various intermediaries she fought an endless battle with the local council over the state of the garden. 'The thieves! I pay my rates, and what do I get? A drop of water. A light at the end of the street like a memorial candle. And what do I ask for? Hyde Park? Buckingham Palace? Tell them all I want is they should put in a few flowers. And tell them about the broken pram and the bike and the mattress. The dustmen all ruptured themselves or something?' A pause for breath then, darkly: 'Tell them I know who put the mattress there. That Mrs O'Halloran. The dirty cat.

'And one day that tree will fall down. You mark my words. We'll all be killed in our beds.' (It was taken for granted that the innumerable catastrophes we were doomed to suffer would come in the middle of the night.)

'The way we have to live . . . If only my husband, God rest his soul, was alive. To have to suffer in a place like this. It's like being buried alive.'

Our flat, in the basement of number 18, was indeed dark and musty; a shadowy obstacle course of shabby furniture, bric-à-brac – and photographs. Someone had once told my mother that to destroy a photograph brought bad luck. She chose to extend this to embrace a failure to display a photograph. Consequently the walls and shelves were covered with overlapping studio portraits of members of the family, faded and out-of-focus holiday snapshots, pictures of friends to whom one could no longer give names, self-conscious wedding groups, remote cousins clutching school prizes and babies on rugs. Even the lavatory was lined with photographs, including people with whom my mother was no longer on speaking terms and a vast, melancholy and noseless rabbi in a glassless frame. As a child his appearance caused me no little unease, until I came to realize that his nose had been erased by the swinging of the handle on the lavatory chain.

Within an hour of my parents moving into the flat the sashcord of the lavatory window broke and the window slammed down on my mother's fingers 'Like from the butcher's chopper'. To hear her tell of it (as she did with some frequency and in long, lurid and elaborately mimed detail) the lavatory was knee-deep in blood for a week, and only divine intervention (plus quarts of iodine, four bath towels and several bowls of hot soup) saved my mother's fingers from amputation before she died of blood poisoning, a heart attack and aggravation. She would display the backs of her hands and say: 'I could have been killed, even crippled for life. I could have sued that lousy landlord for every penny. Look at those scars.' In fact, while the pain lingered, the scars had long been erased by time, but I was taught the advisability of head-nodding sympathy on the day I said that I could see no scars and my mother cried: 'How dare you call me a liar, you ungrateful beast?' and kicked me savagely in the shins – until there came the excruciating realization that she was wearing bedroom slippers, which she then used to beat me about the head.

The incident of the sashcord set the pattern of my mother's relationship with our landlord, Harry Jaye: a mild, myopic and unhappy little man who wore plus-fours and a bowler hat and seldom shaved. He had a precise fetish-like habit of keeping coins of specific denominations in certain pockets: half-crowns, waistcoat top left; florins, waistcoat top right; shillings, waistcoat bottom left; sixpences, waistcoat bottom right; with other coins occupying his jacket pockets and notes distributed around his trousers.

Harry Jaye suffered from an agonizing pain somewhere in the area of his stomach which he found impossible to describe, and his efforts to have it diagnosed and cured kept him in ragged poverty. Thus his demands for the payment of rent arrears involved nothing personal. 'For my part I don't care. If I had my way I'd say forget them. But mine stomach! The agonies! The sufferings! And the prices these specialists charge! For myself I want nothing, Mrs Ashe. It's all for the stomach.'

My mother would say: 'All right, so you want the rent. You want the money I owe. Do you think I like owing money? You fancy I enjoy it? Don't I want you should have a nice stomach? So all right. Suppose – just suppose – I pay every farden I owe. Just suppose, for the sake of argument. So will you then get rid of the damp, give the flat a coat paint, do something about the mice? Will you fit a new sink in the kitchen and make sure the electricity works proper? Change the gas stove? Fit a new bath? The rust in it is so thick, only the other day I tore a piece of skin as big as a *schnitzel* from my backside (if you'll pardon the expression). I could sue you. You know that? I could report you to the council. If I went to the police and the sanitary inspector they'd sue you for every penny. The damages I'd get! Thousands! Remember with the sashcord? Eh? You remember?'

'Am I allowed to forget?'

'But do I sue? And for why not? Because I'm too soft. Too decent. Not like some I could mention. So just say: if I was to pay what I owe, what would you do for me? Just say.'

Impasse. On the one hand Harry Jaye knew it was highly unlikely that my mother could pay her rent arrears. But just suppose (for the sake of argument) that she did have the money. What then? Jaye was aware from bitter experience that if he said, no matter how cautiously, that he would do his best to start on decorations and repairs my mother would utter a triumphant: 'Wonderful! So do them . . . Then I'll pay.'

A long, bitter and noisy argument would end with my mother feeding him tea, cakes, bowls of soup and quarters of cold roast chicken, and he would go away no richer, but with a full and even more protesting stomach.

Following his departure came the full fury of my mother's bitter despair. 'To have to be nice to that . . . that toerag. He should have a black year! In the earth he should be! Fire should eat his guts! . . . If only your father was alive. To have to go on my bended knees and beg to that . . . that stinkpot. That Cossack. If your poor father was alive, would we be here at all? Do you know where we'd be?' (I did know, but it was pointless interrupting her in mid-passion.) 'At the seaside, that's where we'd be. At Westcliff. In a proper house . . . Such lovely houses they got there. With gardens and roses . . . And the air! So strong you can actually feel it doing you good. So pure. So fresh. Sands, and when the tide goes out, mud. Full of goodness to make mud packs for mine arthritis . . . I should have sued that lousy landlord when I had the chance. Now it's too late.' A sigh and a shrug. 'But I suppose things could be worse. At least we're not in Germany or the workhouse. Just the same it's terrible to be without money. Like they say in Yiddish: "God loves the poor – but helps the rich". Anyway, what's the good of talking?'

While others dreamed of The Land of Israel, my mother longed for Westcliff-on-Sea; that characterless and depressing sprawl on the muddy gloom of the Thames estuary. If it offered others a brief, summertime escape, for my mother it was an obsessive end in itself: a composite Shangri-la, Zion, Utopia and Islands of the Blest, where everyone lived wealthy, arthritis-free lives in flower-framed houses which had neither landlords nor damp basements.

'I was at Westcliff for mine honeymoon. In Palmerston Road at Mrs Goldberg's. You wouldn't remember. They played *The Desert Song* at The Palace in London Road.' Tears now as she sat in rocking remembrance of the days 'When I had a seventeen-inch waist and not a grey hair on my head. In those days I was the family beauty. Were the others jealous!' Knuckling away the tears: 'We also used to go to Westcliff for the day; sometimes by train, sometimes by charabanc. Picnics we'd have . . . Westcliff . . .'

A slow smile. 'I'll go outside for a few minutes. It may not be Westcliff, but even this stinking air is better than none.'

On fine days my mother would take a kitchen chair and carry it across to the garden: a short, fat, large-eyed woman with grey hair and red cheeks, dressed invariably in bedroom slippers and a flowered apron over a black dress. Under the elm tree she would join her cronies for a furious exchange of self-recrimination, reminiscence, speculation, accusation and gossip (heard or improvised).

There was Golde Kemensky, wild-haired and old, whose father had been a wonder rabbi in some obscure Jewish village in Galicia – a worker of miracles whose disciples came from Warsaw and Lodz on pilgrimages to his court. The youngest daughter, however, joined the revolutionaries, and rather than accept an arranged marriage, eloped with a socialist bookbinder.

It was to Mrs Kemensky that the group turned for political guidance. She was a babbling cascade of outrageous opinion embroidered with monstrous misinformation and half-remembered incidents from her revolutionary youth, to which the others listened gravely as they knitted, shelled peas or darned socks.

At the end of a speech Mrs Kemensky might turn to my mother and ask: 'Mrs Ashe, tell me – am I right or wrong?' My mother's reply was the one she invariably gave when faced with something she did not understand: 'For my part I don't care one way or the other – so long as it's good for the Jews'.

All my mother's coterie in the garden were, like herself, widows – except the squat, moustached Hettie Lewis. For this my mother never forgave her. Mr Lewis was crippled and helpless, but after hearing the latest clinically detailed medical bulletin my mother would say with warm resentment: 'But at least you've a man about the house. You don't know how well off you are.' Only when her husband died was Mrs Lewis accepted by my mother as a really close friend.

Then there was Pearl Weinberg with her craggy, leathery face and body of a heavyweight wrestler. Her husband had been gassed during the Great War and on medical advice had given up his trade as a baker for an outdoor occupation: selling poultry from an open-fronted shop in Petticoat Lane. Mrs Weinberg took great pains to emphasize that it was 'A proper shop with rooms at the back where we lived. Not just a stall. More like a house almost, or a cottage.' Since the death of her husband, and the onset of varicose veins, a

brother and one of her sons ran the business while she had come
to Daffodil Square to sit, an elastic-stockinged Buddha, knitting
black angora cardigans and hoping vaguely that one day she might
remarry. She still retained the defensive aggression of the market,
and the other women were reluctant to argue with her: apart from
her considerable lung-power she was the source of free chicken
portions and giblets.

The other member of the group was Naomi Malik, a tall,
thin woman with a sharp tongue and peroxided hair. She was
the youngest of them and the wealthiest, renting two floors of a
house which she filled with a hoard of lodgers. It was known that
she let her own bedroom and slept in an armchair in the kitchen.
Her explanation was a back ailment; a condition that prevented
her from stretching out at full length without suffering agonies
of such a nature she wouldn't even wish them on Hitler, Mrs
Kemensky said the truth of the matter was that she was grasping
and mean; Mrs Lewis' fancy was that she slept in the chair because
its cushions were filled with money; Mrs Weinberg's view, shared
by my mother, was that Mrs Malik didn't sleep in the chair at all –
she went out at night to visit a man.

To prove this, my mother attempted to keep watch, but while
she considered it nosey and vulgar to stand on the doorstep, the
angle of view from our basement flat prevented any lateral inspec-
tion of the street. This inability to confirm her theory made my
mother all the more certain that it was correct and strengthened
her belief that Mrs Malik was cunning.

Although my mother disapproved of Mrs Malik – her dyed hair
('Not nice on a Jewish woman'), the fact that she took a folding
canvas chair across to the garden ('Such airs and graces'), her
employment of a char once a week to help clean the lodgers'
rooms ('Who does she think she is? Rothschild?'), and the fact that
Mrs Malik smoked in public (a sure sign of lax morals) Mrs Malik
remained my mother's dearest friend.

'Mrs Ashe,' she would say, 'when I pass away you're going to
have my teapot. I've told my daughter Betty that when I go the
teapot is for you.'

My mother would become very angry. 'What sort of talk is this?

Who's saying anything about dying? May you live to be a hundred and twenty.' But when I returned from delivering a plate of *strudel* or cheese cake to Mrs Malik I learned to anticipate the inevitable question by saying: 'Mrs Malik says thank you . . . And the teapot's still there.'

Mrs Malik kept the teapot locked in a glass cabinet in her dining-room: a hideous oblong of mauve earthenware with a Corinthian spout and legs, decorated with gilt tulips and veined with grey cracks.

My mother's obsession with it did not mean that she was in any way covetous. On the contrary she was ridiculously generous considering that our life at this time was an endless spiral of debt. It was simply that a promise was a promise – and one that could realize forlorn dreams of solvency.

'Just think, Simon,' she would say to me. 'Just think. A teapot that size. There must be a hundred pounds in it. Even two hundred. We'll move from this . . . this sewer. Go and live by the sea at West-cliff. Have a real garden with roses and carpets in every room. Pay the bills. Buy clothes. Buy a new wireless. A gramophone. Pay the family back the money they've lent . . .'

After the dreams, remorse for having them. 'Why am I talking like this? It's like wishing her dead. God forgive me.' Then, inevitably: 'If only your poor father was alive. If only he'd lived another few months. Then things would be different . . . A few more months and we wouldn't be beggars . . . What have I done to deserve it? Why am I being punished? What for?' A few more months and we wouldn't be beggars did not mean that had he lived, my father, a tailor's presser, was expected to have made his fortune, but was a reference to his intention of becoming a Freemason. My mother was convinced that had he done so, and then died, his widow and children would have received sufficient largesse to have kept us in sybaritic luxury for the rest of our lives.

Dreams, remorse – and reassurance. 'Anyway, what's the good of talking? She's a young woman. May she never die.'

But Mrs Malik did die. In the spring of 1937 she was knocked down in Kilburn High Road by a butcher's van. ('But not a Kosher butcher, God be thanked.') My mother was deeply upset by her friend's death, but it was impossible to prevent thoughts of her inheritance from intruding upon her grief.

'To die like that. In such a way. And so young. Such a good woman. Never did anyone a bad turn. So generous. To think that only last week she was reminding me of her teapot . . . *The teapot!* God in Heaven! Is it still there?'

Back at Mrs Malik's after the funeral, performing the ritual of saying 'I wish you long life' to the family mourners, we saw the teapot in its accustomed place. My mother was so overcome with relief she took Mrs Malik's daughter, Betty, by the hand and said: 'I wish you long teapot'.

Next morning Betty brought the teapot. And that was all she did bring.

My mother screamed that she had been robbed. 'It's that filthy daughter of hers. That Betty. The thief. May she have a black year! May her children be orphans! Blue she should turn and the fish eat her guts! May her eyes drop out!'

I suggested calling the police.

'Them!' she waved a fist in the air. 'They're all in it together. Is this what I pay rates for?'

My sister, Ruth, pointed out that since the dust in the teapot was thick and undisturbed it was unlikely that it had ever held any money. 'And who said anything about money in the first place?' she added. 'A teapot, not the Bank of England.'

'Detective,' my mother mocked. 'Shylock Holmes.'

'Sherlock,' I corrected.

'Whose side are you on?' she demanded. Rolling her eyes to the ceiling: 'Even my own son turns against me.' She aimed a blow at my head, then realized that her hand was holding the teapot. 'Take it away,' she screamed. 'Throw it in the dustbin. I never want to see it again.'

I took the teapot and put it in the dustbin. An hour later my mother asked: 'Simey, where's the teapot?'

'Like you said, in the dustbin.'

'The dustbin? How can you do such a thing? It might be valuable. An antique. Worth thousands.'

'Hitler should live so sure,' said my sister.

'Why not take it to Feiner's and have it valued?' I suggested. 'Sell it.'

My mother beat me savagely about the ears. Then for good measure she kicked me in the shins and waved her fists at me. 'Sell? How can you say such a shocking thing? To sell a present. A present from Mrs Malik. A dead woman. Why has God tortured me with such a son? Sell! How can you talk like that? Filth! Atheist! Enemy!'

So I fished the teapot out of the dustbin. My mother washed it with the care she would have given a holy relic and placed it on the mantelpiece in the kitchen, even moving my father's photograph an inch or two in order to make room for it.

And there it remained. In the years that followed she would look at it from time to time and sigh, accepting that even if Betty Silverman had robbed her of its contents it was all part of some grand plan: God's punishment for some unknown, unnamed and unmentionable sin.

One afternoon, about a month after Mrs Malik's death, I came home from school to find a stranger in the square: a thin woman with a long grey face topped by a great busby of white hair on which was balanced a pancake of mauve velvet. Her ankle-length dress was of bright blue satin over Wellington boots, and the extraordinary picture was completed by long canary-yellow gloves.

My mother called: 'Come over and say hello to Mrs Cooperman!'

I approached and said hello. Esther Cooperman beamed at me, patted my cheek and took a grubby peppermint from the pocket of her dress. 'If you're a good boy you'll get another one.' (Since the distribution of grey and chipped peppermints was to be Mrs Cooperman's invariable reward for youthful virtue, she was probably responsible for much of the juvenile delinquency in and around Daffodil Square during her residence there.) I put the peppermint in my pocket, mumbling something about keeping it until after tea.

As my mother told me later, Mrs Malik's landlord had converted her two floors into three flats, one of which Mrs Cooperman was to rent. It had not taken long for four such skilled and persistent cross-examiners as Mrs Kemensky, Mrs Lewis, Mrs Weinberg and my mother to learn that Mrs Cooperman had been born in Stamford Hill and that her parents came from Poland; that her husband, Leonard, was a watchmaker who worked for a firm in Bond Street; that she suffered from heart trouble and bunions; and that she was moving to Daffodil Square now that her youngest daughter had married a lovely boy in the gowns and so her present flat in Golders Green was too large for just her husband and herself.

This much had been established before my arrival. During the peppermint ritual Mrs Kemensky cracked her knuckles and wrinkled her nose with nervous impatience. Now she said: 'So it will mean a good saving money, you coming here. I mean, after all, Golders Green! A classy area. And like you said, your husband works in Bond Street. Also a classy area. A workman there earns good money, no?'

I flinched as Mrs Cooperman's violent negation threatened to send her beret spinning, discus-like, towards my head. 'Money we did have. That I'm not denying. But now? Who's got money? As for saving money, how can I now my Daphne's married and not bringing in? Tell me, if I had money would I move here? You are nice ladies, but would you pretend this was the Promised Land? Do you ladies have money?' (In unified reflex the other women shrugged off a question not worthy of a spoken reply.) 'So if you live here and don't have money, how come I should live here and do have money?'

'Anyhow,' said my mother bitterly, 'at least you got a husband, God be thanked.'

Mrs Cooperman appeared not to have heard. 'If you mend a watch, you mend a watch. Bond Street or Bethnal Green, what's the difference? It isn't the workman gets the money, it's the bosses.' She cleared her throat and looked hopefully at her companions. 'Any of you nice ladies want to have a watch repaired? Or buy one maybe? My husband can get wholesale . . . No? You didn't mind my asking I hope.' Again she cleared her throat. 'Or maybe just a watchstrap. Watchstraps we got plenty. The last man my husband worked for went bankrupt. Worse than bankrupt – broke. So instead of wages he gave him a gross assorted watchstraps . . .

Watchstraps! What can you do with watchstraps? I ask you nice ladies, what can you do?' Her hat trembled as she rose to her feet. 'I must be going. My Leonard's waiting. You're all nice ladies and I look forwards to seeing you again when I move in next week.' After a lengthy ritual of goodbyes she walked off, her hat bobbing up and down on the coiled spring of her hair, her preposterous colours exaggerated by the bleak drabness of the square.

Mrs Lewis: 'A funny woman.'

Mrs Kemensky: 'Such clothes. A real poppy show.'

My mother: 'At least she's got a husband.'

Mrs Weinberg: 'That's true. But just the same, trying to sell us watches within five minutes of seeing us. Like a pedlar.'

Mrs Kemensky: 'My cousin was a pedlar in Lodz.'

Mrs Lewis: 'Next thing you know she'll have a stall here in the square.'

Mrs Weinberg: 'She's got the voice for it. A real market voice like I used to hear outside mine shop.'

Mrs Kemensky: 'And she didn't seem altogether clean, somehow. You know what I mean? Not dirty, but not altogether clean. You understand me?'

My mother: 'A gross watchstraps. I wonder if my brother would be interested. You know – Mendel. The businessman. I'll go see him Sunday . . . But you're right. She is a bit . . . well, unusual. But as I always say, you must speak as you find. She might be a nice respectable woman for all we know. On the other hand, better one Mrs Malik was still here than all the Bond Street watchmakers. Poor woman, may she rest in peace . . . But what is to be, will be . . . Anyway, I can't sit here talking all night. Simon, take the chair and go tell Ruth to put on the kettle . . . But I must say those clothes are a bit common with all the colours of the rainbow. On the other hand, how can you judge? Like it says: "Clothes are only skin deep". So who's to know?'

I carried her chair back to number 18 while she lingered for a further exchange of views about Esther Cooperman.

Two

MY MOTHER was incapable of making decisions. Whether it was a question of gassing us all rather than face eviction and the workhouse, or whether to buy veal or chicken for Sunday's lunch, the cry was the same: 'I don't know what to do for the best. I don't know which way to turn. If only your father, God rest his soul in peace, was alive. Who can help me? What shall I do?'

Sometimes she would seek the advice of her cronies, but if the problem was too personal for discussion under the elm tree there was only one course of action: consult Mendel.

Mendel, the eldest of my uncles, lived with his wife Zillah and my grandmother, Cissie Abrams, in Zanzibar Terrace, a narrow, cobbled row of damp disintegration between Commercial Road and Cable Street, just north of London Docks. With them, on the three floors above Madam Koski's Superior Corset Salon, were Mendel's four children and another uncle, Benjamin.

Uncle Mendel was a tall, fat, laughing man with a booming voice, broad nose, wisps of black hair combed carefully if ineffectually over his baldness, a neck permanently pebbled with boils, a fiercely waxed moustache and spats. Uncle Ben was as tall as Mendel, but thinner; untidy and dandruffed, with a broken nose that had set sideways and a curious, flat-footed shuffle of a walk.

Granny Abrams adored Mendel, but was withering in her contempt of Ben. I recall a memorable outburst when she came to tea one Sunday; a passion inspired by the sight of my mother sewing lengths of elastic into pairs of garters. 'Elastic, eh? You remember during the war, Minnie? The half-inch elastic? Remember?' Her voice trembled with emotion. 'If you wanted to buy a tiny piece half-inch elastic in the East End you couldn't buy except from my Mendel. Not a farden's-worth except by my Mendel! Not that much! Everyone came to Mendel for elastic. Remember? She sat nodding her head, enjoying the recollection of her son's business acumen. Then, as one memory led to another she suddenly spat and shouted: 'And all Ben could do was win medals!'

Ben, under age, had joined the Army in 1915 and was awarded the Military Medal at the Somme when he rescued a wounded officer under fire. He was mildly shell-shocked in the process and this manifested itself in bizarre outbursts which I, as a child, regarded as hysterically comic. Once he was only just saved from arrest when caught running down Wentworth Street in his underwear and medals shouting 'Hang the Kaiser!' and on another occasion caused a panic at a local synagogue when he interrupted the Sabbath morning service with the cry: 'Put on your gas masks – the bastards are using phosgene!' Generally, however, he was quiet and self-contained, spending long periods staring at the dining-room wallpaper and periodically attempting to pluck the tulips with which it was patterned.

My grandmother's feelings towards Ben's Army service did not reflect a lack of gratitude towards the country that had given her refuge. Indeed, three other sons had served in the war, but as she put it that Sunday: 'To go in the Army is bad enough. If they take you to the barracks what can you do? And when they want you they'll take you soon enough. But to go from your own free will, to *ask* to join – this is a sane man? A disgrace! And to save the life from an officer yet. Isn't it the act of a madman who wants certification? A madman? Who gives the orders to start the pogroms and kill the Jews if not the officers? So mine own son behaves like a *verstinkener* Cossack and saves his life. Is this what God gave me children for?'

My mother, who had heard it all before, made shushing noises and said: 'Don't upset yourself. Ben's a good boy. He means well.'

I said: 'But Granny, what about Hitler? Shouldn't the Jews fight him, I mean volunteer to fight him, if there's a war?'

My mother struck me across the nose with a garter. 'To contradict your own grandmother! You should be ashamed. Get out of here.'

If Ben was the black sheep of the family, Mendel was its genius. While my other uncles worked as tailors' cutters or pressers, cabinet-makers, barbers, taxi drivers and the like, Mendel was 'The businessman. The dealer'. He spent his life buying extraordinary bargains – job-lot rolls of unperforated toilet paper; shirts with one sleeve longer than the other ('There must be a million cripples crying out for such shirts'); eleven-inch footrules; Albanian cigars salvaged from a flooded warehouse ('A touch of glue and you'd take them for Corona Coronas'); leaking chamber pots; Hebrew/ Croat dictionaries – which he would sell after gargantuan efforts for minuscule profits.

He was, in fact, the classic dupe, the true salesman's eternal victim. Anyone who found himself with the unsaleable on his hands homed unerringly on Uncle Mendel, while Ben earned pocket money (and a hernia) pushing barrow-loads of improbabilities to and from Zanzibar Terrace. It was true that Mendel had held a vast stock of half-inch elastic at the beginning of the Great War, but I discovered that this was accidental: he had bought it in 1910 and it had lain decomposing in Madam Koski's basement until there was a sudden, fortuitous shortage.

The eternal optimist, Mendel was convinced that his next deal would be the really big one; of such staggering magnitude it would enable him to realize his supreme ambition: to join his Aunt Hannah in New York. When my grandparents fled from Poland to England, Hannah and her husband, Mark Feiner, went to America, and although there had been no contact between the sisters for many years, it was taken for granted that Mark Feiner had amassed a considerable fortune.

'A millionaire,' Mendel would shout. 'It stands to reason. Look, at the Troxy last week I saw this picture with wassername . . . Joan Crawford. She was secretary in a New York office from an estate agent. Not the boss, mark you – he was the one she nearly married but this service G-man from the FBI wasn't dead after all. She was just a secretary doing typing. But the flat she lived in – by my life the bathroom alone was as big as the Albert Hall. This flat had fitted carpets, cushions on every chair like an eastern Harlem – even curtains on the lavatory window.

'And her clothes! Every time you saw her she was wearing something different. Even a mink coat. A mink – so sure as I'm standing here. A mink coat. On top of all this (may God punish me if I'm telling a word of a lie) a motor-car . . . So if a secretary can live like this, how does the rest live? I'm telling you, they're *rich* in America.

'Look . . . Just suppose, for the sake of argument, just suppose that Uncle Mark was also just a secretary. Just suppose. By English standards she'd be a millionaire already. But why should a Yiddisher man be a secretary doing typing? I mean, it stands to reason. So he'd be *more* than a millionaire by English standards. It's logic.'

To which Granny Abrams would reply: 'Maybe not a millionaire. But rich, yes – otherwise we'd have heard soon enough . . . Then again they might be dead, God forbid. She was younger than me, but neither of them can be chickens now.'

'In that case there's bound to be cousins. But don't worry, we'll find out for ourselves.' Twisting his moustache-ends into needle-sharp points: 'You'll see. Moishe Bergman's got a consignment oranges from Palestine. Each so big you'd think they was pregnant. They'd go straight to the Corner House: except they got a bit squashed in the ship coming over. But so full of juice each orange would fill a bucket. Worth a fortune. You'll see. This time next year, please God, we'll all be in New York. Just wait.'

The family waited. In the meantime Mendel held court like a Hasidic rabbi, graciously advising members of the family on their financial, spiritual, moral and medical problems – and treated by them in return with infinitely more respect and veneration than they accorded their official religious and medical representatives.

Deals that went wrong in no way modified this reverence: the family remembered only the half-inch elastic. In any case, Mendel was never to blame: the man who sold him the goods was a thief . . . the man who bought them was a cheat . . . the man who refused to buy them was a rogue. Sometimes Mendel was able to utter the most terribly acceptable cry of all: 'Anti-Semitic robber!'

When we visited Zanzibar Terrace to discuss Leonard Cooperman's watchstraps, Uncle Mendel was at his most ebullient. While I played Ludo with my cousin Herschel, Ruth giggled and whispered with the girls, Aunt Zillah prepared lunch and Mendel told my mother and Granny Abrams of his latest purchase: a crate of assorted glasses from a recently closed Chinese restaurant. 'I got them cheap because they're a bit chipped, a bit cracked,' he revealed, 'but they're a bargain. A gift. Worth a fortune.'

'Worth a fortune?' said my grandmother. 'Broken glasses? How come?'

'That's where being a businessman comes in,' said Mendel, giving an upward brush to his moustache-ends. 'Fleischmann who sold them to me also thought I was potty; a madman. But it's him that's the idiot. As soon as he mentioned the glasses it came to me. And yet I'll bet a million pounds you can't guess what it was.' He looked at us in turn. 'There, what did I tell you? So it's this.

'At Jewish weddings, at the end of the ceremony, you always break a glass with your foot, no? To commemorate the destruction of Jerusalem – or is it to celebrate its rebuilding? So anyway, the glass is done up in paper or cloth, isn't it? So what difference if the glass is chipped a bit or cracked? Who needs a new Dresden cut-glass crystal just to stamp on? It stands to reason. So what I'll do is wrap each glass in a page of the *Jewish Chronicle* to give a religious touch, then tie them up nice with string and sell them to all the synagogues in London. I'll make a fortune.' Mendel clapped his hands. 'Just wait and see. We'll be in America in no time, you mark my words.'

'You'll make so much money just from these glasses?' my mother asked timidly.

'Of course not just from these glasses,' said Mendel scornfully. 'But it's a start. After all, there's synagogues all over England, all over the world. The day will come when from all over the world I'll be bringing in broken glasses and exporting them again wrapped and packaged. It stands to reason that there's a fortune in it. But there must be a beginning, a start . . .

'How did Rothschild start? I saw this film with George Arliss so I can tell you how he started. A moneylender in Frankfurt. By my children's lives, a moneylender. That's all, a moneylender. So you lend your first sixpence and make a penny profit and you've got sevenpence to lend. Sevenpence, eightpence, a pound, a thousand pounds. From that original sixpence has come hundreds of millions of pounds. Hundreds of millions I tell you, just from sixpence . . . Like Cunard. All you need is one liner and the rest is easy. It stands to reason. Like Lipton. From one packet of tea he's now got thousands of shops.

'It's about time we had our chance. It's only right; only fair.'

My grandmother burst into laughter, displaying a trembling set of dazzling false teeth, 'Like it says in the Talmud: "To be patient is sometimes better than to have much wealth".'

Mendel frowned down on her. 'For how many thousands years have the Jews been patient, and what good has it done them?'

'But the Rothschilds are also Jews, no?' said Granny Abrams. 'And Littman's a Yiddisher name. Cunard I don't place, although Mrs Mordisch say there's even Irish Jews. Is Cunard an Irisher?'

'He's American,' said Mendel impatiently.

'But he had to come from somewhere,' said my grandmother. 'All Americans come from somewhere: Russia, Poland, Lithuania – somewhere. So why not Ireland?'

Mendel banged a fist on the table. 'And from Zanzibar Terrace they can't come?' he roared.

'But you've come already,' said Granny Abrams. 'From Poland.'

My mother shouted: 'Watchstraps!'

Disconcerted, Mendel and my grandmother stared at her.

'Watchstraps. A gross watchstraps.'

Mendel's eyes lowered to a frown. 'What watchstraps? How come watchstraps?'

My mother's explanation included a lengthy lament for Mrs Malik, a vivid description of Mrs Cooperman, and an assurance that she had no interest in the matter one way or the other.

Mendel considered. 'You know nothing about these straps? For example, whether they're ladies' or gents'? How much she wants for them?'

My mother threw up her hands. 'Like I said, it's not my business to interfere. All I know she says her husband's got a gross watchstraps. More than that I know nothing. I only wondered if you're interested. After all's said and done you're the businessman, the dealer. Suppose they was stolen? You'd know at a glance. I'm only repeating what she said.'

'Quite right, Minnie, quite right,' said Mendel soothingly. 'A gross watchstraps. Say at tuppence each makes two shillings a dozen. Twenty-four shillings the lot . . . So allowing for my time and trouble and Ben's bus fares . . .' he lapsed into frowning, calculating silence. Finally: 'Yes, I might be able to do business. I'll pop in tomorrow and see her.' He laughed. 'I'll pay you a commission. Here – ten bob.'

'Don't be silly,' said my mother.

'Who's being silly?' said Mendel. 'Business is business. Take.'

My mother took. At that moment Ben shuffled in. 'Hello Minnie . . . Simey . . . Ruth. How are you? Keeping well?' He stared for a moment at the lamp standard, head to one side. Then, to Mendel: 'I couldn't get old *Jewish Chronicles*. They didn't have. I tried all over. Even as far as Lewin's. No *Jewish Worlds* neither. So I got a couple bundles old *Catholic Heralds*. All right?'

Mendel stood still and silent for perhaps twenty seconds. Then his face contorted with fury and he held out unsteady hands towards his brother's throat. '*Catholic Heralds!*' he screeched. '*Catholic Heralds!* How come *Catholic Heralds* in a synagogue? For Jewish weddings he brings *Catholic Heralds*. Why not *Mein Kampf*? Why not *Action*? Why not . . .' He lowered his hands in disgust. 'Oh bloody, bloody.'

'Such language in front of the children,' said my mother.

'Not nice,' said Granny Abrams.

'Bloody, bloody,' Mendel repeated defiantly.

'At least the *Catholic Herald*'s a religious paper,' said my mother. 'It's not as though it was the *Daily Mail* or some dirty book.'

'Dirty books. That's all I'm short of,' said Mendel bitterly. A long, thoughtful silence. Then: 'After all Catholics, Jews, Pro'stants – what difference? They're all religious. They're all . . . well, holy, aren't they? It stands to reason. After all, Christ himself was a Yiddisher boy wasn't he? So what difference *Catholic Herald* or *Jewish Chronicle*? In any case, folded paper – who's going to read? Who's going to see? Does it make sense, at a wedding ceremony to sit down and read the newspaper? Who ever heard such a thing? What difference what newspaper? It's the thought that counts.'

'Of course the thought,' said my mother.

'What else?' said Granny Abrams.

'Just the same,' said Mendel, shaking a finger at Ben, 'if that lump of cabbage had done like I told him we wouldn't have to make a mockery of things. Tonight I want every one of those glasses wrapped and tied. D'you hear? Every one.'

Ben grinned and took a pack of playing cards from his pocket. 'You want I should show you a new trick I learned?'

Mendel's cry of despair half-drowned his wife's call from the kitchen: 'Sit down all. Dinner's ready.'

'Everything I got to do myself, every tiny little thing,' Mendel grumbled as he helped his mother to the table. 'If we was in America would I have as my staff just one no-good blockhead? Remember the picture with Bette Davis and wassis-name? You know, the one with the moustache. Anyway, if he pressed a button or lifted a telephone hundreds people rushed in at his beck and call. Hundreds. May God blind me for life if I'm telling a word of a lie. Shoeshine boys, secretaries, barbers, bookmakers, bankers – just at the press of a button. And what have I got? Him!'

Aunt Zillah came in with the chopped liver.

Lunch with the Abrams was, as ever, long and noisy. The conversation was concerned mainly with family news and gossip, including the information that Dora Choen's son, Joe, had left school and was to start work as a trainee printer. This was Zillah's cue to pinch Herschel's cheek and say: 'I've nothing against printers, but my boy is going to be a doctor, aren't you, dolly?' Herschel scowled. 'You should think of making your Simey a doctor, Minnie – if he's got the brain.'

'Doctor,' my mother sneered. 'So where's the money coming from? I can't even afford a bottle of Lysol – not that I need any, thank God. But you – you have got the money?'

'By the time he leaves school there'll be money,' said Mendel loftily.

'He'll pass scholarships,' said his wife.

'Maybe you can get a doctor to take him in and teach him the trade,' suggested Granny Abrams. 'Ask from Dr Lee.'

Mendel gave her a pitying look. To me: 'What do you want to be when you grow up? What are you good at?'

I shuffled uncomfortably. 'Well, I like writing compositions. Perhaps I'll be a writer.'

Uncle Mendel grimaced: 'Writer, *schmiter*! Listen, if you had an order for a few gross words I'd say "OK, go write them". It stands to reason. But in the meantime you've got to have a trade. Me, I'm different. I'm a businessman. A dealer. But that needs special talent. Better you should learn a trade.

'It stands to reason. Take a barber. All he needs is a pair scissors and a comb and he can earn a living anywhere. In America, for instance, they live like kings. I saw at the pictures with Paul Muni as a barber – like the Duke from York he was living. Or a tailor. A needle and cotton and a pair scissors and you'll always earn money. After all, everyone needs trousers, don't he? It stands to reason. On the other hand, if not a trade, a rabbi. Everywhere in the world there's Jews and they all need rabbis. Take my advice, be a rabbi.'

Aunt Zillah said to me: 'A rabbi also needs brains. My Herschel could be a rabbi. But are you top of the class like him?'

I shook my head. In truth my form position invariably hovered somewhere in the bottom quarter, which was perhaps as well, for unless there was a dramatic change in our economic situation it was certain that I would have to leave school at fourteen and find some sort of work. While my mother was certainly unhappy about this, she accepted its inevitability. Now she spoke vaguely, and with complete lack of conviction, of 'there's time enough yet' and of 'going into the gowns or the wireless', but I knew she took refuge behind the desperate hope that when the time came the problem would be solved with blinding brilliance by Uncle Mendel. 'Anyway,' she added gloomily, 'what difference what job he takes? There's going to be a war any minute and we'll all be blown to smithereens. Not, mind you, that it needs a bomb for our rubbish dump of a square to fall down. Sometimes I'm terrified even to belch, and you know how dangerous it can be to hold things in.'

'Remember the case of the woman in Paris?' asked Mendel. 'How she didn't want to break wind in front of the Prime Minister and an air bubble formed? It blew her insides out and for miles around Paris was like a battlefield. You remember?'

'You believe such rubbish?' said Granny Abrams. 'Who ever heard such a thing?'

'I read in the papers.'

'Bubbles!' my mother shrilled. 'Who cares about bubbles? How do bubbles find Simon a job?'

Mendel sniffed. 'About jobs you may think I know nothing, but bubbles I read about in the paper.' He folded his arms and stared aggressively at my mother and Granny Abrams.

My mother took a deep breath, but before she could speak my grandmother said: 'Catering. Let him go in for the catering. In the catering at least he'll always eat proper.'

My mother's eyes opened wide, then narrowed. 'You mean he don't eat proper now?'

Granny Abrams flung open her arms in a gesture of appeal. 'I said such a thing?'

'All right, all right,' said my mother. 'Anyway, Adolph Wiseman's boy went in for the catering. To learn to be a chef. They wanted he should pay his apprenticeship. So tell me – if I had enough money to spare for Simon to learn to cook food I'd have enough money to buy food, in which case I'd cook it myself and he wouldn't have to work at all. No?' When the others had acknowledged the logic of this my mother turned to me, eyes moist, and patted my shoulder. 'Jobs, ambitions . . . Just grow up to be a good boy and I'll be satisfied. If people ask, tell them that's your ambition.'

An embarrassed silence was broken by my grandmother. 'And how you getting on, Ruthie? You working good?'

My sister, two years my senior, had left school about six months earlier and was now a trainee milliner at some sweat shop behind Tottenham Court Road. She shrugged at Granny Abrams's question and said sulkily: 'It's all right I suppose.'

'You make nice hats?'

Ruth grimaced. 'Make hats! All I do is run up and down fetching needles, matching cottons, unpacking felts and making tea.'

My mother said: 'I keep telling her a thousand times that you got to learn. You got to practise. Learn the business. Anyway, running up and down stairs is healthy. Builds blood.'

My sister rolled her eyes in elaborate disgust. 'Build varicose veins more like. I want to be a secretary and learn shorthand-typing, not millinery.'

'What's the point?' asked Mendel. 'Where you are they pay you while you learn. But stay at school to learn shorthand and you don't get paid. So isn't it better to have a job that brings in a few shillings every week? It stands to reason, no?'

'But Uncle Mendel,' said Ruth, all innocence, 'isn't it a good thing to learn shorthand-typing for when we go to America? I mean all those mink coats and things?'

Mendel took it in his stride. 'It's not the same, is it? England's England, America's America. Even the name's different. Here it's shorthand-typing, over there it's wassername. For the time being you're in England. When you get to America you can do different.'

'A waste of money,' said my grandmother. 'For a boy I say yes, learn a trade. But for a girl? What for? So making hats you learn to use a needle and cotton and that's good. But otherwise? So long you can cook and make a home what else do you need? One day, please God, you'll find a nice boy, settle down. What good will all the typing be then?'

'If everybody thought like that who'd do the typing?' asked Ruth.

My grandmother sniffed. 'Who cares? Let *them* worry.'

'Listen to what your grandmother's telling you,' said Mendel. 'Keep with the millinery. Then you'll find a boy, fall in love . . .'

'Mendel!' my mother shrieked. 'How can you use such talk in front of the children?'

Ruth blushed. 'Anyway, I'm only fourteen.'

'I married at sixteen,' said my grandmother. 'And your grandfather, may his soul rest in peace, was also sixteen. A fine man. A religious man. From Warsaw. I remember the first time I saw him. At the engagement ceremony. Tall like . . . like a giant. Hair like silk and eyes like . . . like Minnie's. A lovely man.'

Ruth said: 'You only met him for the first time just before the engagement?'

'So?'

'But how did you meet him?'

'Like everybody. My father arranged. What else?'

Herschel shook his head. 'To marry without knowing? In business you wouldn't buy before seeing, would you?'

Uncle Mendel took his son by the neck and shook him until his teeth rattled. 'Idiot! The father did the inspecting, no?'

'And believe me,' said Granny Abrams, 'it was the best way. Parents know what's good for their children far better than the children themselves. Nowadays it's all rubbish.'

Ruth asked: 'B-b-but did you love him?'

'The rubbish you talk,' said Granny Abrams. 'He was a good man. He looked after his family, he was a good Jew. He did like it's written in the Talmud: "I have never called my wife 'wife' but 'home'". What more do you want? Love? Of course there was love: love for a good husband.'

'But supposing you hadn't loved him,' Ruth persisted.

'Why shouldn't I?' replied my grandmother, half puzzled, half annoyed. 'He wasn't a drunkard, a trouble-maker. He wasn't a thief or a liar. He never cheated anyone from a farden. He was good to his children. So what was wrong with him?'

I asked: 'What job did he have when you married?'

'Aaaah! Your grandfather was a good man. A real Jew. In those days it was part of the marriage contract for the father to take his son-in-law into his home for five, ten years – whatever was agreed. The reason was so he could go on with his study of Scripture and The Law. Like it says, the best thing a man can do is learn. So he lived with mine parents, may their souls rest in peace, and for three years he spent his days and nights learning and praying. Day and night. We wanted he should spend all his life learning, but things changed. We had to go to Warsaw, Lublin, Lodz – all over we moved until we settled in Cracow. So how can a man learn? Instead he had to take up working.' Tears ran down the parchment of her cheeks.

'Don't give yourself aggravation,' said Zillah.

My grandmother stared at her. 'It's such a terrible thing to cry for mine husband? You mean you wouldn't cry for yours?'

Sensing trouble, my mother said: 'Children, it's time to go home.'

Three

On the bus taking us back to Daffodil Square my mother announced a murderous attack of heartburn. I nudged Ruth and whispered: 'The chicken.' She frowned her disagreement. 'Potatoes.' My mother clutched her bosom. 'The agony! The pain! Like a red-hot knife cutting me in half . . . Serves me right. When I saw those potatoes I could tell there was something wrong with them.' (Ruth dug her elbows into my ribs.) 'The colour was peculiar. God alone knows what she cooked them in. My chest! Like a dagger. A pain I wouldn't wish on my worst enemy. Every time I go to that woman I pay for it. One day she'll kill me with her cooking – if you call it cooking. A woman her age should be able to cook a potato. Is it so difficult to roast a potato? My chest . . .' And so on until we arrived home when my mother realized it was time for supper. The thought cheered her enormously. 'A drop of soup will do us all the world of good. A nice bowl hot soup and we'll all feel better. Simon, you lay the table; Ruth, you cut bread.' She even hummed a few bars of *Sonny Boy* as she took the saucepan from the larder.

Food was my mother's universal panacea. *Lokshen soup* (chicken broth with a form of home-made *vermicelli*) was held to be particularly efficacious: a sort of Jewish penicillin. Colds, bruises, broken engagements, menstrual disorders, corns, bankruptcy, arthritis, headaches, broken bones, infidelity, boils, cancer: 'What you need is a nice drop of *lokshen* soup. It'll do you good. Better than all the medicine' – and a quart bowl would be filled to the brim and placed on the kitchen table.

My mother's faith in her catholicon was demonstrated the following morning when our breakfast was interrupted by a rattling of the letter box followed by an anguished howl: 'Mrs Ashe! Come quick! I've had another of my dreams!'

Startled, I sprayed a mouthful of tea across the tablecloth. Ruth dropped her knife and fork with a plate-cracking clatter. My mother's face drained of colour, her mouth fell open and a segment of smoked haddock trembled at the end of a quivering fork. She tried to speak, but no sound came.

'Hurry,' came the voice. 'For pity's sake come quick.'

My mother managed to croak: 'Who's that? What is it? What's happened? Say something!'

Ruth said: 'That's Mrs Cooperman.'

'How can it be?' asked my mother, her voice normal now. She saw the fork in front of her face and gulped down the haddock. 'How come Mrs Cooperman at this time of the morning? She's not supposed to move till next week.'

I said: 'Yesterday's what Mrs Kemensky told me.'

'People don't move on Sunday,' said Ruth.

'Why not?' my mother demanded. 'What difference what day of the week?'

'Mrs Ashe! My dreams!' came the agonized yell.

' . . . But you're right. It is her voice.'

My mother went to the front door. A moment later Mrs Cooperman, breathless in dressing-gown and hairnet, stumbled into the kitchen and half fell into a chair. In Yiddish she groaned: 'Demons! I'm possessed of demons.'

My mother spat three times to ward off the Evil Eye, then said: 'I thought you wasn't moving before next week.'

Mrs Cooperman shivered. 'A dream. A nightmare. I can't tell you. Demons. Lilith and Samael. The Angel of Death. The King of Darkness . . .' Grasping my mother's hand: 'I dreamed about legs – may you be spared the same. Men's legs (God forgive me). You know what that means according to the Rabbi Klothboltz? You know? You understand? A death in the family, that's what it means. Death and destruction before the full moon. Dust and ashes.' Hands over her face, she rocked in the chair muttering to herself.

With an unsteady hand my mother poured Mrs Cooperman a cup of tea. 'Drink this and you'll feel better. And what's all this with legs and Rabbi Kloth-whatever his name is?'

'You don't know?' said Mrs Cooperman incredulously. 'A nice lady like you don't read Rabbi Klothboltz' Book of Dreams?'

My mother gave a contemptuous snort (although I saw she had

her fingers crossed). 'Dreams? So don't everyone dream? And do we all drop down dead?'

'But he knows. A holy man. The sage of Zucow. He was related to the Alter family from Gur. From all over – even the Tsar Russia – they sent dreams to be explained. I've got his book. It's been in my family for generations. I know what I'm saying. I was a Klothboltz myself before I married my Leonard.'

'I don't know what you're talking about,' said my mother, touching the wood of the table. 'Drink your tea and tell me about these dreams of legs. How come you always dream of legs? And always men's legs? Never chicken legs or table legs?'

Mrs Cooperman emptied her cup in one noisy gulp and embarked on a barely coherent description of the spectres and symbols that invaded her sleeping hours – followed by lurid inter-pretations of their meaning as detailed in Rabbi Klothboltz' Book of Dreams. Sometimes an image or object was not listed by the rabbi (one-eyed nuns, for example, or liver-sausage sandwiches, Maurice Chevalier, cowboy films, the Prince of Wales or watch-straps), but Mrs Cooperman found suitable parallels. Whatever the dream, the signs pointed invariably in the same direction: the humiliating and painful death of Mrs Cooperman before the next full moon.

By the end of her recital my mother's uneasiness was dispelled, and her reply to Mrs Cooperman set the pattern for the exchanges on subsequent breakfast visits. 'The next full moon you say? So you've nearly a week to go. Time for a nice bowl soup.'

'Soup? This time of the morning?'

'All right, a nice middle of fried plaice. It won't take a minute to warm up the oil. Lovely fresh fish.'

'For God's sake, Mrs Ashe, this is a time to talk about fish?'

'So what you want I should talk about? The funeral arrange-ments? All right. I'm told Cohen from West Hampstead does a lovely affair. Very tasteful. And if you haven't any family or enough friends he'll supply mourners. Such mourners! I'm told on good authority that at one funeral not long ago they cried so much they flooded the grounds and the fire brigade had to be called. Marvel-lous cryers he's got. Mind you, Cohen charges a lot of money.

Although I'm told he does do cheaper funerals and still with the mourners. Only for the cheap ones they don't cry – they laugh.'

'Mrs Ashe! How can you make jokes? How can you make a mockery of mine dreams?'

'What you want I should do? Take them serious? To believe such rubbish? An intelligent woman like you . . . Have another cup of tea and a slice salt herring . . . I once dreamed I was the Duchess from Kent in Buckingham Palace. So what happened? In case you haven't noticed, I'll tell you – I'm no longer Minnie Ashe from Daffodil Square but the Duchess Kent from Buckingham. Dreams! . . . Have some cheese cake . . . Dreams. A lot of mad talk . . . Take a biscuit. I made them special.'

'Food! All you talk about is food. How can you at a time like this?'

It was time for Ruth to leave for work and me to go to school. We left the house as Mrs Cooperman wailed: 'But I don't want any chopped liver,' and my mother replied: 'But it's marvellous for dreams. So sure I should live I read only the other day in the *Evening Standard* . . .'

Just as my mother had an unwavering belief in the remedial qualities of food, so she was convinced that anyone not actually engaged in the process of eating was in imminent peril of death. In consequence the oven and gas rings burned white hot to produce roast chickens, *gefulte* fish, *strudel*, shoulders of lamb, *borsch*, salt beef, steamed and fried middle cuts of plaice or halibut, chopped liver and stews.

For years I assumed that all the world breakfasted on smoked salmon or some form of salt, pickled or smoked herring, followed by a pair of kippers or bloaters, or a whole smoked haddock with two fried eggs, the meal rounded off with an assortment of jams, cheeses and cakes.

Lunch, tea and dinner were proportionately vast and eccentric. Ruth responded admirably to this diet: she weighed about eight stone. My mother, who equated overweight with health, was delighted with her, just as I was despaired of. I ate as much as my sister, probably more, but remained skeletal. Periodically my mother would lament: 'It's not natural. There's something wrong with you. Perhaps you've got a worm. Tomorrow we'll go see Dr Solomons.'

My mother had no intention of taking me to the doctor. His name was employed as a threat, an alternative to the bogy-man, for my mother was certain that it was my own fault if I was not fatter. 'You do it on purpose, just to aggravate me.'

So I ate even bigger meals – but remained skinny. My mother wept, recognizing the signs of an early death.

Apart from feeding her children, the food was distributed to friends, neighbours, relatives, tradesmen, and the inevitable army of scroungers attracted by the beckoning fingers of aroma that curled across London.

A superb cook herself, my mother was arrogantly contemptuous of other people's gastronomic efforts. 'Zillah a good cook? Since when? Her food is rubbish. Filth . . . and such small portions.'

Most of my uncles, aunts and cousins had improbably large appetites. While my mother was a compulsive cook they were compulsive eaters. If their gluttony seems now to have verged on the obscene, at the time it filled my mother with fierce pride and myself with fascinated wonder. I recall an occasion when Uncle Dave and his wife Lilly came to tea (the centrepiece: middle cuts of halibut with egg and lemon sauce), and they went on eating for so long that by the time they had finished, supper was ready to be served (chopped liver, barley soup and roast veal). They left at midnight after a farewell snack of *gefulte* fish, cheese cake and cocoa. As the door closed behind them my mother said: 'What marvellous eaters. Such healthy appetites. Lovely! For people like that it's a pleasure to cook.' Later, piling plates and dishes into the sink: 'God knows what we'll eat tomorrow . . . But you can't begrudge your own flesh and blood a cup of tea, can you?' Finally, as the last spoon was wiped and Ruth and I were sent to bed: 'Anyway, they pay for it.'

We were indeed living on the charity of my uncles and aunts. There were no fixed allowances: five shillings or a ten-shilling note would be handed over with varying degrees of ostentation during family visits. Even on this erratic basis the size of my mother's family should have guaranteed us a reasonable income, but a number of factors ensured that we were always in debt.

For one thing it would have been physically impossible to have visited or entertained all my mother's army of brothers and sisters weekly, and the number seen was again reduced by the fact that life with the family was punctuated by fierce quarrels, usually short-lived (and followed by outraged denials by my mother that they had ever taken place), but of sufficient frequency to shrink our income still further. The dominant factor, however, was the enormous percentage of our money that went on food: even when we were the guests my mother would take fruit, home-made cakes and chocolates to a value far in excess of the money she brought away.

My mother never became conditioned to her state of poverty and pride-swallowing dependence on the fitful benevolence of her family. There were long hours of weeping and wild threats of suicide and the workhouse, punctuated with flashes of Yiddish philosophy: 'Things could be worse, I suppose. I could be one of my creditors.'

The only really long and vicious quarrel that my mother had with a member of her family was with my cousin Ada, daughter of her eldest sister, Sarah. Aunt Sarah, the pock-marked widow of a salt-herring pickler from Bessarabia, developed a wasting disease which I never heard referred to by name; only as Aunty Sarah's Thing, as ambiguous an ailment as that which plagued Harry Jaye.

The breach came when Aunt Sarah and Ada arrived for tea and Sarah announced that she would have only a glass of Russian tea and a dry water biscuit.

My mother's response to this challenge was automatic: 'You'll have a piece of fried fish. I cooked it specially.'

Aunt Sarah: 'I can't, Minnie. As sure I should live I'd give a thousand pounds for one mouthful of your fried fish. But I mustn't. I saw the specialist yesterday about mine Thing and he said no more fried fish.'

My mother: 'But it's good for you. It's fresh. Marvellous for the eyesight. I read it in the paper. And so fresh it was alive when I bought it.'

Ada: 'Aunt Minnie, she mustn't eat fried things. The specialist . . .'

My mother: 'Specialist! What does he know? What can be bad about fried fish? Made in eggs and flour and nut oil. It's all pure. All fresh.'

Sarah: 'I'm sure it is. But no fish.'

My mother shrugging: 'More fool you . . . All right, no fried fish. Then a drop *lokshen* soup. It's strong. Builds blood. By my life you'll have tiny bowl soup.'

Ada: 'She mustn't eat anything with fat in it.'

My mother tapped at the table with a fish knife: one of many recognizable danger signals. 'Fat? What you mean, fat? What do you think: I take handfuls of fat in a saucepan and call it soup? Pork fat I suppose. How can you say such a thing? How can you be so wicked? It's all pure chicken. All goodness. There are starving people who would go on their hands and knees for such soup. And you say it's fat.'

Ada: 'All I'm saying is that there must be some fat. That's all.'

My mother: 'So I'll strain it . . . Anyway, what's wrong with fat? Look how skinny she is.'

Ada: 'The doctor said no *lokshen* soup. Because of Mummy's Thing.'

My mother, trembling: 'All right. So no soup. No fried fish. But a piece of *gefulte* fish she will have.' Before Ada could reply my mother rushed to the larder and returned with a plate on which, set in the jellied richness of their own juices, were two huge ovals of *gefulte* fish – a spiced, minced and boiled amalgam of carp, bream, pike and other fish. Aunt Sarah's inherent gormandism got the better of her. With an ecstatic groan she picked up a fork. Her daughter snatched it from her hand, crying: 'Aunty Minnie! What are you trying to do? Kill her?'

My mother clenched her fists. 'Kill her?' she screamed. 'You think it's poison? Is that it? How can you say such things. To call me a poisoner. May you never marry for such talk. You should have your mouth washed out with carbolic. May God punish you with a black year. Poisoner she calls me! Yon wicked girl. You should be ashamed of yourself.'

Aunt Sarah, feebly: 'Minnie . . .'

My mother: 'It's no good you taking her side. She's a wicked beast.'

And so it went on for another ten minutes until Ada, desperate, forcibly dragged her mother from the flat – without even a glass of Russian tea and a dry water biscuit.

From that day my mother refused to visit Aunt Sarah. When they met at family functions such as weddings and funerals my mother, making certain Ada was within earshot, would ask loudly: 'Anyone trying to poison you lately? Anyone been feeding you pork-fat soup? . . . You're looking thinner. You sure Ada is giving you your dog biscuits?'

Between these meetings my mother suffered long periods of tear-soaked misery. 'Not to see my own sister. My own flesh and blood. It's a shocking thing. It's not natural. And don't you think your grandmother is suffering? Isn't she eating her heart out with aggravation? And me? Am I made of stone?'

'Then why not go and see Aunt Sarah?' I asked.

'How can I with that . . . that creature there? That mischief-maker. That stinker. It's all her fault. She's the one behind it all.'

'Why not invite Aunt Sarah here?'

'She'd come without Ada? Not on your life she wouldn't. A plague should take that Ada! Her teeth should fall out! Such wickedness to tear apart two sisters. Why has God punished me with such a niece? What for? . . .' And she would soothe the pain in an orgy of cake-making or vegetable peeling.

Aunt Sarah lived on. Devoted to her care, Ada's youth yellowed. It was perhaps twenty years after their quarrel (or, more accurately, my mother's quarrel) that Sarah finally died: frail and emaciated, kept alive by the doctors during her last years to be the victim of indescribable agonies.

We joined the mourners at her flat off Whitechapel Road. The rabbi who was in attendance said to my weeping mother: 'God gives, God taketh away. She was a fine woman. I will say a special prayer for her.'

Lost in her grief, my mother replied absently and instinctively: 'A nice bowl of *lokshen* soup would do her more good.'

Mrs Cooperman's first breakfast visit proved an irresistibly rich
vein for my mother and her friends. Mrs Lewis was certain that
Mrs Cooperman was indeed possessed of an evil spirit and said that
the rest of us should wear amulets to ward off its sinister powers.
'Sometimes the demon moves from one person to another. It's
from Satan and can do shocking things. I had a cousin who had the
Evil Eye on her – may we be spared the like. The way she behaved!
Tore up holy books, cursed her parents, ate pork and bacon and
God knows what else besides. They had to lock her up until Rabbi
Bloodstok got rid of it. The doctor said it was a brainstorm, but
the rabbi said it was an imp, a demon.' She spat three times and
whispered to herself in Yiddish. 'The Rabbi Bloodstok said these
spirits are fallen angels, born to Lilith from Adam. They cause
disease and make you go mad and drive out your religion. You
end up heathens, like mine cousin. And you know why they can
take you over in such a way? Because you haven't been a good Jew.
And the Rabbi Bloodstok said that since none of us is perfect it can
happen to any of us. You follow? I'll get amulets. It's the best thing.
I'll ask from Iron Foot Yossell next time he calls round. What do
you say, Mrs Ashe?'

My mother shook her head. 'I don't know what to say. On the
one hand who can believe in it? On the other hand, perhaps one
should be on the safe side. What do you think, Mrs Kemensky?'

The old woman gave a wheezing hiccup of a laugh. 'Spirits! Evil
Eyes! Amulets! Such talk makes me sick. I think I'm back again in
Galicia. Back with mine father, the Rabbi of Gobol, may his soul
rest in Paradise. A holy man. From all over Poland disciples came
to his court. They worshipped him almost as if he was Messiah.
The miracles he was supposed to work! And the knowledge he
had! There wasn't a holy book he didn't know backwards. The
study he made of Cabbala, Zohar, the Midrash, the Books of
Enoch and Ezra, the Commentaries of the Rabbis, the Books of
Creation, the Book of Brightness – everything he knew. And what
did it all add up to? Nothing with nothing, that's what. Superstitious nothing. He read, he argued, he talked, he ate his heart out
trying to understand it all, and the men and women came in their
thousands to visit him. But the hare lips remained hare lips, the

barren women remained barren, the demons stayed where they were, and no one was any the wiser to the meaning of anything. And still they believed he was a saint, a worker from miracles.

'So that was in Poland. They was ignorant. They knew no better. I was the same until I run away from it all. I had all this religious poppycock knocked out of me when I was still young, thank God. Politics is the answer, not God. Not Jews, not Christians, not anything else. Revolution is the answer, not amulets.'

My mother asked: 'Revolutions would get rid of Mrs Cooperman's dreams?'

Mrs Kemensky gave a pitying sigh. 'It would teach her not to believe in rubbish and go and see good doctor. A mind doctor. There's specialists for this sort of thing. A good dose salts is better than all the amulets. If you got constipation – God forbid – you take senna pods, not prayers. A cut finger you bandage, no? Not take a ritual bath. So what difference a head that goes wrong . . . Amulets! A good hiding is what she needs.'

'Or a bowl *lokshen* soup,' said my mother.

Mrs Weinberg asked: 'So you think Mrs Cooperman is mad, Mrs Kemensky?' Without waiting for a reply: 'For my part I don't hold with all this talk of evil spirits and amulets. My poor mother, may she rest in peace, had one – but did it stop her dying from cancer? And books of dreams! Who ever heard such a thing! There's only one way to find out the meaning of dreams – tea leaves. There was a Miss Katz, and she was marvellous with the tea leaves. From the leaves at the bottom of your cup she could tell you anything. Dreams were her speciality. But a book of dreams? Who heard such rubbish?'

At this point Uncle Mendel arrived on his way to see Leonard Cooperman's watchstraps. My mother told him of Esther Cooperman's visit and of her friends' theories. He frowned, twisted his moustache-ends and lit a cigarette. 'Evil spirits, you say? Is it likely? Is it logic? Does it stand to reason? I don't argue that they don't exist, mind you. I saw that film not long ago with Boris Karloff and Lionel Atwell. There was this gold coin, worth a fortune, but whoever had it was driven mad. There was this curse on it. I suppose you don't happen to know if Mrs Cooperman's got any gold coins?' He looked at my mother hopefully. 'No? Even so, evil spirits because she's not a good Jew? If that was true half the Jews in London would be spending their time shouting through each other's letter boxes. It stands to reason.' Mendel puffed at his cigarette and pondered. Then with a roar: 'It's the food she eats! It's what she eats. For my part I have terrible dreams if I eat pickled cucumbers and *lokshen* pudding late at night. Isn't that so, Minnie? Eh? It's the food.'

My mother's eyes flashed. 'I dream, too. And is it because of my cooking? Are you saying my food causes nightmares?'

Mrs Kemensky, nodding: 'I think your brother's right, Mrs Ashe. Your cooking isn't her cooking. Who knows what goes on in her kitchen? It makes more sense than all the talk of devils and the Evil Eye.'

Mendel, beaming: 'There you are! Mrs Kemensky is the daughter of a rabbi, so she should know. There's no doubt about it; it's the food.'

Mrs Lewis, sulkily: 'Say what you like, I'm going to get an amulet.'

My mother, self-consciously: 'Maybe there's no harm in it – just to be on the safe side.'

Mendel grimaced. 'Do what you like. But you mark my words: the answer's the pickled cucumbers.'

Mrs Lewis, Mrs Kemensky and Mrs Weinberg left. 'I must go, too,' said Mendel. 'See the husband about the watchstraps.'

'First a cup of tea. Then I'll come with you,' said my mother.

'Come with? What for?'

'To introduce you . . . Anyway, I want to see what her place looks like. But a cup of tea first.'

'Just one cup.'

'You'll have a piece of cheese cake. I make it specially.'

'All right. Just one piece.'

My mother prepared the table: pickled and salt herrings, cream cheese with radishes and spring onions chopped into it, jam, white bread, rye bread and black bread, smoked salmon, anchovies and sardines, an assortment of cakes and biscuits – side dishes to a huge slice of cold fried fish.

'I said I only wanted a cup of tea and a slice of cake.'

'It's nothing. A mouthful of fish won't hurt you.'

'But I've just eaten, and I've got a big supper tonight. Also fish.'

'So? This is teatime. Eat something.'

'I give you my dying oath I'm not hungry. By my life I couldn't eat anything except one piece of cake.'

'So sure I should live I made this fish specially for you. At least taste it.'

'On my children's lives I won't.' (By this time his responses were hardly articulate as they filtered through great mouthfuls of food.)

'Have half a piece.'

'You want I should swear my children's lives away? May I never move from this chair alive if I eat it.'

'A mouthful.'

'May my name be forgotten if I lift the fork.'

'Don't say such things!'

And so it went on as side dishes emptied and tempers snapped: my mother screaming, purple in the face; Mendel banging the table and spluttering segments of radish. Finally:

'It'll get wasted. I'll have to throw it in the dustbin. May God strike me dead this minute if I don't throw it in the dustbin.'

'You mustn't waste food in such a way.'

'Then eat it.'

'Well . . . Just half.'

The formalities having been observed, the fish was eaten, the bones sucked clean, and we went off to see the Coopermans.

Four

LEONARD COOPERMAN was a tubby little man in a skull cap with a broad face, a neatly trimmed triangle of beard and thick pebble spectacles. Across the waistcoat of his well-pressed black suit stretched a heavy gold watch chain, while a diamond twinkled on his wedding ring, gold flashed from his teeth and a pearl pin held his tie in place. He was smoking a Turkish cigarette from an amber holder and wore white cotton gloves – to protect his hands, he later explained, for the delicate art of watch repairing.

Although he greeted us with extravagant enthusiasm, fussing around my mother and treating Mendel with a solemn courtesy that made my uncle's chest strain at its shirt buttons, nothing came of the watchstrap deal. Leonard Cooperman asked three shillings each for them because ('And may my name be forgotten by God if I lie') they were made of real crocodile skin, while Mendel insisted ('And may I drop down dead this minute and then be covered in hair') they were American cloth worth tuppence each at the most – threepence for the sake of generosity since Mrs Cooperman was a friend of his sister.

My mother was clearly on edge, fearing a quarrel between her brother and the new neighbours, but Mendel lost interest in watchstraps. Instead he admired Mr Cooperman's suit and so, via half a dozen tailors they both knew, they turned to Harry Winkle who sold *Savile Row Misfits – Made For Peers of the Realm* from a stall in Berwick Street Market. In Mendel's view the suits were made in Japan, complete with labels bearing the Royal Cypher and the name and address of the King's tailor. 'Them Japs do it all the time,' he fumed. 'You ever see those films with Charlie Chan? They even built a town called Usa so they could stamp their rubbish Made in USA. Usa . . . U-S-A . . . Get it?'

In Leonard Cooperman's view the suits were from Savile Row, but stolen. 'Just imagine, Mr Abrams. Consider. Visualize. The

shame. The humiliation. The woe. You are walking along Picca-
dilly or the Burlington Arcade or Pall Mall. A police constable
confronts you. "Sir," he says, "did you buy that suit from Harry
Winkle's barrow in Berwick Street Market?" You say you did. Why
not? There's nothing to be ashamed of in wearing a suit made for
a peer of the realm. "A-ha!" he cried, "it was stolen from Messrs
Murgatroyd and Winterbottom. Remove it. Take it off. At once.
This instant. It is the law." So you take it off. In the middle of Park
Lane as you are escorting your good lady to tea at the Ritz. Appreciate the horror. The grief. The vexation. And he marches you to
Vine Street in your underwear and you are not only charged with
receiving stolen property within the meaning of the Act, but also
with indecent exposure.'

'What a shocking thing!' my mother exclaimed. 'You could
catch your death of cold.'

My mother had been only half-listening to the conversation:
she was far more interested in the Coopermans' sitting-room
with its walnut veneer table, chairs and sideboard, cut moquette
sofa, sewing machine, large mahogany-framed mirrors, mantel
clock and grandfather clock, and the gramophone on top of an
upright piano. Now, as Mrs Cooperman, in a crimson cloche hat
and yellow dress, brought in tea and cakes, she said: 'You musical,
Mrs Cooperman?'

'Not so much me as my Leonard. We got a lovely collection
records. My Leonard gets cut-price. The piano I don't play, but it's
nice to have one, no? Classy.'

'I, too, got records,' said my mother. 'But no gramophone.
She took a cake. 'Valuable records. Worth a lot of money. But no
gramophone. Maybe I could play them on yours some time.'

'Any time,' said Mrs Cooperman.

'The food of love,' said her husband.

'The food of love?' my mother echoed, staring startled at her
cake.

'Music, Mrs Ashe, music,' said Leonard Cooperman.

My mother grunted, felt the cake's texture, sniffed and took a
cautious bite. "Very nice, Mrs Cooperman. Light like a feather. I
see you're very fond of almond essence.'

'Not essence,' said Mrs Cooperman, 'real ground almonds. My Leonard gets wholesale. If you want some, just ask.'

Mendel banged his fist on the arm of his chair. 'Pickled cucumbers, Mrs Cooperman. Take my word for it – pickled cucumbers.'

Both Coopermans stared at my uncle. 'What cucumbers?' asked Leonard.

'Don't eat pickled cucumbers at night, Mrs Cooperman,' said Mendel. 'I know from experience.'

'I never eat cucumbers, day or night, Mr Abrams. Never. They give me indigestion.'

'No? In that case the *lokshen* pudding.'

'*Lokshen* pudding?' said the bewildered Mrs Cooperman. 'I haven't made for donkey's years. My Leonard isn't all that fond of it. But why suddenly cucumbers and *lokshen* pudding?'

'They cause dreams.'

'Dreams?' said Mrs Cooperman, puzzled. 'Dreams? . . . Aaaah, *dreams*! Take no notice. I get nervous, that's all. Isn't it so, Lennie—'

Her husband nodded vigorously. 'Yes indeed. My Esther's very sensitive. Delicate. Easily upset. Highly strung. She takes things to heart. She told me, Mrs Ashe, how good you were to her this morning. I appreciate it.'

My mother shrugged. 'So long there's nothing to worry about it's all right. So long it's not dangerous.'

Mrs Cooperman reddened. Her husband patted her hand. Silence – until Mendel said: 'Mrs Cooperman, seeing your sewing machine gives me an idea. A wonderful idea. Them watchstraps. Why don't you sew them together and make handbags? Crocodile bags – if they are crocodile – can be worth a fortune. Harrods would buy all you can make. It stands to reason. You could become a big manufacturer.'

Leonard Cooperman shook his head. 'Not for me, Mr Abrams. I'm a watchmaker. A worker. A toiler. An artisan. What little talent the Lord blessed me with is in my fingers. I'm not a businessman.

'Selling the watchstraps is different. That I must do to make up my wages. As it says in Leviticus: "The wages of a hired man shall not abide with thee all night until morning". But me, I didn't get my wages at all. Instead I got watchstraps, and as you know it says in the Talmud that it breaks many laws to give a worker goods instead of wages.'

'But one must make allowances. The man went bankrupt. It was the will of God.'

Mendel snorted. 'The will of God that a man should go bankrupt! If a man's not a businessman he's not a businessman. Why drag God into it?'

'What my brother says is true,' my mother added forcefully. 'How can everything be the will of God? Is it the will of God I should lose my husband and live like a beggar? Is it His will your wife should have her dreams or the Jews should be persecuted by Hitler? – may he have a black year. A funny God we got, according to you.'

Leonard Cooperman gave a sad little smile. 'This,' he said patiently, 'is the destiny of the Jews. It is our fate, written in Heaven, to wander the face of the earth until Messiah comes and leads His people to the Promised Land.' Wagging a finger: 'But . . . but . . . He will only come when we down here are ready. And we get ready, we prepare, by suffering. It is our destiny, Mrs Ashe. It is our historic destiny to suffer. But there must be joy in our suffering, Mrs Ashe. Joy. Joy to be chosen as the instruments of God's will.'

Slowly my mother nodded her head. 'Believe me, if suffering is the way to get to Heaven they must be reserving me the best hotel they got.' She gave a mocking laugh. 'But joy as well, yet! A fat lot of joy I got in my life. What's there to be so joyful about? I should make a song and dance because that way I'll get to Heaven? In the meantime a fortnight at Westcliff wouldn't do no harm.'

Mendel thrust out his lower lip and nodded sagely. 'Me, I'm not a good Jew as I'd like to be. My father was a good Jew. A whatchercallit – a scholar. In the synagogue he was given a seat on the east wall. But in this day and age it isn't so easy. When you're competing against the rest of the world you've to do things their way. It stands to reason.'

Leonard Cooperman sighed. 'Sometimes I think we'd have been better off if our parents had stayed in Poland and Russia. There was persecutions, pogroms, but at least they could live like proper Jews. They used to say the West had only impure ideas; that it would be the ruin of the Jews. Maybe they weren't so wrong. They lived poor and died under the Cossacks, but they died good Jews.'

My mother's eyes flashed. 'There were no bad Jews? And if there were they didn't die? Like, I suppose, Hitler – may his kidneys fester – asks if they're good or bad Jews before he kills them. So some will go to Heaven. Marvellous! Wonderful! But in the meantime is it such a crime to want to live?'

I sidled from the room and went in search of one or another of my friends. I did not have to go far: Sholto Popplewell was in the square lazily tossing stones at the pigeons.

He was a tall, thin-faced boy with sharp, restless eyes, a twitching mouth and an endless fund of dirty stories, the point of which I seldom grasped (and, looking back, I doubt if he fully understood either). On this occasion he had with him a small, black-bound book with red-edged pages called *The Works of Aristotle*. The Victorian printing was small and over-inked, almost impossible to read, but Sholto was interested only in the illustrations: line drawings, sinister in their clumsy execution, of the cross-section of wombs showing the foetus in varying stages of development; male and female genitalia; a wide variety of monster births, and similar information which 'Every Married Lady and Gentleman Should Know . . . Compiled by an Eminent American Professor . . . Approved by Bishops and the Medical Profession . . . Not Suitable Reading for the Unmarried or the Young'.

I shook my head in disbelief and walked away. I knew there was no truth in suggestions that my origins had anything to do with gooseberry bushes, the doctor's black bag or the stork, and I was aware that women's bellies did come into it somehow – but I refused to believe that there could be any connexion between my presence on earth and this grotesquery.

The problem nagged at me all that night and most of the following day – until, upon my return from school I mustered my courage and asked my mother: 'Where do I come from?'

My mother, who was preparing tea at the time, flushed and trembled. 'What do you mean, where you come from? You're here, aren't you? Isn't that enough?'

'But you've got to come from somewhere,' I persisted. 'You've got to be born.'

In her agitation my mother poured hot water over a tray of biscuits. 'Look what you've made me do!' She swung a blow at my head. Attempting to dodge it I knocked a freshly sliced salt herring to the floor. 'Get out of here!' she screamed. 'I've no time for your mad talk.' (Any subject that she did not wish to discuss with her children brought the response 'I've no time for your mad talk' as automatically as 'Bless you' to a sneeze.)

'I only asked where I came from.'

'How should I know? Now leave me in peace. And no more mad talk.' I backed out of the kitchen as my mother knelt on the floor, her grey hair falling over her face as she grabbed viciously at segments of herring.

I took the problem to Ruth. She burst into tears and ran towards the kitchen, howling: 'Mummy! Simon's being filthy.' I fled from the house and went in search of Herbert Levinson who knew the answer to everything.

If anyone asked what his father did for a living, Herbert replied, on parental advice: 'He's a cigarette manufacturer.' This was true in that Jack Levinson collected dog-ends which he re-rolled in a Rizla machine and sold at five a penny – an occupation which provided a valuable conversational source for my mother and her friends. Firstly it was agreed that everyone who smoked in public (threw cigarette-ends on the pavement) was consumptive – 'So what sort of work is this; spreading disease? He's a monster. A Finklestein. He should be reported to the council.' It was known 'for a fact' that he had an arrangement with all large West End hotels, cinemas and theatres to collect their cigarette-ends, and it was also known 'on good authority' that his wife and children worked day and night without food or sleep manufacturing cigarettes – another matter about which the council should be informed. It was agreed among my mother and her cronies that half the cigarettes smoked in London had their origins on the pavements of Swiss Cottage and Kilburn or in West End ashtrays. 'Some must have been rolled over and over, a thousand times. They must be hundreds of years old already.'

Herbie was my own age, but since he spent most of his time peering myopically into gutters and along pavements he was already so round-shouldered people touched his back for luck. I found him in Maida Vale clutching the inevitable carrier bag in which he collected his cigarette-ends. 'Where you come from? Everybody knows that,' he said contemptuously. He launched into a long and lurid explanation punctuated with sudden downward swoops and cries of 'Look – an Abdullah Turkish', or 'Marvellous – a whole half Black Cat'. According to Herbie, the process of reproduction involved rituals of such an ingenious and dramatic nature that the survival of the human race must have depended upon tireless contortionists of remarkable anatomical construction and with mental processes of a singularly horrific nature.

I also sought advice from Mervyn Tsimmus, the rabbi's son, but his only comment was: 'Like the rest of us, you come from God. Where else?'

On my way home I encountered Mrs Kemensky and asked her for confirmation of this last assertion. I should have known better, even at that age.

The old woman, bent and toothless, gold-rimmed spectacles balanced halfway down a carrot of a nose, gave a gasping, asthmatic laugh like the dying gasp of a soda syphon. 'Come from God?' she mocked. 'If there was a God would you have been born into this world at all, with its misery and wickedness? God? You should go on your hands and knees and thank God there isn't one.'

When the facts of life were finally mine I was at a loss to understand my mother's reluctance to admit their existence, since the family was a huge one and there was almost always one or another of its members involved in some stage of the breeding ritual: betrothing, marrying, aborting, carrying, miscarrying, bearing or circumcising.

For my mother the family was real, yet abstract; an attitude as well as a fact, in the manner of The Monarchy or The Empire. Its size was such that since my mother bore only two children Granny Abrams considered her barren: in the family a woman had to have a minimum of four children to qualify as a mother. The fact that my father died soon after my birth in no way modified this tenet of faith.

Granny Abrams was certainly a mother. She had produced thirteen children, eleven of whom had reached maturity, married and procreated at a prodigious rate. The resultant confusion of aunts, uncles, cousins, second and third cousins, cousins various times removed and tenuous relatives by marriage persists to this day when an aged stranger will stop me in the street and be mortally offended in that I don't recognize him as Alf Bloom who is in the gowns and whose nephew by marriage married my second cousin, Eva. 'Fancy not knowing your own family. You should be ashamed of yourself.'

Because the family was defined to embrace such distant and complicated relationships there were members whom even my mother did not know, or had forgotten. Thus the drama of Miriam Minsk.

She came one day to visit Pearl Weinberg who had been a friend of her now dead daughter, Rosie, and stayed to join the other women for a talk under the elm tree. At one point the conversation turned to the probability of war and my mother mentioned that her parents came from Cracow, and that she had uncles, aunts and cousins there whom she had never seen but who would certainly be put into concentration camps if the Germans invaded.

'What name would they be?' asked Mrs Minsk.

'All sorts of names I suppose. My mother was a Glickstein before she married. My father, God rest his soul, was Aaron Abramson before they came to England. Now its Abrams. More English.'

'Abrams, *Schmabrams!*' said Mrs Lewis. 'For my part if you've got a face like the map of Jerusalem what difference if you call yourself George Fifth? Someone will maybe believe it?'

Mrs Minsk waved an impatient hand. 'Please do me a favour and let me get a word in edgeways . . . You say your mother was Glickstein. Not Cissie Glickstein?'

My mother looked hard at the old woman and nodded.

'Tell me. Did she by any sort of a chance have a brother, Laban? A printer from books?'

My mother frowned, puzzled and suspicious. Then she nodded again. 'I've heard talk of him. But how would you know?'

Excited, Mrs Minsk wriggled in her chair and tapped a finger against the side of her nose. 'And there was another brother, Meir, at the slaughterhouse. And a sister. What was her name – the tiny one with the moles? Aie, aie, I'm getting so old I can't remember . . . When you get to my age you need a memory, but you get robbed of it . . . Leah. That was it.'

My mother sat pale and quivering. 'What is this? Witchcraft?'

Mrs Minsk banged her hands on her knees. 'It's the strangest coincidence that ever happened. Coincidence? What am I saying? It's a miracle. A miracle from God.'

Angry now, my mother shouted: 'What are you talking about?' More calmly, as the truth came to her: 'You mean you knew them in Cracow? You remember from all those years?'

'Remember? Listen. Your uncle, Israel the milkman, married Esther Schwartz. Esther was my third cousin on my father's side. So how would I forget? . . . Don't you see? We're cousins!'

Mrs Weinberg, Mrs Lewis and Mrs Cooperman burst into tears. Mrs Weinberg spluttered and gasped as though being strangled. Mrs Lewis' crying was quiet and controlled, accompanied by delicate sniffs, gentle sighs and thick rivulets of mascara. Mrs Cooperman, on the other hand, was a weeper of the old school: the lusty, lung-torturing, bosom-clasping, rocking-on-the-heels bawler who really comes into her own at Jewish weddings. Then Mrs Kemensky: her wheezing croak unnervingly like her laugh. Inevitably, my mother joined in: massive sobs of joy as distinct from her monotonic wail of misery. Finally Mrs Minsk's face crumpled into a cobweb of folds and wrinkles, and her weeping was the most disturbing of all: absolutely silent.

Next morning, a Sunday, my mother took Ruth and I to Granny Abrams to confirm Mrs Minsk's story. Apart from other considerations, my mother was fiercely proud of the family and wasn't going to let anyone join it solely on the strength of their own say so. (When a relative announced his or her intention of marrying, my mother was the principal counsel for the prosecution when it came to arguing the undesirability or unsuitability of the match.

She may have seen the prospective bride or groom only once or twice, but this in no way inhibited her or tempered her onslaught. 'How do I know? I know, that's all. I feel it. Isn't that enough?' Fortunately for the continuance of the family it seldom was enough.)

At the mention of Miriam Minsk's name, Granny Abrams swayed as though about to faint. 'She still alive? I don't believe it.' She collapsed into an armchair and it was fully three minutes before she could speak, during which time my mother just stared at her, hypnotized, while Ruth and I clung to one another, terrified.

When Granny Abrams opened her mouth again it was to say 'No, wait a minute. I do believe it. The devil looks after his own.' She spat three times to ward off the Evil Eye. 'She should be dead, mind you. Dead and buried and rotting.' At this point she went off into a long stream of Yiddish of which I understood only a few familiar phrases: burying alive, rats in the bowels, suffocation, fits, boils in the mouth, leprosy and the angel of death.

In English she continued: 'When I first knew her she was Miriam Rosenfeldt. The daughter from a mad dealer in grain. When she married that no-good Minsk they came to Cracow. He couldn't find work as a bookbinder so your father – may he be happy in Paradise – gave him a job in the workshop. We was in the tailoring then. We treated them like our own. I should have so many thousands in the bank as meals they ate with us. God in Heaven!'

'So what happened?' asked my mother.

'What happened? Don't ask what happened. One night when we was all asleep in bed that Minsk breaks down the door, steals every inch of cloth, every yard of lining, goose irons and scissors, and they run away with the money. That's what happened. To England they run, only I'd always thought it was to America.'

'But perhaps the wife, Mrs Minsk, knew nothing about it.'

My grandmother's look was withering. 'That idiot could think of it by himself? He'd have the nerve? She put him up to it. She was behind it all. She was always the one with the brains . . . So you're surprised I'm sorry she's not dead already?'

My mother bit her lip. 'How come I've never heard you tell this story before? All the years you never mentioned it once.'

'I shouldn't have told you now if you hadn't said her name.'

'So why the secret?'

Granny Abrams sighed. 'Because,' she said wearily, 'how do you think things were for us? Did we have money in the bank? Were we the Tsar or Count Potocki? We owed everybody money, and on top of that no stock. So what could we do? . . . I'll tell you what we did. We took a leaf from that Minsk's tree. Aaron got a job with Pinkus and stole *his* stock. Then *we* run away to England.' She smiled at the memory.

As a sort of conditioned reflex to her shocked astonishment my mother turned and smacked my face. 'You shouldn't be listening.'

My grandmother sat for a while, smiling and silent. Then: 'So Miriam's still alive. All these years we never heard a word. She's the same age as me. What does she look like now?'

'How can you compare? She looks twenty years older than you. She's an old woman. The same age? I don't believe it. You could pass for her daughter.'

'So that's good. And the husband?'

'Mrs Weinberg said he passed away when he was only fifty.'

'Serves him right,' said my grandmother with some satisfaction. 'Miriam . . . Fancy . . . After all these years.'

She sat nodding, her lips moving silently, her thoughts many years and miles away. Finally she grunted and said briskly: 'Minnie, why don't you bring her for a cup of tea next Sunday? Make some of your *gefulte* fish and maybe a bit of chopped herring and a few biscuits. Eh? Bring her over.' She lifted her skirt. Between her dress and her linen petticoat she wore a canvas apron divided into two pockets: her bank. She fumbled in one pocket and pulled out a ten-shilling note which she gave to my mother 'towards the fish'. Then remembering, she searched in the other pocket until she found a sixpence 'for Ruthie and Simey'.

I was never to see my mother as bewildered as at that moment. Taking the ten-shilling note she stared at Granny Abrams and said in a voice that was almost hysterical: 'Bring her over? You want I should bring her over? But you . . . After all you've said? After all she's done, you . . . you still want to see her?'

My grandmother shrugged and spread her hands. 'What else

can you do? After all, she's one of the family, isn't she?'

I did not attend the reunion since it was thought that the uncertainty of its outcome made the occasion unsuitable for children. My mother left home nervous and irritable, complaining of palpitations. She returned with heartburn (Aunt Zillah's red cabbage) and mild bewilderment.

'I thought there would be blue murder, but after a few minutes they kissed each other! They said to let bygones be bygones. After all, as Mother said, it was a long time ago. She was young. People make mistakes. Now your grandmother thinks it's funny. You should have seen her laugh! She said you got to see the funny side of it . . . So there you are. Who's to argue? If she wants to be friends, who am I to say otherwise?' My mother looked at me challengingly, as though daring me to contradict her. 'And it was such a pleasure for your grandmother to find someone still alive she knew in the old days. Someone she could talk to about old times. Then they started crying. Oh, how they cried! About the old days, the people they knew, the people who died.' My mother gave a long groan of a sigh. 'Laughing, then crying – the history of the Jews.

'It's a strange business, just the same. Like they say in Yiddish: if you live long enough you'll see everything . . . But she seems a nice enough woman, so let it all be forgotten. Forgive and forget. Live and let live.'

'But she was a thief,' I said. 'That can be forgiven?'

My mother glared at me. 'When you was a baby you wet the bed. You want I should remind you all your life? We all make mistakes. Now she's sorry. What more do you want? Blood? In any case, if your grandmother is prepared to forget who are you to interfere? You become God Almighty all of a sudden? So no more mad talk. Understand?' To make certain I did understand she struck me across the head.

Angrily I shouted back at her: 'What about Aunt Sarah and Ada? Why don't you forgive and forget there?' I prepared to run from the kitchen but my mother assumed what Ruth and I called her Queen of Sheba pose: body erect, shoulders back, chin up, eyes half closed. 'That,' she said, in her haughtiest voice, 'is different. Neither your aunt or your cousin has said sorry. There's been no apology.' Reverting to normal: 'So shut your big mouth in future, you cheeky know-all.'

During supper Ruth said to my mother: 'It's weird how things work out. I mean, if Mrs Minsk hadn't done what she did and Granny hadn't done what she did, they might never have come to England, I mean, we might still be in Poland. We wouldn't be English, but Poles.'

My mother put down her soup spoon and sat for a moment absorbing this. 'I hadn't thought of that,' she said finally. 'It hadn't crossed my mind. So in a way what the Minsk woman did was a *good* thing, no? Just imagine if we'd been born in Poland! Where would we all be now?' She sat clicking her teeth in wonder – until she suddenly collapsed into a fit of wild, body-quivering laughter. She tried to speak but it was perhaps five minutes before she was able to explain: 'I don't know *where* we'd be, but even if we was in prison or the workhouse or in hospital or eaten by rats or being murdered in our beds we'd be enjoying every minute of it. We'd be as happy as angels. If you don't believe me, go ask Mr Cooperman.'

Five

INCLUDED AMONG my mother's natural enemies were all landlords, Lithuanians and council officials, policemen, our neighbour Angus McKenzie – and Jack Hobson, the local vet.

My mother's hatred of the latter sprang in part from the fact that she insisted upon calling him Jacobson and was outraged when he denied being a Jew. 'When I asked him which synagogue he goes to he said he's a Gentle. Gentle! With a name like Jacobson? Who's he kidding? So every Jew in Germany should say he's a Gentle. "Me Rabbi Jacobson? A diabolical liberty! I'm Rabbi Gentle." So maybe Hitler would give him a five-pound note. Let that lousy vet go tell Hitler he's a Gentle. Let him tell Mosley.'

I attempted to explain. 'His first name is Jack. His second name is Hobson. Jack . . . Hobson. Not Jacobson.'

'So you take his side! An anti-Semite in my own house! For what is God punishing me? That's all I want to know: what for? Just say.' She was silent for a moment as though awaiting an answer. Then, to me: 'Now get out of here. And no more mad talk. No more, do you hear?' – with a mighty backhander across my face by way of emphasis.

The main reason for my mother's detestation of Jack Hobson was that he had been paid 'good English money' to doctor our cat, Itchky, but had patently failed to do so. 'Otherwise why should he stay out all night like he was some sex maniac? If a cat is doctored it stays home. It doesn't want to be a dirty stop-out. It's got respect. But if it wasn't doctored proper, you can't blame the cat, can you? After all, it's got its feelings. It's only human. It's that lousy vet that's the blame.'

Motivating these outbursts was my mother's pathological fear of mice. She was convinced that a vast army of them, each as large as a greyhound, lurked somewhere beneath the floorboards and that one day, the moment the cat disappeared through the front door or the window, they would strike. 'We'll be eaten alive in our beds. Then that lousy vet will be sorry. I'll sue him for every penny.'

Sometimes, seeing the cat calculating the distance between itself and licentious freedom, my mother would ask Ruth or me to close the window – the request made in Yiddish so that the cat wouldn't understand.

She spent her waking – and supposedly sleeping – hours listening for noises under the floorboards, periodically banging on the lino with a coal shovel to keep the mice at bay. To the resultant complaints from the neighbours my mother had one stock reply: 'Go complain to the lousy Gentle, the rotten toerag.'

As an added precaution mousetraps, enticingly baited with salt herring, chicken bones and stewed prunes were laid indiscriminately about our flat: in the lavatory and in wardrobes, under beds and chairs, on shelves and tables. I cannot remember them ever catching a mouse (proving to my mother that the vermin of Daffodil Square were possessed of a singular cunning), but I do recall a succession of bruised, bleeding and near-amputated toes and fingers.

One thing was certain: if the mice could dodge the traps they could surely have evaded Itchky, a slow-witted, slow-moving tabby who lived in fat and salivating melancholy on a diet of cheese cake, chopped liver, *strudel* and *lokshen* soup.

On the rare occasions that Itchky was ill my mother refused to consult another vet, but cured him herself with huge portions of soup and dismissed with a neck-swallowing shrug the astonished praise of our neighbours. 'After all, it's all goodness. It's pure. So why shouldn't it make him better?'

The most militant complainant against my mother's mouse-scaring tactics was the kilted Angus McKenzie, a long, lean, bloodhound-faced civil servant who lived on the second floor. Although the occupants of the flats on either side of us and on the ground and first floors grumbled with weary, almost formal, regularity at the muffled thuds that filtered through to them, it seemed that because of some acoustical freak my mother's lino-beating reached McKenzie, not as a distant drumbeat, but a plangent, ear-shattering reverberation that made him imagine he was living inside a nightmarish belfry. McKenzie protested that while this was bad enough during normal waking hours, to have to endure 'that Kosher cacophony' at 3.30 in the morning 'was beyond the endurance of a decent Christian body'.

The Scot grew progressively more truculent until one morning, as we were going out, he shouted from his window: 'Shut yer blewdy row, yer noisy waman! Can't a body have some peace and quiet? Go back to yer own blewdy country and make yer noise there!'

My mother screamed in reply: 'How dare you, you wicked man! This *is* my country. I was born here. I'm English. You're not. So go back to *your* country, you dirty foreigner!' McKenzie's face turned blue before it disappeared behind the curtains.

He then tried to organize a petition among the other, non-Jewish residents in the square, but most were involved with more important problems, were unaware of my mother's activities with the shovel, or disapproved of the motives behind McKenzie's agitations. He was not a popular figure in the neighbourhood. His next move was to write a letter to Harry Jaye in which he took great pains to point out that he had nothing against my mother personally, since some of his best friends were Jews, but . . . Whereupon our landlord wrote back giving McKenzie a month's notice to quit.

It was not the easiest of months. McKenzie took to wearing a black shirt and tie with his kilt, tied to his sleeve a homemade brassard decorated with a lightning flash in a circle, and when the women were under the elm tree he would goose-step around the square giving the Fascist salute and shouting 'Madagascar for the Jews!' or 'Go back to Palestine!'

'I wish we could,' said Mrs Lewis, and reported Angus McKenzie's behaviour to the police, They said they could do nothing about it: for some technical reason it did not constitute a breach of the peace. My mother was not surprised. 'The police,' she said contemptuously. 'They're all in it together. Didn't I always say so?' Mrs Kemensky consulted a man who once nearly worked for a solicitor. He spoke vaguely of injunctions, actions in the civil court and solicitors' letters, but argued that since McKenzie would be

leaving soon it would be simpler to be patient and await his departure. 'Lawyers!' my mother sneered. 'They're all in it together.
Didn't I always say so? . . . The dirty toerags. The robbers. Stink-
pots. Buried in the earth they should be – police, lawyers, the lot.
A black year they should have. Their children should be born blind
and crippled.'

But all her invective and fury could not hide her basic bewilderment. 'Everywhere there's Hitlers, anti-Semitism, persecution,
pogroms. Even in my own street . . . Why? What for? What have
we done to deserve it? What have we done? Am I such a wicked
woman to have to suffer like this? Are my children criminals? . . .
Aie, aie, aie . . . If only my husband was alive he'd know what to
do. But I'm a widow – a punishment in itself. But a punishment
for what? If only I had some idea what I done, what I'm being
made to pay for. I ask a million times. But who can answer? . . .
So am I supposed to be trodden on by that Mosley in a skirt? Am
I a doormat? There must be something to be done. Some way of
stopping him . . .' A cry of triumph. 'Mendel! He'll know what to
do. I'll ask Mendel. I should have thought of it before.'

I was filled with foreboding.

When I first encountered anti-Semitism at school I became involved in several fights, all of which I lost. I did not tell my mother
the reason for these beatings, since I did not wish to add to the
aggravation, heartburn and palpitations brought on by my torn
and bloodied appearance. Instead she assumed I had been fighting
because I was: 'A wild animal. A ruffian. A Cossack. One day you'll
kill yourself, just to annoy me. As if I didn't have enough to put up
with.' And I would receive a further salvo of blows upon my head
and shoulders. So I asked the advice of Uncle Mendel when we
were out for a walk in the East End one afternoon.

He stopped and ruminated. 'Beatings yet. That's bad. But don't
be ashamed, you understand? There's nothing wrong with being
a Jew. I've been one myself for years. It stands to reason . . . But
if you fight and always lose, that's not good either. You don't win
ever? Not even once?'

'How can I?' I protested. 'At school there's a few Jewish boys.
But there's hundreds of them. Thousands.'

'Thousands?' My uncle stroked his moustache and we walked on in silence through Old Montague Street and Wentworth Street, up Brick Lane into Fashion Street. There Uncle Mendel stopped and gave an excited bellow. 'I've got it, Simey; I got it! Now listen careful. What I want you should do is this. When any of these bastard anti-Semites insult you I want you should reply this to them: "I am a Jew, and proud of it, too". Make them ashamed from themselves. You understand? Make them feel small. "I am a Jew, and proud of it, too." Got it? I want you should repeat it until you got it by heart perfect. Say it.'

I whispered: 'I am a Jew, and . . . er . . . proud of it, too.'

'Louder!' Mendel thundered.

'Here? In the street?'

'So why not? In Commercial Street of all places you *are* ashamed of being a Jew? So say it.'

I said it in my normal speaking voice.

'Louder!' Mendel thundered.

'I am a Jew, and proud of it, too!'

'That's better. Now again.'

People were looking at us. I shut my eyes, held Uncle Mendel's arm and yelled it over and over, not daring to open my eyes until I heard him turn the key in the front door at Zanzibar Terrace.

At school during the next few days, whenever I saw my enemies approaching, I uttered the mighty and desperate cry: 'I am a Jew, and proud of it, too' – and was rewarded with the most savage thrashings I was ever to suffer.

Now my mother was to raise the subject of McKenzie's anti-Semitism with Uncle Mendel and I paled at the thought of the slogans we would be required to howl across Daffodil Square, and trembled at the possible outcome.

But there was to be no defiant doggerel from Mendel. Instead my mother unburdened herself to Uncle Ben when he dropped in on his way back from Willesden where he'd collected a hundred glass lavatory seats for his brother.

Ben listened, motionless and silent, his mouth half open until my mother's story came to its breathless end. Then, in a quiet, emotionless voice he said: 'The pig-dog. The Mosleyite filth. The dirty rotten bum-boy.' He lighted a cigarette. 'He works during the day and only starts in the evenings and weekends, is that it?'

'If the weather's nice and we're outside.'

'It's evening. It's nice. Maybe he's there now.'

'And if he is?'

Ben said calmly: 'I give him a good hiding. Hit him. Bang, bang! He'll remember all his life. Break every bone in his body. Cripple the lousy dog's dropping.'

I went wide-eyed with excitement and wonder: this was a side of Uncle Ben I had never encountered. My mother was appalled. 'Fighting? Like a common hooligan? God forbid! I'm sorry I said anything. Fighting, yet! Don't you dare do such a thing. So sure I should live I won't let you. I take my dying oath on it.'

'Why?'

'It's not nice, fighting like a ruffian. It's . . . well, it's not nice. What about the neighbours? You'll cause ructions. Anyway, you could get hurt. McKenzie (may he get cancer) is a young man. Big like a horse. Strong like an ox. You got a hernia, remember?'

Ben clenched huge fists. 'Don't worry, the work I do needs strength, believe me.'

'Please Ben, no. Wait better until we've talked to Mendel.'

Ben looked slyly at my mother. 'And he'll tell you about a picture he saw with Rin-Tin-Tin . . . Leave it to me.'

'You're mad.'

Ben grinned and nodded his head. 'That's what they say. I'm the dummy. Potty. So let me get on with it.'

My mother bit her knuckles. 'You'll get killed. There'll be police, ambulances. You'll be arrested. Go to prison. Fighting like a common guttersnipe.'

Ben patted her shoulder. 'I don't know this McKenzie. He don't know me. He don't know I'm your brother or nothing. So a perfect stranger hits him. Goes away. Who's the wiser?'

My mother took Ben's hand. 'Darling, I know you mean well. But he'll be moving soon. For thousands of years the Jews have put up with anti-Semitism. We can't wait another fortnight?'

Ben gave a sad smile. 'When he moves he won't be anti-Semitic no more? These people don't change . . . Teach a lesson he won't forget in a hurry. I know better than you, better than Mendel. They say I'm a bit soft. A bit missing up there. But these *scheisspot* Blackshirts I know from Ridley Road, Cable Street, Clissold's Park. You got to hit back. Bricks they use. Socks filled with sand. So hit back. Bang, bang! A lesson. Bang, bang! Then they'll know.'

Tears came to my mother's eyes. 'All right, do what you want. But first have something to eat. A drop of barley soup. I made from three pounds of bones. Strong like iron.'

'Later,' said Ben.

'But you mustn't fight on an empty stomach. It's dangerous.'

'Later,' Ben repeated, and went to the front door.

We trooped after him. My mother took Ruth's arm. 'You boil a kettle of water and prepare iodine, bandages, boracic lint – everything. And put a light under the soup.'

Ruth protested: 'But I want to see what happens!'

'Meanwhile your uncle bleeds to death! No arguing. Do like I say.'

Grumbling, Ruth turned back. My mother paused a moment, then followed her, reappearing with a rolling pin. By the time we reached the top of the area steps Ben was shuffling round the square. I followed him while my mother went to join Mrs Lewis and Mrs Kemensky who were sitting under the elm tree; one knitting, the other peeling potatoes.

Ben went round the square half a dozen times, with me trailing a few yards behind and the women chattering and gesticulating, until McKenzie appeared from number 18, tying his brassard to his arm. When it was fixed he raised his arm in the Nazi salute and began goose-stepping.

Ben reached in an inside pocket, took out his row of Great War medals and pinned them to his lapel. He did not vary his pace until he came to McKenzie when he stopped and said: 'You don't do that salute proper. Sir Oswald wouldn't like. You do like this.' And his right fist came up from his thigh in a mighty uppercut.

As Ben swung McKenzie must have leaned forward: the blow did not connect with his chin but with his mouth. The Scot uttered a dreadful scream and fell back, his body absolutely rigid, so that had his head hit the pavement he would almost certainly have smashed his skull. But he skidded round on one heel and fell face first into a bush, where he lay twitching and gurgling.

The women ran across to us.

Mrs Kemensky: 'A pleasure to watch, Mr Abrams; a real pleasure.'

My mother: 'Ben, what have you done? Is he really dead?'

Mrs Lewis: 'Serve him right if he is.'

Ben: 'He's all right, that's all. Bang, bang! I'll kick in a few ribs.'

My mother shrieked: 'God help us all!' She grabbed Ben's arm to drag him away and screamed again. 'Your hand! What's the matter with your hand? What is it?'

Ben lifted his arm. Embedded deeply in his knuckles, red with blood, were McKenzie's upper dentures. Ben stared at them, fascinated. 'Teeth, yet.' He winced as he pulled them free, causing the blood to pour down his fingers. He put the teeth in his pocket ('Maybe Mendel can sell them') and tied a dirty handkerchief round his hand.

'Come quickly,' my mother cried. 'Come and let me put on iodine. Bandage it proper. Drink a bowl of barley soup. I made it special. Full of bones. Come . . . Come . . . Better than all the medicines. All pure. Hurry, there isn't a second to lose.'

'Don't be silly,' said Ben. 'Here when he wakes up? If he sees me come from your place he'll know. I'll go to a chemist and get a bandage. Don't worry . . . You sure I shouldn't kick him a few times?'

'You must have disinfectant on that hand,' my mother howled. 'With a pig like that who knows what he eats? What poisons he carries in his mouth? It could get in your blood and cause consumption. I read in a book.'

Ben pulled himself free. 'I must go. He's moving.'

There was indeed a rustling in the bush. Ben went to his barrow and pushed it along the road. The rest of us scurried to the entrance of Mrs Kemensky's house and clutched at each other as we watched McKenzie stagger to his feet, sobbing and gasping, blood dribbling down his face, soaking his shirt. He limped towards number 18, moaning, and half-fell through the front door.

Mrs Kemensky pointed a trembling finger. Uncle Ben had stopped at the corner to watch McKenzie. Now he stood rigidly to attention, saluted with his bandaged hand and roared: 'Hang the Kaiser!' His salute became a wave, he picked up the handles of his barrow and disappeared around the corner.

It took my mother many hours and several bowls of soup to recover her composure. When she was near-normal I said: 'Uncle Ben's a very brave man, isn't he? Strong, too.'

My mother's eyes sparkled. 'Why not? He's your uncle, isn't he? Mine brother, an Abrams. So why shouldn't he be brave?' She gave a long and weary yawn. 'What a day! I never want to live through another like it. Fighting, yet, like common hooligans. I never thought there'd be such ructions outside my own doorstep.' She giggled. 'Try saying "Madagascar for the Jews" with no teeth. Just try . . . Ben gave him what for, eh? Your uncle gave that McKenzie bunions, no?' She bit her lip. 'On the other hand I hope there's no trouble. That's all we're short of – the police coming round, writs, court cases, the council. That's all I need, as if I didn't have enough aggravation.'

'Don't worry,' said Ruth. 'You heard what Uncle Ben said. McKenzie doesn't know him. He doesn't know he's your brother. So how can you be sued?'

'He'll find a way,' said my mother grimly. 'These swine-dogs always find a way . . . And we'll be the ones to suffer.' She grumbled on until, exhausted by the events of the day, her words dissolved into grunts and she dozed off in her chair. When she awoke she refused to go to bed, but insisted upon keeping watch all night with a poker on her lap.

The next day began with a visit from Mrs Cooperman whose sleep had been disturbed by a dream which contained not one, but two, symbols – safety pins and elbows: a combination so dreadful, so satanic and evil that Rabbi Klothboltz had been unable to bring himself to write down the full measure of its awful meaning.

My mother was in no mood for Mrs Cooperman's dreams. 'I got more important things to worry about. That McKenzie's gone out to work – so at least he's not dead, more's the pity – but suppose he comes back with a gang? It's still not too late for him to go to the police. So don't drive me potty with your dreams. It's what's going to happen while you're awake you should be worrying about.'

Mrs Cooperman shook her head. 'Don't worry. Nothing will happen.'

'Talk is cheap,' my mother retorted. 'And in any case you don't live here with that madman over your head. I do. I'm the one who'll suffer. And the children. It's my door that'll be broken down, not yours.'

Mrs Cooperman was quick to grasp the implications. 'Yes . . . Well . . . I must be going. My Leonard will be wondering what's happened to me. You're a nice lady, Mrs Ashe, but I must see my Leonard off to work.' She was already halfway through the door.

My mother called: 'At least you've got a husband to look after you.' She turned on Ruth and me, 'Go to work! Go to school! You'll be late. So hurry! Don't worry about me. So what if they kill me? I'll be better off out of it. It'll teach you both a lesson for the way you've treated me. When I'm dead you'll be sorry for the aggravation you're giving me.' She raised an arm. 'So what are you waiting for? If you come back and find I'm crippled for life just put me in the Home for Aged Jews or the workhouse and go stay with your grandmother (not that she hasn't enough to put up with) . . . So what are you hanging about for? Go!' With fierce cries and savage gestures she drove us from the flat.

I spent a worried morning at school and at lunchtime borrowed a penny from Sholto Popplewell in order to return home by bus. My mother was not in. It was raining, so no women sat in the square. By ringing doorbells I eventually found them all in Mrs Weinberg's front room, drinking lemon tea and eating biscuits.

McKenzie had returned. With three other men and a van. My mother had locked herself in the lavatory with a rolling pin and a bottle of iodine, and emerged only when she heard the unmistakable sounds of furniture being brought down the stairs.

'Done a bunk,' Mrs Weinberg explained to me. 'A flit.'

Mrs Kemensky asked: 'I wonder what rent he owes?'

My mother sniffed. 'Let the lousy landlord worry. So long he's gone . . . And to think it's all the fault of that filthy vet. If it wasn't for him none of this would have happened . . . Just the same, if he does owe rent then for once I feel sorry for that *verstinkener* landlord.'

She felt sorrier when he told her of McKenzie's parting gesture: he and his friends had smashed the washbasin and lavatory pan, scratched swastikas through the enamel of the bath, painted circled lightning flashes on the walls of every room, and had emptied their bowels and bladders on the floors. Tears filled Harry Jaye's eyes. 'It's not so much the money to put it right – although where's that coming from? – it's to think people can act in such a way. The effect on mine poor stomach I don't dare think about. The way I feel now I could do away with myself.'

'Have a bowl of *lokshen* soup,' said my mother. 'It works wonders for the stomach. Believe me, like they say in Yiddish: "Your health comes first – there's time to hang yourself later".'

Harry Jaye nodded gloomily and picked up his spoon.

'And to think,' said my mother for the thousandth time, 'to think that Jacobson is a Jew himself and was part of it. Can you imagine such a thing?'

Automatically I muttered: 'Hobson. Jack Hobson' – as I did that evening when my mother put the question to Leonard Cooperman.

'Perhaps he isn't Jewish,' said the watchmaker. 'Maybe his name really is Hobson. After all, what's in a name? as Shakespeare says. Do you know, dear lady, that in Scotland – or is it perhaps in Wales? – they've got Isaacs what isn't Jewish. They've also got Cohens, only they call themselves Cowans. So why shouldn't a Hobson be a Hobson?'

Unable to follow his reasoning, my mother frowned but said nothing.

'What's in a name?' Mr Cooperman repeated, warming to the subject. 'Yours was maybe Ashkenazi? Jews have funny names, Mrs Ashe, for all manner of reasons. Some make them more English when they come over here. Then again there was the time when Jews weren't allowed to have no surnames. Imagine! Consider! No surnames! But it was the law of the land years ago on the Continent (I'm not talking of England now, of course). So when they was allowed surnames some took their religious names like the Cohens and the Levys, and others the jobs they did like the

Silvermans, the Goldschmidts, the Schneiders, the Millers, the
Podeschwas. You understand me? Others took names from their
streets, like the Rothschilds. The name means Red Shield. They
lived in the Street of the Red Shield. Did you know that, Mrs Ashe?
So visualize! Ponder! The Rothschilds. The Royal Family among
Jews started with no surname. Impossible? But true. So what's in
a name?

'Then some took their father's names like Aaronson or
Mendelson or Abrahamson. Abraham-son. Son of Abraham. Do
I make myself clear?'

My mother uttered a loud and triumphant 'Ha!' and pointed an
accusing finger. 'So Jacobson isn't the son of Jacob? And even if it's
Hobson – and I'm not admitting anything, mind you – so isn't that
the son of Hob? And isn't "hob" Yiddish for "have"? So he's got a
proper Jewish name either way you look at it, no?'

Mr Cooperman appeared not to have heard. 'Then, sometimes
when they came over and arrived at London Docks, and the police
couldn't understand the names on their papers (they was written
in Polish or Russian or Yiddish) and the Jews themselves could
speak no English to answer the questions, so the immigration
made up names for them. And such names! You would not believe,
Mrs Ashe! You would not credit! You would not accept! I tell you,
Mrs Ashe, so sure my father's soul should be happy in Paradise,
there's one man living to this day in Higham's Park with a name
you'd never believe. Never!

'When he comes over his name was plain Simcha Bavecher, but
some clever dick on the boat, some smart alec, some know-all, tells
him to call himself by a more English name. Just what it was he
forgets now, but let's imagine, let's suppose for the sake of argument, let's pretend it was Smith or Robinson or Stanley Baldwin
or Jones. Say Jones. John Jones. So he's John Jones. OK? Only when
he reaches London he's so excited! After all, Mrs Ashe, he's away
from the pogroms, the Cossacks, the Jew-baiting. He's in England.
Freedom! Happiness! Joy! So what happens? In his excitement he
forgets his new name. His mind is a blank. It's gone! Finished! Over!
So when the man asks for it he bangs himself on the head and
says: "Already I've forgotten!" Only he says it in Yiddish: *"Schoin*

fergessen!" And so what happens? The immigration writes it down as Sean Fergusson. And so sure I should live, this little Yiddisher man from Czestochowa, a marvellously orthodox Jew, a button-maker who can't speak from two words of English, has got this Irisher name, Sean Fergusson.'

Ruth and I shrieked with laughter. Unsmiling, head forward, my mother glared at Leonard Cooperman. 'This is supposed to be a joke? If so, I'm telling you I'm in no mood.'

Mr Cooperman looked hurt. 'How can you suggest such a thing, Mrs Ashe? Is it a joke that a decent Jewish man should go through life with such a name? Not even a Jewish name?' He shook his head. 'Like I've said, once the Jews start to lose their Jewish-ness there's only disaster. Satan whispers in a man's ear that he shouldn't have a Jewish name – so now he's an Irisher . . . No, it's true, Mrs Ashe. He's living in Higham's Park at this very moment.'

My mother shrugged. 'So *Schoin Fergessen* changes his name to Sean Whatever, and Jacobson changes his to Jack Hobson. So what have you proved?'

Leonard Cooperman threw up his hands in despair. His wife said she'd put the kettle on.

Six

IN THE process of time and telling the Battle of Daffodil Square was to assume epic proportions, but for a while it was over-shadowed by a far more momentous event: the news that we were going to Westcliff for the day.

Moishe Sox, the son of Miriam Minsk's second cousin by marriage, had taken over a boarding house there, and my grandmother had been invited to visit him. Uncle Mendel, who had met Sox as a result of the famous lunch with Mrs Minsk, was to have accompanied his mother, but he and Sox were no longer on speaking terms: a confused story of a complicated deal involving cups and saucers Mendel supplied to Sox, only the cups fell away from the handles and one of the people at the boarding house had been scalded, but why should Mendel be blamed since the man he'd bought them from said he got them from the brother-in-law of the manufacturer who'd sworn they were as strong as iron, and anyway what did Sox expect for tuppence each, Wedgwood?

So my mother was to take Granny Abrams to Westcliff, and Ruth and I were to go with them, Mendel paying the fares.

The trip was announced on a Wednesday, and while my sister and I were certainly wildly excited at the thought of a day by the sea, for my mother the next three days were an agony of maddening suspense, tearful reminiscence and gloomy forebodings. 'Westcliff, after all these years. It's too good to be true. Something'll go wrong, you mark my words. One of you will break a leg, Just to annoy me. Or the train will crash. Everybody's so anti-Semitic these days you don't know which way to turn.'

There were frenzied preparations, in which particular my mother received much conflicting advice from her neighbourhood cronies. Her instructions finally boiled down to this:

'The seaside is the seaside so we'll want light clothes. Ruth, you wear the blue cotton with the short sleeves and I'll wear my green. But it can still get chilly later on, so we'll take cardigans and scarves just in case. You can never tell, and it's better to be safe than sorry. Simon, you'll take a pullover. Then it might rain, so you two take your Wellingtons and we'll all take our macs and I'll take an umbrella to be on the safe side. We'll take ordinary shoes for walking and you two take your plimsolls for the beach. Then we must take towels in case I want a hot sea bath. You know what I've always said about using strange towels. You never know who might have used them before and what diseases you can catch. Did you know most cancer is caught from towels? Mrs Kemensky told me. Her father was a rabbi so she must know. We also want towels in case you paddle in the sea – so Simon, make sure you wear socks without holes in; for once don't show me up and make me ashamed.'

In the absence of olive oil to ward off sunburn, my mother decided that frying oil was equally efficacious: 'After all, oil is oil.' Aspirin was vital in case of headaches, and a two-pound packet of washing soda was an essential in the event of insect bites – the quantity determined by Mrs Cooperman's warning that some mosquitoes were as big as roasting chickens and only a generous application of soda would save their victims from the most loathsome of unmentionable social diseases: 'After all, they live on blood – and who's to know what some people carry in their bloodstreams, God forbid?' Since my mother had grave doubts about anyone's cooking but her own, bicarbonate was obligatory, and a roll of toilet paper vital because, as my mother put it: 'You never know.'

The journey from Daffodil Square to Moishe Sox's would take nearly two hours – far too long a period to be spent without food. Allowing for the return journey, my mother prepared middle cuts of fried plaice, various sandwiches, *strudel*, cheese cake and biscuits, hard-boiled eggs and a Thermos of *lokshen* soup.

Nervous excitement prevented any of us from sleeping well on Friday night. At six-thirty on Saturday my mother, already dressed, urged Ruth and myself from our beds. 'Hurry up. You want we should miss the train?'

'But the train's not until eleven o'clock,' I protested.

'If I had my way we'd be catching it now. But your grand-mother's not such a young woman. Anyway, don't argue with your mother. Who knows best? Hurry.'

I hurried. I bathed and dressed in fifteen minutes and swallowed my breakfast in great indigestible gulps. My mother managed to squeeze the necessities for our journey into five large carrier bags, and at eight o'clock we were ready to leave. My mother made certain Itchky was indoors and locked the window and door of each room: 'In case from burglars.'

'We've got so much to steal?' asked my sister.

'All right, so we've nothing to steal. So we leave the door wide open with a printed notice: "Burglars come in and make yourself comfy". Is that what you want?'

The morning was warm and sunny, and inspired by the moment of the occasion, and infected with its excitement, my mother's friends were waiting at their doorsteps to wave us on our way, wish us well, and caution us not to forget to bring them back sticks of rock. My sister and I, embarrassed by their noisy shouts and laughter, wanted to hurry away, but my mother led us in slow and majestic procession through the square, acknowledging her cronies with gracious nods and gay flourishes of her umbrella.

Her moment of glory came to an end when the bottom dropped out of one of my carrier bags, scattering towels and smoked-salmon sandwiches over the pavement. The umbrella, at that moment, aloft, whistled down on my shoulder. I howled with pain. My sister ran from the square. My mother shrieked that I had done it on purpose. She stood in the road, arms outstretched, head raised to the cloudless heavens and asked: 'Why? What have I done to deserve it? Once in a blue moon I get the chance of going away for the day and this swine tries to ruin everything. Why? Just tell me. Just say.'

Mrs Lewis came running across with another carrier bag and ten minutes later we boarded a bus for Fenchurch Street Station.

We arrived an hour and a half early. Ruth and I sat eating sand-wiches and cakes on the theory that it would give us less to carry, while my mother went through a throat-clutching, platform-pacing ecstasy of heartache, convinced that Granny Abrams would miss the train. She arrived with twenty minutes to spare, and after Uncle Mendel had given Ruth and myself a shilling each and pressed a ten-shilling note into my mother's hand, we nearly did miss the train: my mother's farewells to her brother could not have been exceeded had we been departing to spend the rest of our lives in some remote and savage Outpost of Empire.

The journey was memorable for my mother's gaily vocal good spirits, which failed to communicate themselves to the other passengers in the compartment who objected to being bullied to look out of the windows at cows, trees, back gardens and horses, resented being asked at five-minute intervals if they thought the weather would hold, and failed to appreciate her nagging pleas that they should share our sandwiches, fried fish and cheese cake which, being all pure, would do them more good than all the medicines. The situation was in no way helped by my grandmother's loud and ear-piercing snores.

At Westcliff my mother jumped from the train almost before it came to a halt, filled her lungs with the steam and smoke pouring from the engine and said: 'Smell the air. I feel better already' – then hurried us to Moishe Sox's boarding house in Cobham Road.

Moishe Sox was small and harassed; his wife Dora, a great and hearty bosom of a woman. Greetings were warm and lengthy: twenty minutes of inquiries about our health, their health, the health of my uncles and aunts, the journey we'd had and how the Sox's were finding business (a long and carefully qualified admission that things could be worse). Then we went into the parlour for a glass of lemonade with Mr Sox while his wife went about her duties in the kitchen.

As Mr Sox poured the drinks he asked: 'You know Westcliff well, Mrs Ashe? You been here before?'

My mother gave him a pitying look. 'Know Westcliff? Do I know Westcliff? Wasn't I here for mine honeymoon? By Mrs Greenberg in Palmerston Road. Is she still there, I wonder. A nice woman. Very religious. Wore a wig. You know her?'

Mr Sox shook his head. 'This is my first season here so I don't know many people. As for the boarding houses, there's so many of them. Every day a new one. The competition! I can only thank

God there's enough Jewish people to go round. Only the other day . . .'

'A little woman and not a bad cook. She had a son who did the ironing. We had the room at the front. Mind you, I'm going back a few years. Maybe it's changed.'

'You mean the room isn't at the front any more?' Sox gave a high-pitched titter.

My mother giggled with him. 'Of course I don't mean that, Mr Sox; of course not. I mean, for instance, is the Palace Theatre still there?'

'Yes, it's still in London Road.'

'And the Kursaal, the hot sea baths, the bandstand? And near the synagogue in Ceylon Road I remember clear as crystal a house with roses. Roses like you've never seen. Big like those cushions. And the smell! Like scent. That's what I like about Westcliff. Everything smells so nice. So pure. And it's all so clean. Even the sea. Every day the dirty water goes out and fresh comes in.'

'Twice a day,' said Mr Sox.

'There you are. And such lovely people. Such nice houses. If only you knew what things were like in my neighbourhood.' She was interrupted by the sound of a gong.

'The meal's ready,' said Mr Sox.

Each course of the lunch, served with much Welsh muttering by an aged and moustached waitress, was subjected by my mother and grandmother to long and doubtful scrutiny, careful dissection, lip-smacking, sampling, thoughtful analysis and sonorous verdicts (all unfavourable).

When it was over Dora Sox came in and asked whether they'd enjoyed the meal.

'Marvellous! A banquet fit for the King of England.'

'Beautiful. I wish I could cook so nice.'

Dora Sox's bosom swelled. 'Now come in the parlour and have a glass Russian tea.' Seeing the sulky expression on my face: 'You don't like Russian tea?'

I shuffled my feet and said: 'I want to go on the beach.' (It had dawned upon me during lunch that Ruth and I would be expected to spend the afternoon accompanying my mother to the sea baths before making a sentimental and tearful pilgrimage to Palmerston Road, the Palace Theatre and any other surviving memorial to her lost youth.)

'Don't be so ungrateful,' said my mother. 'Don't I want to go to the beach? Doesn't your grandmother want to go on the beach?'

'For my part,' said Granny Abrams, 'I want to sit in a chair and sleep a few minutes. You go with the children to the beach.'

'First I want a hot sea bath.'

'I don't want a hot sea bath,' I whined.

'Nor do I,' said Ruth.

'I haven't the strength to argue,' said my mother with an elaborate sigh. 'Go to the beach. Go enjoy yourselves. Don't bother about me. I'll manage . . . But don't forget your Wellingtons and macs and towels, and remember it's dangerous to paddle straight after a meal. You can get cramps and drown from a heart attack.'

Ruth and I rushed from the house (without Wellington boots, macs or towels) and ran down Cobham Road. At the top of the steps leading to the promenade my sister said: 'Don't think I'm spending the afternoon with you. I've got better things to do.'

'Like what? Chasing boys?'

She reddened, said: 'Don't be disgusting' and walked off, head high. (Certainly Ruth was now aware that the division of the human race into two distinct sexes was not just a meaningless caprice of nature.)

'Make certain they're Jewish boys,' I yelled and went down to the promenade.

My first discovery was that I would not be paddling: the tide was out – at Westcliff a circumstance that means an expanse of mud stretching away as far as the eye can see. At the kiosk by the jetty I spent a penny on an ice-cream and walked eastwards towards Southend. I bought a stick of rock, envied the boys and girls who had bathing costumes, went on the beach, collected coloured pebbles (which I soon found too much of a bother to carry), bought another ice-cream and climbed across the cliffs. At Southend I walked as far as the Kursaal, weighed myself, lost tuppence on a pin table and put a penny in a machine to discover What The Butler Saw (a plump woman in camiknickers flamboyantly powdering her nose). It was a pleasant enough afternoon.

At five-thirty I was back at Cobham Road.

I could hear my grandmother snoring in the parlour. Ruth, exchanging giggles in the front garden with a tall and stooping youth, shouted: 'Mum's in the kitchen.'

As I entered the house I recognized a familiar, if unexpected smell: the sweetly warm and heavy odour of hot pastry. In the kitchen I found my mother sitting in a chair, dressed in one of Dora Sox's overalls, her arms covered to the elbows with flour, the kitchen table bowed under the weight of trays of *strudel*, biscuits and cheese cake.

'I . . . I must have dozed off. What's the time?'

'Half past five . . . You been making cakes?'

She flushed. 'Half past five? Already? I don't believe it. It can't be . . . Oh, my God! We've got to catch the train in an hour.'

'Did you have a nice sea bath?'

My mother was near to tears. 'Leave me alone . . . Half past five! . . . You sure?'

'I'm sure.'

'Go tell Ruth and your grandmother we must be ready soon.'

'But what happened?'

Waving her arms, my mother screamed: 'No more mad talk! Do as I say!' She reached towards a rolling pin. I fled from the room. When I woke my grandmother she asked: 'Is Minnie still in the kitchen?'

'Yes,' I replied. 'What has she been doing?'

My grandmother laughed until tears came. Then she told me.

As they drank their Russian tea in the Sox parlour the conversation turned to cooking and the baking of cakes and biscuits. Granny Abrams was overwhelmingly lavish in her praise of my mother's prowess as a pastry-cook, which led Dora Sox to ask for details of her recipes and techniques. Listing the ingredients was simple enough, but when it came to quantities my mother would only say: 'I take a bit of butter, a handful flour, a pinch salt . . .'

'A handful? How much is a handful?'

'A handful is a handful. What else?'

'You mean you don't measure?' asked the astonished Mrs Sox. 'You don't use scales?'

'Scales? Who can afford scales?'

'But how do you know the amount?'

'I know.'

'But how?'

'For twenty, thirty years already I've been baking. So I can tell. From experience.'

'A fat lot of good that does me. To start with my hands are smaller than yours.'

My mother shrugged. 'So you'll make smaller cakes.'

Mrs Sox said: 'I've got to make a few biscuits this afternoon. Perhaps before you go out you'll take a look and see if I do right.'

'So all right, I'll look.'

At this point in her story my grandmother choked red with laughter. 'You know what your mother's like. She hasn't got the patience to watch; she has to do it herself. And once she starts she doesn't know when to stop. So she doesn't make from a small sample biscuit pastry. She makes the biscuits, then she makes cheese cake, then she makes *strudel* and God alone knows what else she makes.' She wiped her eyes. 'But don't you or Ruth say nothing. Let's finish the day in peace and quiet.'

During the journey back to London my mother sat gazing out of the window, her face an unyielding mask of tight-lipped misery. She did not utter a word until we reached Fenchurch Street and were greeted by Uncle Mendel who asked: 'Did you have a nice time?'

My mother managed a smile. 'A lovely place, Westcliff. The air is so pure. And such houses. Moishe Sox has got a marvellous garden, with roses and . . .' She made a gesture of helplessness. 'What's the good of talking? Ask Mother. She'll tell you.'

When we arrived back at Daffodil Square I was horrified to see the familiar group of neighbours gossiping in the square. As they came towards us my mother straightened her shoulders and took a deep breath. There was a barrage of questions: 'So how was it?' . . . 'Did you catch the sun?' . . . 'What did you do?'

My mother raised a silencing hand. 'It was marvellous. A

wonderful place, Westcliff. The air is so strong. So fresh. Houses with roses, and there's the beach, and yet it's only an hour by train from Fenchurch Street.'

'So all right,' said Mrs Weinberg. 'But what did you do?'

My mother gave her a long, unblinking stare. 'What do you mean, what did I do? What do you think I did? What do you suppose people do at Westcliff? Spend the day baking cakes or something?'

Inspired by Mrs Lewis, my mother's friends concluded that her reluctance to talk about her day by the sea was because of the memories it had brought back and they never again mentioned it. As for my mother, even the next visit of Harry Jaye was followed by a long silence broken only by a deep sigh and a mournful: 'I bet she still doesn't mix the flour and the butter properly.'

It was some months before she again voiced a longing for her Paradise on the Thames Estuary.

Seven

MY MOTHER did not forget Mrs Cooperman's offer of the use of her gramophone, although she made no mention of it until one afternoon in the spring of 1938. The women were sitting under the elm, gossiping and arguing, when my mother suggested: 'That gramophone of yours, Mrs Cooperman. Why don't you play some music on it? Cheer ourselves up a bit. What d'you say? If it's all right by you I'll get Simey to bring it over.'

'Bring over?' asked Mrs Cooperman, startled. 'You mean here, in the street?'

'Why not?' my mother replied. 'In the fresh air. Like a bandstand.'

There was astonishment, protests, then giggles as her friends fell in with the idea. The women went to their homes for a selection of records while I brought out two more chairs (one on which to place the machine, another for my mother's records) then staggered across with Mrs Cooperman's ornate, mahogany-cased gramophone.

My mother kept our collection of two records lovingly wrapped in an old prayer shawl in a Huntley and Palmer biscuit tin. Both records were scratched and worn, and chipped at the edges, but were prized high among my mother's few personal treasures. One was Al Jolson's *Sonny Boy* (on the reverse side, *There's a Rainbow Round My Shoulder*); the other Sophie Tucker's *My Yiddisher Momma* (on the reverse side the song sung in Yiddish). No one but my mother was permitted to touch the records or even the biscuit tin, which she carried across the square with a stiff-armed, lip-biting, sweat-beading effort of concentration.

Although she loved music, it brought out the worst in my mother. This began to show itself as she placed the tin on the chair and asked Mrs Cooperman: 'You got a new needle in?'

Mrs Cooperman, patiently: 'I always put in a new needle, Mrs Ashe.'

'You sure?'

'Sure I'm sure.'

'Then I'll play mine records first. They're valuable. Worth money. I don't want they should suffer no damage.'

And so the scratched, worn, but still powerfully bellowed sobs of Sophie Tucker exploded into the dusk, frightening the pigeons and starlings and provoking a sporadic barrage of complaints from other residents of the square.

My Yiddisher Momma never failed to bring tears to my mother's eyes. This worried me. I did not appreciate that the tears were an automatic response to the song's glutinous sentimentality. I knew only that the lyric referred to a mother who was dead and my maternal grandmother was still alive. So why cry? I put the question to my mother.

She went red in the face and grabbed me by my hair. 'How dare you say such a thing? How dare you?'

'What thing?' I howled. 'And let go of my hair. You're hurting me.'

'Don't you deserve to be hurt saying I wish my own mother dead? How can you be so filthy? So spiteful? How can you?' She released her hold of my hair and struck me over the head with the lid of the biscuit tin while her friends, as yet unaccustomed to the effect music had upon her, shook their heads and made half-hearted protestations. My mother flourished the dented lid and shrieked: 'Now look what you've made me do. God in Heaven, why have you cursed me with such a son? Why? Just tell me. Just say, so I'll know what I'm being punished for.'

Finally Mrs Cooperman calmed her with the magic words: 'Mrs Ashe, we're waiting from Al Jolson.'

Tears for Sophie Tucker, a heaving bosom and glazed rapture for the fruity richness of Al Jolson, When the last note died away, an ecstatic groan of a sigh. 'Such a voice. Like an angel. Tell me, isn't it the loveliest voice in the world?'

Mrs Kemensky, Mrs Cooperman and Mrs Lewis didn't bother to reply, but Mrs Weinberg ventured: 'What about Caruso?'

'You're entitled to an opinion,' said my mother with airy munificence. 'Everyone has their own tastes. All I'm saying is that no matter what tastes you've got you have to admit that Al Jolson's got a better voice than Caruso. That's all I'm saying. And what's more,' she added to settle the matter, 'Al Jolson's not only got the better voice but he's also Jewish.'

'That's true,' said Mrs Lewis. 'I read somewhere that his father's a cantor from a synagogue in New York.'

'American Jews I don't count as real Jews,' said Mrs Kemensky mournfully.

'My grandfather, may he rest in peace, was a rabbi from near Frampol,' said Mrs Lewis.

'My *father*, may he rest in peace, was a rabbi,' said Mrs Kemensky. 'Famous through the whole of Poland.'

'I never knew my grandfather,' said Mrs Lewis, 'but there was a man with a marvellous voice. They say it could be heard in the next village. For both villages at the same time he was able to conduct the services.'

My mother was visibly impressed by this awesome example of lung power. 'Two villages!' She whistled, then said: 'Mind you, the Rabbi Tsimmus must have had a good voice when he was younger.' With a doubtful look in my direction: 'He's teaching Simon his *barmitzvah*.'

In the eyes of God I achieved manhood when I reached the age of thirteen, and this momentous event – my *barmitzvah* – was to be celebrated in synagogue during the summer. It involved special religious instruction, hence the services of Rabbi Tsimmus, a white-bearded barrel of a man who smelt of aniseed and wore, irrespective of the weather, a preposterously ancient and balding sable overcoat that reached to his ankles. A poor and pious man, a scholar and something of a mystic, Rabbi Tsimmus was devoted to the search for a deeper understanding of God's will so that, by knowing, he might attain a greater purity of spirit.

Obsessed as he was with this formidable and holy task, Tsimmus had little interest in teaching other than as a religious duty. In consequence his educational methods were direct and uncomplicated: he chanted long and sonorous Hebrew sentences, and having made me repeat them a dozen times would viciously pull my ears if I was not then word and melody perfect. (Even now, seeing someone with unnaturally long ears, I am tempted to approach him and say: 'So you, too, were taught your *barmitzvah* by Rabbi Tsimmus.')

Inevitably, the approach of my *barmitzvah* again raised the problem of my post-school future. As my mother put it one day to Mrs Kemensky: 'If only I knew what was going to happen to him. In fact, what was going to happen to any of us. If only I knew what it all means. If only I could see into the future.' A deep sigh and a long pause. 'Mind you, some people are marvellous at telling fortunes. There was an old woman in the East End who was like witchcraft with the things she could tell from cards. Ordinary cards like you buy from Woolworth's. But the things she could tell you! Anyway, she's dead now, so what's the good of talking?'

Mrs Kemensky: 'You mean you believe in all that superstition? Like with crystal balls and bumps on the head?'

My mother flushed. 'Believe? Who believes? But it would be interesting, for the sake of curiosity, that's all.'

'You'll end up like that one,' said Mrs Kemensky, nodding across the square towards the house where Mrs Cooperman lived.

'God forbid! Anyway, how can you compare? I'm thinking just for fun, for a joke. Curiosity. Nothing to take real notice of. I'm not superstitious or anything like that.'

'Of course not,' said Mrs Kemensky with heavy irony. 'After all, why should you need a fortune-teller for your son? Isn't your brother, the clever one, that Mr Abrams, arranging everything?'

'He will do,' my mother replied hurriedly. 'It's only . . .' (she looked over her shoulder as though half-expecting to find Mendel listening) '. . . well, if only I was *sure*. That's all. A mother wants to know. Is entitled to know. It's only natural . . . But as for believing fortune-tellers . . .' She gave an unconvincing laugh.

For all her denials, my mother was none the less a compulsive toucher of wood and crosser of fingers. She knew the significance of such things as walking under ladders, seeing the new moon through glass, finding a pin, accidentally treading in dog's excrement, Friday the Thirteenth, black cats and leaving unanswered correspondence on the bed. She had an awesome respect for people who could read the messages contained in the patterns made by the leaves at the bottom of teacups, knew the hidden meanings of the lines etched in the palm of the hand and could explain the momentous implications of being born under one sign of the zodiac rather than another. But most of all she admired the gift of being able to foresee the future from a pack of playing cards.

'There are people you can go to, but they sometimes cost a fortune . . . Surely there must be someone who tells the future as a good turn. It would be interesting to know, for curiosity. But who?'

The answer came in the unexpected and bearded shape of Iron Foot Yossell. Short and broad, invariably dressed in a frayed and disgustingly greasy black suit with matching homburg, Iron Foot Yossell, with his two enormous suitcases, was well known in North-West London as a door-to-door salesman of Jewish calendars, memorial candles, amulets, prayer books and other religious accessories. If people did not want his wares they never failed to give him a copper or two: it was felt that his trade had a quasi-rabbinic quality, and there was the pity felt for the disability that gave him his nickname.

Yossell's left leg was so monstrously twisted it was about ten inches shorter than the right. The difference was made up with a clumsy iron framework attached to his left boot. Asked what had happened to his leg he replied that he had had a terrible experience while pearl diving. He would never elaborate upon this, but over the years my friends and I built up a romantic picture of Yossell Teitelbaum diving for pearls off some coral strand in the Pacific and fighting a horrific life-and-death battle with a man-eating shark or giant octopus.

One day I came home from school to find Yossell at the front door talking to my mother. He patted me on the head with a hand like a bunch of ageing bananas and asked: 'You learn good at school today?'

'Not bad.'

My mother said: 'I don't know what to do about him. It's his *barmitzvah* soon and he leaves school next year, but what work is he going to take? If only I knew what to do for the best.'

'What is to be will be,' said Yossell solemnly. 'We must wait and see. Like it says in the Commentaries of Rabbi Pinkus: "Patience is a virgin that very few possess".'

'He said that?'

'I've got a copy here.' He opened his suitcase and took out a tattered book. 'Seven-and-six. Published in real Yiddish by mine uncle, Reuben Pinkus. The rabbi's great-grandson. For you Mrs Ashe, five shillings. Bloom in Stamford Hill (may his eyes drop out) is selling for half a guinea. You want?'

'Do me a favour!' A thought occurred to my mother. 'This Pinkus. Has he anything to do with a Rabbi Klothboltz?'

'Klothboltz I've heard of. Also a good man – but a raving lunatic. Take no notice. For your particular problem Rabbi Pinkus is better. He comforts. He advises. He guides.'

'Will he tell me how to get the money for this week's rent? You know, so sure I'm standing here, I didn't sleep hardly a wink last night worrying about the rent I owe that lousy landlord.'

Iron Foot Yossell tapped the book. 'As the Rabbi Pinkus says, if you owe the landlord money, let him be the one to lose sleep.'

My mother nodded mournfully. 'And when I do doze off for a few minutes I'm frightened to wake up in case he's waiting.'

'So sleep longer,' said Yossell.

'More of Rabbi Pinkus' advice?'

Yossell gave a shy shrug. 'The advice of Yossell Teitelbaum, Mrs Ashe. But as Rabbi Pinkus does say, even from the mouths of baby ducklings can come pearls wisdom – if He whose name I'm not worthy to mention gives me power.'

My mother, suspiciously: 'Power? What power?'

Yossell's teeth bared black and yellow in an embarrassed smile. 'Sometimes I get a feeling . . . A glimpse.'

After some probing by my mother, and much self-deprecatory wriggling by Yossell, it emerged that he was possessed of the rare and remarkable power of interpreting playing cards: a gift inherited from his mother (may she rest in peace), a direct descendant of Baal Shem Tov, the eighteenth-century founder of the Hasidic movement.

At this, my mother almost dragged Yossell to the kitchen for a 'cup of tea and a slice cake'.

Despite her impatience, my mother's natural generosity compelled her to cover the table with food: various herrings and cheeses, fried fish and chopped liver, cakes and jams. Then, to her disgust, she found that Yossell was a remarkably slow and methodical eater. For an hour he chewed his way through dish after dish while my mother, who usually admired nothing more than a healthy appetite, wriggled restlessly in her chair. Finally Yossell picked the last crumbs from his beard, complimented her on her cooking and produced a greasy pack of cards.

An elaborate ritual of shuffling and cutting was followed by the arrangement of the cards into complex patterns. Then Yossell sucked in his breath, nodded a few times and chuckled happily. The omens, he told us, were excellent, promising the rosiest of futures filled with dark strangers, journeys across the water, letters containing good news and the immediate death of Adolph Hitler.

My mother listened with mouth and eyes opened wide, and with only an occasional interruption. 'The rent. You see anything about the rent?'

'Don't worry. Everything's going to be all right.'

'You sure?'

'See for yourself. Look at the three hearts on the seven clubs.'

'That's good?'

'You'd argue with the cards? Anyway, I've got a feeling. Such a feeling as I haven't had since Hitler (may his teeth drop out) started his anti-Semitism. I said it would be bad for the Jews, and was I wrong?'

My mother nodded. 'And Simon here. What do you see about Simon. Do you see a job for him?'

Yossell scraped his iron foot across the linoleum as he twisted in his chair and gave me a long, hard look. 'What job you want to do if you get the chance?'

'I like writing and drawing and things.'

Yossell gave a mighty roar of triumph. Turning back to the table he shouted: 'What did I tell you? What did I say? Eh?' A trembling finger pointed to the queen of diamonds, 'That, Mrs Ashe, is you.' His finger swept across to the jack of diamonds. 'And this is your son. Now what's between them?'

'A lot of cards,' said my mother.

'Of course cards,' said Yossell impatiently. 'But isn't one of them the three of spades. Isn't it?'

'So?'

'So that means art, writing, culture, doesn't it? Rabbis have such cards.'

My mother, alarmed: 'You mean Simey is really going to be a rabbi?'

'Not as a matter of course,' said Yossell. 'But something cultural, that's for sure.' He lifted his finger and waggled it under her nose. 'As Rabbi Pinkus says: "The moving finger moves, and having moved has moved". You understand?'

'Sure I understand,' my mother lied. A pause, then: 'Culture, yet . . . Like with a beard and sandals like an Armenian.'

'Bohemian,' I said.

Instinctively my mother struck me about the head with the nearest weapon to hand – a fish knife. 'Don't contradict, you ungrateful swine!' To Yossell, hopefully: 'Can you be more definite?'

Yossell sucked in his cheeks and gnawed at them. 'I got a feeling like I haven't had since my mother, may her soul rest in peace, got dropsy. I said no good would come of it, and was I wrong? I got a feeling that your son is going to be something to do with writing. Can I say fairer than that?'

'Writing,' said my mother doubtfully. 'Does it cost a lot of money?'

'Don't worry. Everything's going to be all right. All you've got to do is remember the three spades.'

Yossell left soon afterwards. 'Goodbye, Mrs Ashe. And don't worry about the boy. Everything's going to be fine. Just remember the three spades.'

As Yossell limped off through Daffodil Square my mother looked at me oddly. 'A writer yet. Who'd have thought? On the other hand, why not? We've never been a family of idiots. There's your Uncle Mendel – a genius. And am I a mental defective? And your father was a clever man. Not in business, mind you, but in other ways.' She wiped away a tear. 'And he could write. Ah, yes, he could write. To the landlord, the council, the butcher – such letters that brought lumps to my throat like duck eggs.' She brushed away more tears. 'Not, mind you, that letters pay the bills. But they sometimes helped delay a while.' Unexpectedly, she grinned. 'I always used to say the reason was it took them so long to read his writing.' Seeing the expression of astonishment on my face, she kicked my shin. 'So don't stand there like a stuffed dummy. Go down to the kitchen and write something. You heard what Yossell said. Go write!'

'B-but what shall I write?'

'How should I know? If the cards say write – write. What more do you want? Remember the three of spades . . . Wait, I've got an idea. Go write a letter to the lousy landlord. Tell him I'll sue him for every penny if he doesn't do something about the mice under the kitchen floor. One day they'll eat us alive in our beds. Then you can write to the council about the rubbish in the square. And then . . .'

I fled.

And so, in a magnificence of self-deception, my mother passed the responsibility for my future from Uncle Mendel to the three of spades – and made my life an absolute misery during the weeks that followed. If I was not eating, sleeping, studying with Rabbi Tsimmus or at school, and was seen without a pen and paper in my hand, my mother would explode into near-hysteria. Punctuating her words with wild blows, she would scream: 'So what are you wasting your time at? Why aren't you writing? Practise a few words! Write a letter . . . What are you trying to do: disgrace me? . . . You'll be sorry, you mark my words. You'll regret the way you're treating me. When I'm dead from the aggravation you're giving me you'll be sorry for the way you drove me to my grave . . . Or maybe that's the writing you want to do: write inviting people to my funeral. Is that it? You . . . you mother killer!'

The news that I was to be a writer was greeted by my mother's friends with varying degrees of incredulity, cynicism and hilarity. Surprisingly, my mother did not rise to the natural challenge of these reactions: with the sublime serenity of a Joan of Arc who knew what she had heard in the field at Domremy, she ignored the doubters and mockers and bought me a dozen exercise books. 'I want they should all be full up by the end of the week . . . And use small writing – they cost good money.'

Then Uncle Mendel came to tea.

Eight

Uncle Mendel arrived bearing flowers, a complete *wurst*, half a pound of smoked salmon, boxes of chocolates, grapes, bags of nuts and raisins, a cream-sponge from Lyons Corner House, lisle stockings for my mother and Ruth and socks for me.

'You shouldn't have,' my mother protested. 'To spend all this money. How can I thank you enough? . . . Ruth, Simon, say thank you to your uncle. Give him a nice kiss. Don't be ungrateful . . . It must have cost a fortune, all this.'

'Things are looking up,' Mendel boomed. 'And why not? After all the years I've been working it's about time I had a bit of good luck, eh? It stands to reason, don't it?'

My mother began heaping the table with food and for once there was no oath-punctuated 'just a cup of tea' charade. Instead, Mendel smacked his lips and drooled: 'You're a beautiful cook, Minnie.' As he devoured a great middle cut of halibut covered in egg and lemon sauce my uncle explained the source of his windfall.

'Some magazines I got from a man who bought them by mistake. They was called *The French Tongue* and this geezer – he runs a Methodist bookshop – thought they was educational, for schools.' Looking significantly towards Ruth and me: 'I can't go into details, but they turned out to be what's called art magazines. He had to get rid of them quick. You get me?' (My mother shook her head. '*Art*. From *Paris* . . . *Paris*. I sold to a shop off Charing Cross Road. *Charing Cross Road*. You understand? . . . No matter, the deal's over and done with and I didn't do so badly out of it. Not bad at all. Things are looking up, Minnie. We'll be in America with Aunt Hannah yet. You mark my words. Just wait and see.'

He clapped his hands, hummed a few bars of *Anchors Aweigh* and pinched my cheeks. 'And how's the *barmitzvah* boy? You learned it all yet? And you got a nice speech ready? You know you got to make a speech, don't you? I made one myself. So did your cousin Herschel. Remember? (I remembered. It was no difficult feat to recall it practically verbatim since every *barmitzvah* speech followed a set pattern. *Today I am a man . . . Thank parents, grand-parents and regret absence of the dead . . . Thank Rabbi . . . Thank for presents . . . Hope to grow up to be a credit . . .*)

'Talking about Herschel,' said my mother, 'how is he? Has he left school yet?'

'In the summer.'

'And what about his being a doctor? You still set on that idea?'

Mendel moved uncomfortably in his chair. 'The way things are . . . Hitler . . . A war soon . . . The doctoring will have to wait a few months. Until America. It's better over there. In America you got proper hospitals and proper doctors. Physicians. I saw this picture with William Powell and wassername. He wasn't actually playing a doctor, but he had to go to hospital to get rid of the bullet. I mean, what else do you do with a bullet? So anyway, the hospital was spotless. Like . . . like I don't know what. You could have eaten off the floor. And the machines they got! You can't imagine. So this doctor, we see him first of all at his home and . . .'

My mother interrupted: 'So what is Herschel going to do in the meantime?'

'In the meantime he's going to learn the bakery from Ober in Brick Lane. After all it's a trade, like a doctor. Everyone eats bread, don't he? They call it the staff of life, so why shouldn't Herschel join the staff? It stands to reason.'

'Such a pity,' said my mother with over-elaborate sympathy. 'Zillah had such hopes. Such ambitions. And he's such a clever boy. Always at the top of the class. What a shame.'

'Shame,' said Mendel belligerently. 'What's the shame in being a baker? As for being a doctor, what's the rush? Where's the hurry? He's only fourteen, the baby of the family. If he does as well as his brothers I won't complain.' His eyes narrowed. 'And what about Simey here? Next year, please God, he'll be leaving school. You made up your mind to make a rabbi of him like I said?'

My mother shook her head as she poured Mendel's fourth cup of tea. 'God forbid I should argue with you, but he's not going to be a rabbi. He's going to be a writer. Already he's filled six books with words. Isn't that so, Simon?'

'Writer?' said Uncle Mendel, puzzled. 'I thought we'd finished with that idea. Anyway, what sort of words he written?'

My mother grimaced. 'How should I know?' To me: 'Tell your uncle what you've written.'

Embarrassed, I muttered something about a diary.

Uncle Mendel nodded, 'So now you sell it for five hundred pounds to the *Daily Mirror*, is that it? Listen, I know about newspapers from a film I saw with Edward G. Wassisname. The life these reporters lead! Hooligans they are! Drinking all the time, mixed up with women, being shot at by gangsters. And you, Minnie, want your son to be one.'

My mother grabbed me by my tie. 'So that's why you want to be a writer, is it? To drink women and shoot people. You . . . you . . . you filthy swine.'

'I didn't mention newspapers,' I yelled. 'And writing was only an idea. It was Iron Foot Yossell who said . . .'

'Who?' Mendel roared.

'Iron Foot Yossell.'

'That nobody! That no one from nowhere!'

'You mean Iron Foot Yossell Teitelbaum?' said my mother.

'How many other Iron Foot Yossels do you know?'

'But he's a good man. Almost a rabbi. On his mother's side he goes back to Shem Tov the Hasid.'

'That I wouldn't know. But Yossell I do know. I've known him since we was at Jews Free School together. So it stands to reason I know him, don't it?'

'Did you know him when he was pearl diving?' I asked.

'Pearl diving?' Mendel stared at me. 'What's this new madness?'

'His leg. He says it happened when he was pearl diving.'

Uncle Mendel sucked at his moustache. 'Pearl diving? Pearl diving? . . . Wait a minute! Wait a minute! Pearl diving. Of course pearl diving.' He doubled up with laughter.

'In the catering pearl diving is slang for dish washing. You follow? Think about it and it stands to reason. Years ago Yossell was a dishwasher from Schloch's restaurant in Ridley Road. So one day he fell downstairs and broke his leg in half a dozen places. So no one finds him for hours and when they do they think he's drunk and throw him out in the street. So the police find him and lock him up. So when he does get to hospital they want to cut off his leg. Anyway, his father won't let them – something to do with cutting meat on the Sabbath – and instead they bandage him up and send him home. And his leg set like a corkscrew.' Mendel laughed again. 'Pearl diving. It's not a lie, eh?'

My mother banged a hand on the table. 'So what's this got to do with Simey? What about his job?'

'So what's Iron Foot Yossell got to do with finding Simey a job?' Mendel countered. 'What's so special about him all of a sudden?' My mother lowered her eyes and chewed unhappily at a thumb-nail. Mendel uttered a threatening 'Well?'

Reluctantly, every word torn from her like a deep-rooted tooth, she told him. Mendel's reaction was a predictable and violent bellow of spittled rage, mockery, invective, curses and disgust. 'You . . . you take notice of that rubbish?' he ended, assuming his most intimidating, lapel-clutching glower. 'You listen to that dung-eating toerag? Three spades yet! To think an intelligent woman like you believes such things.'

'Who believes?' said my mother feebly. 'It was just for curiosity.'

The bickering continued until Mendel left, his parting words: 'A gangster in the family. That's all we're short of.'

My mother's dilemma was acute. Mendel was one of the few people she was reluctant to defy, yet there was her terror of ignoring the three of spades. But again: what if she did as Yossell advised and her only son spent his life a womanizing drunkard, shot by gangsters? 'If only I knew which way to turn,' she howled. 'If only there was someone to tell me.'

There was now a period of loyalty-divided misery, my mother torn between two fears: defying Fate, as symbolized by the three of spades, or defying her brother, the infallible Mendel. But it did not need tea leaves, playing cards or crystal balls to divine the outcome – although she must have suffered cruel doubts and torments before her decision was reached.

One evening, about a week after Mendel's visit, she came into the kitchen, saw me scribbling in my diary and trembled with fury. 'Writing!' she shouted, beating me with a teaspoon. 'Writing, when you should be learning for your *barmitzvah*. Learn to be a good Jew instead of wasting time with all this rubbish. Go study! You hear?' She shook her head in self-reproach. 'To think I doubted mine own brother, mine own flesh and blood. A businessman. A genius. A man who knows such things. As for that Yossell, I'll never have him in the house again. Never again, you hear? Him and his mad talk ... And even, just supposing for the sake of argument, even if the three spades does mean what he says – and I'm admitting nothing – how am I to know he dealt the cards proper? Maybe he made a mistake. After all, he only does it on the side for a hobby. He's not a professional. So perhaps he was wrong. But would your Uncle Mendel be wrong? Would he make a mistake? I was potty to listen to that Yossell, even for five minutes. Yossell or Mendel – how can one compare? ... Three spades! Fortune-telling! People must be mad to hold with such things. Out of their minds they must be. It just isn't natural, all this superstition. It could be dangerous.'

She spat three times to ward off the Evil Eye.

So I abandoned my diary and concentrated upon my religious studies. Until my *barmitzvah* preparations began, my attitude towards religious education was one of bitter resentment at the waste of evenings that could have been spent at play with my friends. But Rabbi Tsimmus, with his thundering threats of hell-fire now began to put (literally) the fear of God into me, and for some weeks I was sufficiently frightened to say my prayers – and say them loudly to make certain God heard them. My mother was proud of this new-found devotion – among other things it seemed to confirm that I had the makings of a rabbi – until the day I sat at the kitchen table and began to recite the grace before meals. She asked me what I was doing. I told her.

She nodded. 'Prayers in the morning make sense. Who knows? Maybe if you ask nicely, one day God will find time for a minute to answer. And by evening the rent will be paid and my arthritis will be cured. Anyway, it does no harm to be on the safe side. At night also it makes sense. Who wants, God forbid, that the roof should fall in or we should all be murdered in our beds? . . . But prayers before meals you can do without – unless you eat at your cousin Ada's.'

The religious fervour passed and I concentrated on speculating upon the gifts that are essential to a *barmitzvah*. I knew that as a collective gift, Granny Abrams and a group of uncles were to pay Rabbi Tsimmus' fee and for the food and drink at the reception which would follow the religious celebration. I considered this something of a dirty trick, but realized equally that there was no possible alternative if these bills were to be met. Other gifts would certainly include prayer books and items of religious regalia, and there was a reasonable chance that among the more welcome presents would be a pocket watch, a fountain pen and a shaving set.

But I was engrossed with thoughts of the cash I would receive; money that would enable me to buy a made-to-measure, chalkstriped, grey flannel suit. I had seen a sample of such a suit in the window of Montague Burton, The Tailor of Taste, priced at fifty-five shillings: double-breasted with high, square shoulders, enormously broad lapels, a nipped-in waist and wide-bottomed trousers that all but covered the tips of the shoes. Shoes. Maybe those, too; in black patent leather. To say nothing of a shirt that buttoned all the way down the front instead of being pulled over the head.

A glorious dream inspired by having had to wear, for longer than I could remember, clothes outgrown by my cousins.

One morning at breakfast I cautiously mentioned the suit to my mother. 'New suit, made-to-measure,' she echoed, and sat for a while staring at the wall.

'Well,' I prompted, 'what about it?'

She blinked away tears. 'I was thinking of your father, God rest his soul in peace. He always dressed so beautifully. If God had spared him we'd all have new suits . . . If only he could have been here for your *barmitzvah*. When you're in the synagogue I want you should think of your father and sing nice. Like Al Jolson I want you should sing. For once in my life I want to be proud of you. When you sing they should hear you from Kilburn across to Golders Green like Mrs Lewis' grandfather. With all the family there I want they should hear you sing and drop dead from jealousy. Do you understand? Don't just stand there like a stuffed dummy, but make with feeling . . . And loud!' Patting my shoulder: 'You'll be a good boy and sing nice, eh? If you're a credit to me and to your poor father and I think you deserve it, a new suit. Can I say fairer than that? So you'll sing like Al Jolson, eh, sonny boy?' The patting hand became a vice. 'Because if you don't I'll break every bone in your body.'

My thin treble would have barely reached to the other side of Daffodil Square, far less echoed across to Golders Green, but inspired by the suit I filled our basement kitchen with shrill and gasping imitations of Rabbi Tsimmus' powerful vibrato and cadenza passages and his splendid vocal curlicues. My mother smiled her approval, but when I sang in the same manner in the Tsimmus drawing-room my left ear was nearly torn from my head. Lower lip trembling, the rabbi spluttered: 'Why are you making a mockery of God's music?' I felt it prudent not to mention the made-to-measure, chalk-striped grey flannel suit, and told him only about my mother's wish that I should sing like Al Jolson.

Tsimmus combed his beard with his fingers. 'Al Jolson?' He raised his eyebrows and shrugged. 'If God wanted you to have a good voice He would have given you one. If you have not been blessed with a good voice – and you haven't – then to try to get one is sinful. You are wanting to alter God's will. His scheme of things. That is conceit. If God didn't give you a good voice He has His reasons.'

That, in essence, was the verdict of Rabbi Tsimmus, but it took him fifty beard-combing minutes, punctuated with lengthy Biblical references, complicated Talmudic allusions, obscure mystic parallels, involved quotations from the great rabbis of history, and much pulling of my ears.

I passed the information to my mother. She listened attentively, for the judgement of a rabbi is not to be taken lightly. 'All right,' she said when I had finished, 'so it's wrong to expect you to sing like Al Jolson. Who's to argue with the rabbi? Maybe he's right and I'm wanting too much. After all there's only one Al Jolson. Forget Al Jolson (God forbid). You'll make me just as happy if you only sing as good as Caruso.'

My mother began darning a sock, then stopped in mid-stitch. She frowned, troubled, and pursed her lips as she processed some complicated and disturbing thought. Finally she put down her sewing and said carefully: 'So if God wanted you should have a good voice He'd have given you one, eh? That's right, isn't it? That's what the rabbi said. No?' I nodded. Her voice began to rise. 'All right. Fine. Wonderful. So tomorrow you'll tell the butcher – the thief – that if God wanted us to pay our bills He'd have given us the money. Then go tell it to the lousy landlord. After that, go tell the grocer.' With an explosive exhalation she picked up the darning. 'So what do I do? What God wants or what the lousy butcher wants? Go ask the rabbi that.'

I placed sufficient value on my ears not to ask Rabbi Tsimmus any such thing, but I mentioned it to his son. Mervyn Tsimmus scratched an acne-pitted cheek and mumbled: 'God has His reasons for everything.'

I tried out on him an argument I'd heard a few days earlier from Mrs Kemensky. 'Look. Suppose you consider everything in the Universe. I mean really everything. Not just the moon and the stars and the planets, but *everything*. The . . . er . . . The Whole. All right? Now there can be nothing outside of The Whole, can there? Otherwise it wouldn't be The Whole, would it?'

Mervyn looked at me suspiciously. 'So?'

'So if there can be nothing outside of the Whole then God must be inside it – which means He must be smaller than The Whole. In which case He can't be God, can He? So there isn't a God, is there?'

Mervyn uttered a shrill squeak and fled down the street.

I dreaded my next visit to the Tsimmus household, convinced that Mervyn would tell his father of my blasphemous outburst. But it transpired that he was unable to bring himself to repeat such profanities and merely hinted – to his mother – that I had said 'nasty things'.

Rachel Tsimmus was small and wiry, with a long, thin nose and a yellow complexion. She piled her hair in an untidy, loose bun from which hairpins were always falling and had memorably small hands and feet. She smoked heavily, resented the waste involved even when a holder was used, and so took to clasping the end of her cigarette in the prongs of a hairpin. In this way she was able to smoke her cigarettes with no more than a millimetre of wastage, and although I often feared I would smell scorching flesh she suffered nothing worse than a permanent nicotine stain on the tip of her nose.

For some time I assumed that the absence of electric light in the Tsimmus home was due either to poverty or some obscure religious observance. Then I saw Mrs Tsimmus preparing to go out one afternoon.

It was a dry spring day, but the rabbi's wife put on Wellingtons, rubber surgical gloves and a sort of rubberized fireman's helmet. Next, and quite unselfconsciously (although I was staring at her open-mouthed), she swathed her body in a succession of bicycle inner-tubes. They went around her arms and legs, her torso and her neck, and were covered by a vast rubber raincoat. With her tiny feet and hands and long thin nose peeping out she resembled an inflated grotesquery in a Disney Silly Symphony: either a wind would carry her over the rooftops, or one pin-prick and she would explode. With a polite 'Goodbye' she left the house. I stared after her in astonishment until I heard her daughter, Rebecca, say: 'Electricity. She's frightened of electricity.'

'Electricity? B . . . but she's going out of doors.'

'Lightning,' Rebecca explained. 'She's terrified that she might be struck by lightning, but that if it happens the rubber will protect her. Insulation, that's the word. She thinks she's insulated against it. She wanted all of us to dress the same, but Dad says that if God strikes us with lightning He'll have His reasons and it's not our business to argue with God's will.'

'Is that why you haven't any electric light in the house?'

Rebecca nodded. 'Nor a wireless. Not even a torch.'

I absorbed this. 'What happens when you go visiting?'

'She doesn't like it if she has to take off her things. But she has to put up with it otherwise Dad would go wild.' Rebecca gave an emphatic shake of her head. 'But she certainly doesn't like it.'

'Why is she so frightened of electricity?' I asked.

Rebecca Tsimmus' head rocked from side to side like a failing metronome. 'Ask me another. She won't use a telephone or travel by tram or Underground. If I go to the pictures I have to go secretly because the film is screened by electricity.'

'Doesn't your father say anything?'

Rebecca gave a mocking laugh. 'Him? So long as he can study his books he doesn't care whether it's electricity or gas or candles. I asked him once and he said that if God meant us to have electricity He'd have provided it. So I said that if God wanted us to read He'd have put a library in the Garden of Eden. He beat me black and blue and locked me in my room for a week, so I haven't said anything since.'

My friends and I evolved a number of theories to account for Mrs Tsimmus' electrophobia (a word coined by Sholto Popplewell), but the truth was revealed only when Mervyn told his mother of the 'nasty things' I had been saying.

The next time I went to Rabbi Tsimmus for a lesson his wife dragged me into the kitchen and wagged a finger at me. 'You've been saying nasty things to my son, eh? Eh? Hmm? Eh? What? Filthy things. I know what he means: sex. Eh? Hmm? What else would be so disgusting my son wouldn't mention it to his own mother? Eh? Take my advice and cure yourself before it's too late. Hmm? You don't know what might come of it. It's horrible. Take my word for it. I know, don't I? Eh? For the first eleven years of my marriage didn't I have a child every year? Eh? Hmm? Didn't I? And isn't it dirty and nasty? Then I was told by a wise old lady. "Use rubbers," she said. I said: "Why rubbers?" And she said she was told rubbers. They protect from sex with husbands and wives. But why should I need protection from a man who's not only my husband, but a rabbi? Eh? Hmm? What?

'So I made inquiries and found that rubber is a protection against electricity. Eh? So then I realized my husband was too full of electricity. And that's your trouble, young man: too much electricity. So do like I do: use rubbers and have nothing to do with electricity. It works, believe me. Since I started with rubbers I haven't had another child. So take the advice of someone who knows. Eh? Hmm? Wear rubber and all those dirty ideas will go away. The electricity can't reach you; can't get through. Keep away from electricity as much as you can and never be without rubbers. Then you'll grow up like my Mervyn, eh? Hmm?'

I asked, timidly: 'Does he wear rubber? And Rebecca? And the others?'

'I'd like them to,' said Mrs Tsimmus sadly. 'I want them to. I wish they would. But my husband, the rabbi, says no. And he's not an easy person to argue with. But that's no reason why you shouldn't be protected, is it? Eh? . . . Now go for your lesson.'

The next time I visited the Tsimmus house she asked me: 'Where's the rubbers? You've got no rubbers. Why not?'

For some seconds I could think of no reply. Then, inspired: 'Hot-water bottle. I . . . I've got a hot-water bottle under my shirt.'

She made a strangled, choking sound. 'A hot-water bottle! What a clever boy! Why didn't I think of that? What a good idea. Extra protection, next to the flesh where it's most needed. Like rubber knickers. Eh? Hmm? I'll get one this minute. You clever boy!' She ran up the stairs as I made my way to the drawing-room.

Nine

THREE OR four of the Abrams children, including my mother, had been born and raised during a nomadic and glossed-over period in the family history: restless and rootless years brought about by a succession of disastrous business enterprises in Manchester, Sheffield, Leeds, Nottingham and a dozen districts of London, and which ended only when my grandfather returned to tailoring. As a consequence my mother's formal education was erratic and rudimentary, and she finally left school at the age of twelve to gut fish and peel potatoes in the fish-and-chip shop her parents had opened in Bethnal Green.

My mother expressed no regrets at having had no proper schooling. 'After all,' she would say, echoing Granny Abrams, 'I learned what I had to learn – how to run a good Jewish home. Would learning Greek or dates help me make better *lokshen* soup? Would I be a better mother if I know how far it is to Timbuctoo? . . . Believe me, when you work in shops like I did for my poor father – fish and chips, wet fish, drapery, sweets and tobacco, and all sorts of others – you learn more than from all the books. You learn how to buy proper; you learn the tricks these lousy toerags use to try to diddle you. The thieves! . . . Regrets? How come regrets? . . .'

A brooding silence, then a sigh as tears came to her eyes. 'I don't regret nothing. The only thing I don't understand is what God's got against me. I worked hard from the age twelve. I stayed with mine parents when the other girls was gone and married. I know people say I look young, but I was over the age of thirty when I married. I tried hard to make a good home and be a proper mother. And for that nobody can say a word in criticism. I did my best. I tried hard . . . So for what is God punishing me with aggravations like the plagues from Egypt? For what, eh? He takes my husband (may he rest happy in Paradise), and gives me in exchange poverty, a landlord worse than a Cossack, mice, arthritis, anti-Semitic neighbours, an ungrateful son, damp . . . For why? What have I done to deserve it? That's all I want to know. Is it so much to ask? And aren't I entitled to an answer?

'No regrets for leaving school – no. As I say, if I stayed until I was twenty and learned to talk like the Duke from Westminster, would it have made me a better wife? Would it have cured the stones in my husband's kidneys if I'd learned long words? . . .' A sudden angry change of mood. 'Anyway, am I such an ignoramus? A dummy? Don't I know what's going on in the world? Am I so stupid? Don't I read all the papers when I get the chance? Who do you know that reads more newspapers than me? Eh? Just say. Just tell me.'

My mother was certainly an avid reader of the popular Press, particularly the more sensational Sunday publications. Indeed, when she sent me shopping, her instructions about cost, fresh-ness, quality and the need to watch the scales, were frequently supplemented with the injunction: 'Make sure it's wrapped in last Sunday's *Pictorial*, *Referee* and *News of the World*. I didn't get a chance to see them.'

Apart from crime and scandal, compulsive reading included horoscopes (mocking the optimistic, relishing the warnings of doom and woe); recipes (irresistible opportunities here for sca-brous contempt); fashion articles and pictures ('You won't catch me in no two-piece bathing suit, I'm telling you'); and news of the Royal Family (awesome respect). Naturally enough, stories of Hitler, anti-Semitism and the threat of war were read closely and commented upon with near-apoplectic fury, but less direct items – the economic recession in France or a new interpretation of the mathematics of the pyramids – brought either the familiar reflex: 'Is it good for the Jews?' or a bitterly rhetorical: 'So will it cure mine arthritis?'

My mother's newspaper memorabilia was selective and bizarre, carefully stored away in her memory for some useful moment.

'Mrs Lewis, I just don't understand how you can buy ready-made chopped liver.'

'But why not, Mrs Ashe? Rubin makes fresh every day.'

'That may be, Mrs Lewis, but I read in the *Sunday Express* only

the other week – in that Would You Believe It? column by Ripley –
that a woman in India laid a hard-boiled egg. An egg. An ordinary
egg. May I have a death in the family if I lie, but I read in the paper,
in black and white. She laid a hard-boiled egg.'

Mrs Lewis' eyes bulged. 'A hard-boiled egg? How come?'

'You mean how come it was hard-boiled? How should I know?
Maybe because it's so hot in India.'

Mrs Lewis shook her head with some vigour. 'But an egg.
No matter hard-boiled, fried, scrambled, soft-boiled – an egg. A
woman laid an egg. You positive?'

'So sure I'm sitting here I read in the newspaper. You got to
remember funny things happen in India.'

Mrs Lewis clicked her teeth. 'Who would believe it? . . . But
wait a minute! Hold on! What's this got to do with chopped liver
from Rubin?'

My mother gave a triumphant 'A-ha!' and her eyes narrowed. 'So
what I'm coming to is this. On top of chopped liver they put some
hard-boiled egg, no? So think Mrs Lewis: if one woman can lay
an egg, who not others? Why stop at one? For all we know there's
probably thousands of women laying eggs all over India. And how
do we know what happens to the eggs? So take my advice: be on
the safe side and buy no more ready-made chopped liver.'

Or a conversation with Mrs Cooperman during which there
was mention of the resignation of Anthony Eden as Foreign Secretary. 'You know he's Jewish,' said my mother.

'Since when?'

'Since all his life.'

'You really think so?'

'I read in the paper. That's why Hitler (may his bowels drop out)
don't like him. He called him a Zionist something-or-other. I read
in the *Sunday Dispatch*.'

'You're a nice lady, Mrs Ashe,' said Mrs Cooperman scepti-
cally, 'but can you believe what Hitler says (may he go bankrupt)?
According to my Lennie anyone he doesn't like he says is a Jew or
a Bolshevik. Sometimes both.'

My mother gave a one-shouldered, head-cocking shrug. 'Look
Mrs Cooperman, your husband is a very intelligent man. Clever.

But just suppose, for the sake of argument, that the *Sunday Dispatch* was wrong. Just suppose. So does that mean Anthony Eden isn't Jewish? When every picture you see of him shows him wearing a hat. His hat's so famous they even call it the Anthony Eden hat. What they don't understand is *why* he wears it. And the answer – what else? – is that he's a very orthodox Jew. Doesn't every good Jew keep his head covered all the time? But they don't understand. They think it's a joke. The Anthony Eden hat! It's the good Jew's hat, that's what. Otherwise, Mrs Cooperman, just tell me one thing: why should he always keep his head covered? Come on, be honest; tell me just once when you've seen a picture of Anthony Eden in the papers without his hat. And tell me why else he should always wear one if not because he's an orthodox Jew?'

Esther Cooperman turned down the corners of her mouth and thoughtfully probed her left nostril. 'But Eden isn't a Yiddisher name, is it?'

My mother looked pityingly at her friend. 'Mrs Cooperman . . . Your own husband, a clever man . . . Didn't he tell me how lots of Jews had no surnames and had to take their name from where they come from? So Anthony Eden took his from Eden – and in the Garden of Eden wasn't they all Jews? If you don't believe me ask from Mr Cooperman.'

Mrs Cooperman still seemed unconvinced. Impulsively I said: 'Does that mean all cantors in synagogues come from Canterbury?' My mother beat a tattoo on my head with her knuckles. '*Dumkopf!* Mother hater! Gorilla!'

Mrs Cooperman said: 'It was a joke, Mrs Ashe,' and searched in her pockets for a peppermint.

My mother grunted: 'This is no subject for jokes . . . Anyway, as I was saying, it was your own husband – and what a fortunate woman you are to have one – who told me about names . . . But then again he said sometimes people make their names more English. So if his name wasn't Eden maybe it was originally Yidden. Eden – Yidden. Why not? It makes sense. Anyway, what's the use of arguing? If you add up what it said in the *Sunday Dispatch*, and that he always wears his hat, and his name (one way or the other), then take my word for it, he's Jewish.'

Weary now of the conversation, Mrs Cooperman asked: 'So what difference does it make if he is Jewish?'

'Difference? No difference? It won't get rid of the mice. It won't pay the rent. But it's always nice to hear of a Yiddisher boy who's made good.'

Mrs Cooperman nodded. 'My Lennie, a very wise man, said only this morning . . .' But the familiar multiple knock on the front door announcing the arrival of Harry Jaye denied us this pearl of the watch repairer's wisdom.

Our landlord was more than usually melancholy and unshaven. When my mother asked: 'How are you?' he shook his head and replied: 'If there's one thing I've learned in life it's that when people ask how you are the last thing they want is that you should tell them. But I don't mind telling you I'm feeling lousy. The stomach is really giving me billy-o. Sometimes like an enormous hand with nails sharp as needles is grabbing hold of my insides. Then it changes to an ache like a steam-hammer. Then it changes so that my guts . . .'

My mother interrupted: 'I read in the paper an article by a Harley Street doctor – in *The Star* – that very often these pains is only in the mind.'

'The mind is up here,' said Harry Jaye, pointing. 'Mine guts is down there. So how can a pain in the stomach be a pain in the head? It's . . . it's like saying constipation is really . . . really dandruff.'

Mrs Cooperman said hopefully: 'An uncle had baldness caused by dandruff and cured it with some ointment that smelled of what you're suggesting. You know . . .' Her voice dropped to a whisper: '. . . Dung. So maybe you aren't so wrong. It's called Dr Rambler's Unction. From Japan. My husband knows the traveller and can get wholesale. So if you want a few boxes just say. It might help. It's worth a try.'

'I read somewhere that what you just mentioned is good for everything that grows,' said my mother ruminatively. 'It makes food grow (although it's not something I like to think about), so why not hair? Or cancer? They all got roots, no?'

Mr Jaye squeaked: 'What d'you mean, cancer? You think I got a cancer?'

My mother made soothing noises. 'Don't get so aeriated. Just don't rub it on your stomach . . . Anyway, have a cup of tea and a piece yeast cake. It's light from a feather, even if I say so myself. And you too, Mrs Cooperman.' But Mrs Cooperman had to return home to prepare her husband's dinner.

During tea a mischievous twinkle came to my mother's eyes and her lips twitched with suppressed laughter, but she said nothing until Harry Jaye, devouring the half-pound slice of salt beef that preceded the yeast cake, said: 'What I really come for, Mrs Ashe, was not to eat your food, but to ask for some rent money. Believe me lady, I really need it. Last week the X-rays alone cost a small fortune.'

This was my mother's cue. 'Talking about manure, it's like Jack Levinson's cigarettes when you come to think about it (and I can't imagine why no one reports him to the council). I just remembered a story in one of the papers. Manure makes the grass grow. The oxes eat the grass and make more manure for more grass to grow. But isn't it logic that some of the manure must stay in the animal? Otherwise the whole country would be knee-deep in it . . . How much, I wonder, is inside that beef you're eating?'

Slowly our landlord's mouth fell open, he put down his knife and fork and looked at my mother with an expression that combined horrified disgust with a pathetic appeal to be told that he had misheard her. After some seconds he took a deep breath, forced his mouth shut, managed to swallow the beef he had been chewing and said: 'You serious, Mrs Ashe? You really read that in a proper newspaper?'

'It was a joke, Mr Jaye,' said my mother contritely. 'To tell you the truth there was such a story, but there was also a bit more by a professor from somewhere-or-other that there's nothing to worry about . . . And another thing, Jewish people don't eat the hind-quarters of animals so it's all pure, all fresh . . . Eat up, it will do you good.'

'Jokes are no good for mine stomach,' our landlord grumbled. Cautiously he took up his knife and fork, gave my mother a sideways look, received in return a reassuring nod, and resumed eating. 'Yes,' he said, 'there's no doubt about it; this beef is better even than from Tutnik's in Brick Lane.'

'Tutnik!' said my mother derisively. 'He sells horsemeat.'

'Surely not,' Mr Jaye protested.

'There was a case in the papers. This man – I forget his name – from Alie Street off Goodmans Fields. He was arrested by the police for doing his you-know-what in the middle of the road (if you'll pardon me mentioning it). And he got off because they serve horsemeat. He was . . . um . . . acquitted that's the word acquitted because of the horsemeat. Because if you're a regular customer by Tutnik's, they sell so much horsemeat you get a licence to do it in the road.'

Harry Jaye stared at her. 'This was in the papers?'

'In black and white.' A pause. 'Perhaps not in the papers, but as good as in the papers – my brother Mendel told me.'

Harry Jaye shook his head in disbelief. 'Like that McKenzie – and the money it cost to put the flat right after he moved out. Don't talk about it!'

My mother raised her eyebrows. 'Who's talking about it?'

'Me. I've got to talk about it. That's why I'm asking for the rent, Mrs Ashe. My stomach eats up every penny I have. A small fortune. You know, lady, it's so bad that every Friday in synagogue I pray to God for relief . . . Not that anything happens,' he added sadly.

My mother quoted: ' "If praying did any good they'd be hiring men to pray".'

'So in the meantime,' said Harry Jaye pointedly, 'I need the rent. Be reasonable, Mrs Ashe. You got the flat. You live here. So why shouldn't you pay the rent? And please – just for once – don't tell me about the damp and the sashcord.'

'For the moment I've got other troubles,' my mother retorted, 'For example, there's Simey's *barmitzvah* coming up soon. That has to be paid for. So tell me, just for the sake of argument, if I had any money – which I haven't – what's more important: your rent or that I should pay the *barmitzvah*? Isn't God more important, or do you think you're more important? Won't He thank you in Paradise? But won't He be upset if you stop a future rabbi from being *barmitzvahed* because you got a belly-ache?'

'Belly-ache!' said Mr Jaye indignantly, reaching for a fourth slice of yeast cake. 'I wish that's all it was . . . But what's all this about a rabbi?'

'My brother Mendel says. It's all fixed. All arranged.'

'So! . . . Well, well,' Harry Jaye was visibly impressed. 'A rabbi yet. This *barmitzvah* I must come to. I've never been to the *barmitzvah* of a rabbi . . . That's to say if you invite me.'

'Huh! So now you understand. For one thing I'll have to be inviting people back to this . . . this slum with its damp and its mice and its electric that don't work proper – and everybody will know that it's your fault. So come! Make yourself at home! I'll be glad for everyone to know. I'll also invite the sanitary inspector to see for himself . . . On the other hand you'll not have to worry. You'll be the only guest. For how can I afford to invite even my own mother if you're taking from me every penny I own? We're a big family (God be thanked), but the way things are going nobody can come to this rotten *barmitzvah* – nobody!'

When Harry Jaye left, bloated but unpaid, he reached in his waistcoat pocket for a sixpence which he gave me with the request: 'Buy some sweets or an ice-cream – and then perhaps when you're a rabbi you won't forget me, eh? I'm not really such a bad man as your mother likes to think.'

When he had gone I said to my mother: 'I thought the family were going to pay for the cost of Rabbi Tsimmus and the reception.'

'Does the lousy landlord have to know that? Give him an inch and he'll take a mile. And as for wanting an invitation – did you hear him actually ask for one? – don't I have enough trouble knowing who to invite and who to leave out without putting him on the list? If only your father was alive . . .'

The problem of guests was indeed cataclysmic. My mother, impulsive and generous as ever, wanted to invite everyone who qualified for an invitation, no matter how remotely: the legion of uncles, great-uncles, aunts, great-aunts, in-laws, cousins, second cousins, dubious cousins by marriage; my friends, my mother's friends, my sister's friends – and anyone else who expressed an interest in the event, either genuine or motivated by thoughts of a free meal. But there were two drawbacks to this simple expedient: the size of the bill that would be imposed upon my grandmother and uncles, and the impossibility of accommodating such a multitude in our small basement flat. Who, then, to invite; who to leave out? It did not take long for my mother to decide that if there was a solution to the insoluble, only one man could provide it: Mendel. So the problem was taken to be discussed over tea at Zanzibar Terrace.

Mendel's view, expressed with noisy, cup-rattling vehemence and much sharpening of his moustache-ends, was: 'Immediate family. Just Simey's grandmother, uncles, aunts and first cousins. And finish.'

My mother: 'I ask advice and you come out with rubbish. Immediate family! Talk is cheap. So what about Dora Cohen? So all right, she's *my* cousin; only Simon's second cousin. But she's always been very close. She told me she's looking forward to the *barmitzvah* and is going to give a nice present. So what do I do? Say don't come? Say keep your present? Spit in her face?'

Granny Abrams: 'All right. Enough already. Invite her.'

My mother: 'But what of her brothers and sisters? If you invite one you must invite the others. It's only fair. Only proper. No? And the Kings and the Levys are also his second cousins. What about them? Don't they count?'

I asked, cautiously: 'Can I invite my friends? Just my best friends? Herbert Levinson, Mervyn Tsimmus, Izzy Glick, Sidney Felton . . .'

'Friends!' cried my mother, striking me across the nose with a stick of celery. 'So we've all got friends. Haven't I got friends? But are they more important than our own flesh and blood? Our own family? . . . Mother, say something.'

Granny Abrams began to eat a piece of *strudel*. My mother threw up her hands. 'So what do we do?'

Mendel: 'I told you what we do. To Dora you have to explain. What else do you want? Hire the People's Palace for the day? Get Monnikendam to do the catering? As things are it's not going to be a cheap affair. A good job I've got some *schnapps* from that deal I did with Harry Lewin. From Spain, from a ship sunk in the bombing. A real bargain . . . It'll cover drinks for people.'

My grandmother swallowed the *strudel*, said: 'For my part I like *kümmel*, and reached for a portion of cheese cake.

'*Schnapps! Kümmel!*' my mother shouted. 'What about the people?'

'Immediate family,' said Mendel.

My mother banged the table. 'How can you ignore Dora Cohen and the Kings and Levys? And what of the Myers and Colemans? Are they strangers? Dirt? I'm telling you, as sure I should live, if they don't come I don't want nobody should come.'

'And I'm saying may I drop down dead this minute if they come.'

'By my children's lives they will.'

'May God strike me deaf, dumb and blind if they do.'

'May I never leave this room alive.'

'May I . . .' Mendel stared at my mother, astonishment on his face. 'Who's paying for this bloody *barmitzvah*?'

'Keep your stinking money. I'll manage.'

'How?'

'That's my business.' Tears now. 'If only my poor husband was alive. Would I then have to come crawling on my hands and knees like some lousy beggar? And to my own brother, yet. If I take a penny from you God should punish me with a black year.'

And so it went on, the table banged until the crockery danced, a crazy tympanic accompaniment to the wild duet of Mendel's boomed baritone and my mother's hysterical soprano. Finally Granny Abrams, the chorus master, raised her hands – the compulsive matriarch. The voices died away. 'Enough already. Now I'll tell you what to do.' In Yiddish, which I did not understand, she outlined some compromise scheme which, from the sulky expressions on their faces, displeased both my mother and Uncle Mendel. But they agreed to it, and after a final exchange (each determined to have the last word) we returned to Daffodil Square.

On the bus back to Kilburn my mother said: 'It's strange to think that of all the people to ask there's no one from your poor father's side. Not a brother, a cousin, not no one.' (My father had come to England as a young man with his brother Nahum. The intention had been for them to find jobs and a home and then send for the rest of the family. The war came, Nahum died in Flanders, and my father's letters to Poland went unanswered until in 1920 a message came from a distant cousin saying that the family had been slaughtered during the pogroms that followed the liberation of Poland by the Germans.) 'When you don't know people you can't miss them,' said my mother. 'But when your own family turns against you it would be nice to have an in-law of some sort to turn to for advice.'

During supper my mother brooded and hardly spoke, her quarrel with Mendel still rankling. But when we had finished eating she said with sudden cheerfulness: 'Well, what is to be will be. Simey you practise. Ruth you wash up. Me I'm going to write the invitations.' At bedtime she was in sufficiently good spirits to tell me I could invite my friends to the *barmitzvah*, and began humming *Sonny Boy*. There was no accounting for her change of mood, and Ruth and I were both vaguely troubled by it, but her excellent humour continued until the great day arrived.

I was as near word and melody perfect as I was ever likely to be – and the presents had arrived. They included an Ingersoll pocket watch from the women in the square (supplied by Leonard Cooperman at cost price), the expected prayer books and items of religious regalia, safety razors, a Platignum fountain pen, propelling pencils and a trilby hat. The cash, handed to my mother for safe keeping, totalled six pounds ten shillings. Never did a happier youth stand on the threshold of manhood.

As we walked to the synagogue my mother, chatteringly nervous, repeated over and over: 'You'll sing nice, eh? For my sake. For the sake of your poor father. And loud. Make with the lungs . . .'

At the synagogue we were greeted by Rabbi Tsimmus who gave my right ear a friendly tug.

With the usual Sabbath morning congregation supplemented by the people attending my *barmitzvah*, the synagogue was packed. As I looked at the males in the well of the building and the women in the balcony, I glimpsed faces I half-remembered as being vaguely of the family: the Cohens, the Kings, the Levys, the Myers, the Colemans, and a dozen others. So Granny Abrams had forced Mendel to capitulate. (I could almost hear her saying:

'It's Simey's *barmitzvah*. If Minnie wants to invite people, why not let her? If everyone gives a few more shillings will it make such a difference? Will it turn us into Rothschilds? Be big. Be a man. Like Rabbi Jochanan says in the Talmud: "He who gives becomes rich".' And Mendel, with a sigh and a shrug, reluctantly agreeing.)

Certainly Uncle Mendel was not his usual ebullient self as he sat beside me. Normally a passionate and emotionally vocal worshipper, his prayers and responses were automatic and muted, with dark, secular undertones.

When my moment came I repudiated Rabbi Tsimmus and sang as my mother wanted me to sing. Perhaps they didn't hear it in Golders Green; certainly no one dropped dead with envy; but I sang from the heart and when I glanced up at the balcony tears of joy were streaming down my mother's face.

When it was over more tears, kisses, handshakes, slaps on the back, congratulations. The mob surged back to Daffodil Square where it was indeed demonstrated that even by occupying the bedrooms and kitchen there was insufficient space for all our guests. Fortunately it was a warm and dry day and the overflow moved to the garden in the centre of the square. Tables and chairs were set among the abandoned prams and mattresses, builders' rubble and other debris, and food and drink were brought across by a relay of female cousins. Then came Mrs Cooperman's gramophone, but this time no Al Jolson or Sophie Tucker. Instead the neighbours were treated to a selection of Hebrew melodies and Yiddish folk music. Inspired by the jollity of the occasion and Uncle Mendel's *schnapps*, the guests danced on the dust-spitting ground, much as they or their parents must have danced in the villages of Poland and Russia. The residents of the square accepted it in good humour, watching from their windows or the pavements.

The day came to an end. A few people stayed on to help with the washing up, and when they left I sat in the kitchen with my mother and Ruth, bloated with food and exhausted after the accumulated excitements. 'Well,' I asked, 'did I sing nicely? Like Caruso?'

My mother threw out her arms. 'Caruso nothing. It was like Al Jolson. Isn't that so, Ruthie?'

My sister grimaced. 'Al Jolson's cat more likely.'

My mother shrugged. 'Take no notice. It was lovely. Like real singing.'

'So I can have the new suit?'

She dropped her eyes and shuffled uncomfortably. 'You really want a new suit? You really need?'

A great icy hand grasped my heart. 'What . . . what do you mean? You . . . you promised.'

My mother nodded. 'I know . . . but what could I do? The extra food had to be paid for.'

'But Grannie Abrams and Uncle Mendel and Uncle Aaron and Uncle Noah and the others were going to pay.'

'They left half the people out,' my mother said impatiently. 'You know that. You were there. But I had to act proper, didn't I? I had to invite people. Otherwise there'd be bad feeling. Such talk, we'd never hear the end of it. You know what they are, the mischief-makers.'

I was puzzled. 'But won't my uncles pay the extra?'

My mother sat erect in her chair. 'I should go begging? That'd be the day! They can keep their money. Not that they've got any, mind you, but they can keep it.'

'And my *barmitzvah* money . . .'

'You know how much money I owe around here. The butcher, the grocer, the greengrocer, the fishmonger, the baker.' She shook her head wearily. 'And I had to have a few flowers . . . So anyway, they wouldn't let me have no more credit, so what with the uncles' money and a pound here, a pound there . . .' Her voice trailed away.

'You mean it's all gone? My money's all gone?'

My mother fished in her pocket and handed me a crumpled ten-shilling note. 'Here, take.' She pushed the money into my hand.

'I . . . I . . .' But there were no words left. Only tears. They poured out in a great, explosive, contagious torrent, and for some twenty minutes the three of us sat there howling out a long black anguish of the soul. Finally I lurched from the table and dragged myself up the stairs to my bed.

In the morning I wept again, then examined the ten-shilling note. The made-to-measure, double-breasted, chalk-striped, grey flannel suit was a dream. Here was the reality – a larger sum of money than I had ever owned in my life. Perhaps, I reasoned, if God had wanted me to have a new suit He'd have made certain I got one. I would raise the point with Rabbi Tsimmus.

That afternoon I took Herbie Levinson and Sholto Popplewell to tea at Lyons followed by a western at the State, Kilburn. There was just enough money left with which to buy my mother a new, unscratched and unchipped record of Al Jolson singing *Sonny Boy*.

Ten

WHEN MY mother and her friends were not gossiping, arguing, eating or listening to gramophone records, and the weather did not allow them to sit outdoors, they might gather in one or another's home to play cards for farthing stakes: Sevens, Rummy, the Polish *Klaberjacz*, or the German children's game, God Blesses The House of Cohen. They all played atrociously and cheated outrageously, but dishonesty was no longer a cause for quarrel or reproach. There had been so many disputes, accusations and acrimonious exchanges early on that the cards sessions would have ended altogether had not shady play become, by tacit agreement, accepted into the rules. As Mrs Kemensky explained to Mrs Cooperman who, when a newcomer, protested at a piece of flagrant chicanery by Mrs Lewis: 'It's only a game, missus. We play for the fun, not the fardens. And it adds more fun – no? – to have our little tricks. If you don't spot them it's your fault. So keep awake.'

My mother's style of play was fascinatingly distinctive. She had read in a newspaper an interview with a professional poker player who was reputed to have made a million pounds from the game, and who argued that the cards one held mattered less than the bluff one employed. So she hummed nonchalantly or yawned with elaborate indifference when she had good hands, gave what she hoped were happy little cries when they were bad – and deceived nobody. Unable to concentrate, she played with reckless impatience, was for ever forgetting the rules, and revealed her hands still further by continually asking such questions as: 'Do three fives count, or must it be four?' or 'Does the ace come after the king or before the two?' When she lost money my mother accepted the fact with lip-compressed fatalism: it was merely another manifestation of the Divine anger she had so mysteriously provoked. But the remarkable thing (and she expressed as much disbelief as anyone) was that despite her curious methods of play she usually showed a modest profit at the end of an afternoon. She would gaze at the farthings in her hand and say wistfully: 'If only every one was a hundred-pound note . . .' then wink and smile at the inevitable banter: 'Money goes to money' . . . 'Don't spend it all at once' . . . 'I don't suppose you'll talk to us now'. For some reason one cliché brought not grins but wrath: when Mrs Weinberg quoted 'Lucky at cards, unlucky at love, Mrs Ashe.'

My mother's face went blotchy with rage. 'How can you say such a thing, Mrs Weinberg? Love! With my poor husband (may he rest in peace) still warm in his grave. And at my age of life! It's not . . . it's not decent, such mad talk. I'm very upset.'

Mrs Weinberg wriggled her wrestler's shoulders. 'It's natural for a woman to be married. It says so in the Bible. (If it doesn't, it should.) And you're a young woman, Mrs Ashe. Younger than me. If I got the chance to marry a respectable man I'd seize it like a shot. Isn't it better than being a widow? Your husband's been dead how long? Eleven, twelve years? You're not so terrible to look at. I've seen worse women than you married two, three times. So why is it such a crime to want Mr Right to come along?'

My mother's eyes moistened. 'It's disgusting . . . It really upsets me. Love! Marriage! Believe me, Mrs Weinberg, if my poor husband was here you wouldn't dare say such things.'

Another irritant, this time shared by all the women, was a visit by Iron Foot Yossell, during a card session. He disapproved of gambling ('As Rabbi Pinkus says: "Let lying dogs sleep, for Rummy is the root of all evil".') but this did not deter him from offering a ceaseless torrent of advice and criticism, nor from trying to sell them packs of lucky playing cards blessed by a saintly old man in Bethnal Green.

Having sworn that Yossell would never again enter our home it was perhaps fated that the next card session in our flat was interrupted by his arrival. ('What could I do?' my mother pleaded later. 'Slam the door in his face? After all, he's an old man, a cripple. A religious seller from Bibles. So what harm in giving him a cup of tea?') He ate, drank, sneered at the play, quoted Rabbi Pinkus ('Listen to the voice of the Almighty, for as He makes the kings and queens of the earth so He also makes the aces and the knaves'), tried to sell copies of the works of that learned man, then got round to the lucky playing cards.

My mother asked: 'What's the bargain being lucky for farthings? If we was playing for five-pound notes it would be different. Then it would be worth while. Win a few hundred pounds. Move from here to Westcliff. Have a nice house with fresh air and a new lavatory. But lucky cards for farthings: why bother?'

'Lucky cards!' Mrs Kemensky scoffed. 'Superstitious rubbish. If we was all to play with the cards, so we'd all be lucky, is that it? None of us would lose. Is that what you mean?'

Yossell searched his beard as though for a reply, but before he found one Mrs Weinberg said miserably: 'So if we were all lucky at cards, and so we did win fortunes, money still won't buy happiness.'

Mrs Lewis: 'Would it be such a terrible thing to be unhappy in the Ritz Hotel instead of Daffodil Square?'

My mother: 'Even in Buckingham Palace still isn't Paradise. I read in the *Daily Mirror* that Queen Mary suffers from bunions, like Mrs Cooperman here. You'd think that with all her money she'd be able to find a Harley Street specialist who could cure her of a little thing like bunions. But my brother Mendel told me that no one, not even the King himself, is allowed to touch the Queen's feet. It . . . it's some form of treason. So the poor woman has to suffer.'

Mrs Lewis: 'Suppose she has an operation?'

'I asked Mendel the same question. For that they have a special doctor. But the Archbishop and the Prime Minister has to be present with the dukes and other people. They made a picture about it. But for bunions – nothing. So who can say that even the Queen from England is happy?'

Mrs Lewis: 'Some people must be happy.'

Mrs Kemensky, thoughtfully: 'It's strange, you know; really strange. You talk about being lucky; you talk about being happy. My father the rabbi, may his soul rest in peace, used to say that the only time you can tell if a person's happy is when he's dead. For it's only when he's dead that you can see his whole life. He'd ask: "How can a man be happy when he doesn't know what miseries tomorrow might bring him? So while a man still lives, don't say he's happy; say he's lucky."'

Mrs Cooperman shook her head. 'That don't follow. Suppose, God forbid, a man is knocked down by a bus tomorrow – but until the bus hits him he can be a happy man.'

Mrs Kemensky glared at her, 'There wasn't no buses in Gobol, clever dick! . . . And who are you to argue with mine father? A rabbi famous throughout the whole of Poland. The Sage of Gobol.'

'My grandfather was a rabbi,' said Mrs Lewis. 'His voice could be heard . . .'

'We know all about your grandfather,' said Mrs Kemensky testily. She turned to Yossell. 'Maybe you understand what I'm talking about.'

Yossell nodded wisely. 'In the words of Rabbi Pinkus he advises that a man must repent the day before his death. And when asked how a person is supposed to know which day he is going to die, he says that you must consider every day to be your last. You must always be prepared for it.'

Unexpectedly, Mrs Cooperman said: 'Pinkus, *Schminkus*! That's from the Talmud. My Lennie told me.' Yossell opened his mouth to reply, but she continued: 'Anyway, why all this talk about death? May we all live to be a hundred and twenty.'

My mother shook her head. 'With a war coming any minute?'

'There won't be no war,' said Yossell Teitelbaum firmly. 'I got a feeling. Such a feeling as I haven't had since Rouse murdered that man in the burning car. I said no good would come of it, and was I wrong?'

'And if there is no war,' said Mrs Lewis bitterly, 'I suppose Hitler (may he have piles) can get on with what he's doing?' She gave a long, sad sigh. 'Sometimes I wonder if it was such a bargain for the Jews to be the ones chosen by God.'

Mrs Kemensky: 'Don't worry, missus: if God hadn't chosen us the world would have done so.'

My mother gestured across the table. 'Please, just for five minutes, can't we forget wars and death and Hitler? Haven't we got enough aggravations without making ourselves more miserable?' She rubbed her hands. 'Anyone fancy another game?' The women shook their heads. My mother sat with her head cupped in her hands, then said cheerfully: 'Maybe we can go to your flat, Mrs Cooperman, and listen to some music to liven ourselves up a bit. I got a new record from Al Jolson singing *Sonny Boy* my Simey bought for me from his *barmitzvah* money.'

This brought a chorus of compliments from the women. Yossell gave my head a heavy pat. Mrs Cooperman handed me a greyer than usual peppermint and said: 'Yes, let's have some music.'

They filed up the area steps into the street. My mother led the way clasping the biscuit tin containing her records and demanding: 'You got a new needle, Mrs Cooperman? Mine records are very rare, very valuable . . .'

I thought I would visit Herbie Levinson who was spared dog-end collecting in the wet weather, but as I left the house my mother spotted me and called: 'I just remembered something. Be a good boy and go round to the butcher and tell him I want a shoulder lamb and a boiling chicken for the weekend. You know we got the family coming Sunday.'

Once my *barmitzvah* was over my mother had behaved as though there had been no row with Mendel. My uncle had been equally silent on the subject, but while in her usual fashion my mother had convinced herself that the quarrel had never taken place ('A tiny argument. A discussion. Nothing from nothing'), I learned from Herschel that Mendel's lack of comment followed a severe lecture from Granny Abrams which contained the telling point: 'Minnie's done what she wanted, she hasn't asked for a penny piece above what you and the boys said you'd give – so what's it got to do with you that she invited half London?'

So Mendel, Zillah, Ben and Granny Abrams came to a lunch of *lokshen* soup and roast lamb the following Sunday, and my mother was able to tell them of the drama of the Men from the Council.

They arrived while I was at school the morning after the card game: six or seven workmen led by an important-looking official in a bowler hat ('Probably the Mayor'). They came equipped with picks and shovels and poles and other equipment, and for a brief, glorious moment my mother imagined they had come to clear the builders' rubble, household rubbish and other junk that now spread beyond the perimeter of the garden towards the elm tree. ('And about time, too. All that filth is dirty. You don't know what you might catch from it. The amount of rates I pay it wouldn't bankrupt them to put in a few flowers. Maybe roses like at West-cliff . . .') But they made no attempt to remove the debris and other muck: they clambered over and around it and began taking various measurements, stretching white tape between a rectangle of poles.

My mother's excitement turned to an unbearable curiosity. She was desperate to know what was going on, but was nervous of the man in the bowler hat ('After all, supposing he really was the Mayor?'). Mrs Weinberg had no such qualms. She marched up to him and questioned him closely while my mother waited restlessly by the elm tree.

It appeared that he knew nothing about removing the rubble – that wasn't his department. He knew nothing about planting flowers – that was yet another department. All he and his men had been told to do was to take measurements in case it was decided to build an air-raid shelter in Daffodil Square.

In her own words my mother was 'flabbergasted. It was as though all the breath had been knocked out of my body. An air-raid shelter! Here, in the square. I couldn't believe it.' When she did believe it there were a dozen questions that demanded imme-diate answers, and despite protests about her varicose veins Mrs Weinberg was sent back to the man in the bowler hat. But beyond assuring her that whatever work that was performed would not involve chopping down the elm tree, he would say nothing: he had no time to waste, did Mrs Weinberg know how many squares there were to be measured in Kilburn? and the best thing she could do was go to the Town Hall.

'The Town Hall!' my mother fumed to Mendel before our visi-tors had had time to sit down. 'A fat lot of good that'll do. The Town Hall! If those people meant anything they'd have done something before now about flowers, about another lamp post, about the paving stones at the corner that could kill you every time you cross the road. The Town Hall! They're all in it together, the anti-Semitic dogsbodies. A black year they should have! Warts

they should suffer, and their children have blackheads and withered arms! . . . You know, Mendel, I was so aggravated I walked
over to that man in the hat and gave him what for. Mayor or no
Mayor, I really told him off.

'I said to him that even if they're not going to cut down the tree,
so what about the roots? Everybody knows about roots, how dangerous they are. They grow for miles in all directions. They're
probably under every house in Kilburn, an enormous tree like
that. So if you cut through the roots to dig your holes, the tree will
be lopsided and fall down. And with my luck it'll fall here, killing
us all in our beds. And even if it falls the other way the cut roots
will shrink and all the houses resting on them – especially the basements – will collapse into God knows what. So I said to him:
"You'll kill us all off; do Hitler's dirty work for him, you rotten lot."
Oh yes, I told him all right. And when the basements do collapse,
what about the mice? There's only the floorboards between us and
being eaten alive.

'So anyway, I asked him what sort of shelters they were
building. Trenches, like during the war? I told him, Ben, that from
you I knew about trenches. I told him my brother was a brave
man, a soldier who won medals. So many medals you're in danger
of being blinded unless you wear sun glasses. From you . . .'

Granny Abrams: 'Medals, *schmedals*! For saving the life of a
verstinkener officer! Cossack!'

'. . . I told him about shelters. He couldn't bamboozle me. Rats,
lice, mud up to the armpits you get from trenches. So I don't only
have arthritis, but me and my children will also get rheumatism,
pneumonia, ingrowing toenails. The rotten child-killers! And lice
yet. That's all we're short of.

'And what about lavatories? And cooking in these trenches? To
get bombed on an empty stomach is dangerous – ask from Dr Lee.
And what are they going to do about chairs and tables? Another
thing: there's valuables I got to find room for – mine gramophone
records, photos, the silver knives and forks and the candlesticks.
Mrs Malik's teapot . . .'

'The cat,' I added, 'for the rats.'

My mother hurled an ashtray at me. 'Don't interrupt, you . . .

you Mayor-lover! Let them find their own lousy cat. Let them get one from the Gentle. Itchky I need here for the mice. It's their shelter, let them provide the cat. I got enough to do without supplying cats . . . So like I was saying, what if it rains or snows? Do they provide umbrellas in these trenches? And how do we sleep? Does each family have its own trench, or do we sleep together like wild animals in the zoo? Oh, I asked him all right. Sleeping together like that: it's not decent. It's dirty. You don't know what you can catch. Consumption, like from that Mr Tingler at number 9, spitting all the time (someone should report him to the council, to the sanitary inspector). And cancer is also catching from people, and so is baldness – I read in the paper only the other day . . .'

She stopped, breathless; radiating an eye-sparkling, bosom-heaving self-satisfaction. Then: 'So how are you, Mother? Mendel? Zillah? Ben? The children all right? Business?'

Granny Abrams asked: 'So what did he say, this man in the hat?'

Joy became gloom as my mother's shoulders sagged and her face grew long. 'He said to go ask at the Town Hall. But what else would you expect from such a dirty toerag?' She looked hopefully at Mendel: 'You fancy going to the Town Hall for me? After all, you're a man. A businessman. You can talk to them. To you they'll listen.'

'True,' said Uncle Mendel, toying with his moustache. 'A widow they take liberties with, but I'd give them no nonsense. They're all the same, these town halls, even in America. Did you see this film with Sylvia Sydney and Wassisname Cagney?' He paused and looked craftily at my mother. 'Of course, I don't mind going to the Town Hall. But they can't just build air-raid shelters for no reason, Minnie. The orders got to come from high up. A general, maybe even the King himself. So who's to argue with the King?' Mendel's expression was now one of deep cunning. 'If they're going to dig these trenches it's more logic to move out. It stands to reason.'

'Move out!' my mother exclaimed. 'Talk is cheap. Move out! Where move out?'

Mendel pursed his lips. 'You always fancied Westcliff.'

'Westcliff! What sort of joke is this? Westcliff! Chance would be a fine thing.'

'Talking about Westcliff,' said Granny Abrams, 'did you hear about Mrs Sox?' My mother shook her head. 'She died last September (may it never happen here). Mendel heard the other day.'

My mother's natural reaction to news of a death, no matter how remotely she knew the deceased, was a gasping intake of breath, moist eyes and a respectfully whispered: 'What a shocking thing; it gives me the shivers.' On this occasion she added: 'How? . . . What happened?'

Mendel's head shook as though he would rather not discuss the passing of Dora Sox. 'Her heart. She used to think she had wind. Was always complaining about it. Took bicarbonate by the ton, but it wasn't no good. It wasn't the wind, it was the heart. And what's good for the wind isn't necessary the same for the heart. It stands to reason.'

'The heart,' said my mother, appalled. 'At Westcliff I didn't think such things happened.'

'Poor Moishe Sox,' said Mendel.

'Poor Dora Sox,' said my mother hotly. She frowned. 'How come you heard of this? From Mrs Minsk?'

'From Sox.'

'You friends now?'

Mendel shrugged. 'Business. I happened to have a few gross bottles lemonade to get rid of. So I got in touch with Sox through Fleischmann.'

'Lemonade,' said my mother, surprised. 'You deal in food now?'

Mendel scratched tentatively at a boil. 'Not exactly. But they come cheap from this warehouse in Hackney because the labels had all come off. Some is lemonade, some is white vinegar. Until you open you don't know which is what. So what do you do?' He looked at us in turn, but as usual his question did not allow time for an answer. 'I'll tell you what you do: you sell to a boarding house where they got need for both. What turns out to be lemonade they sell to the customers; what's vinegar they use for pickling herrings, no? If you got a good business brain you got to make these snap decisions.' Snapping his fingers by way of illustration: 'In America a million, a billion dollars can depend on these snap decisions.'

I tried, unsuccessfully, to make my fingers snap and said: 'I can't do it. I suppose I'll never be any good at business, eh, Uncle Mendel?'

My uncle gave me a friendly wink. 'Don't worry; for you we got other plans, haven't we?'

My mother expressed admiration at her brother's ingenuity and business knowledge. 'But Mrs Sox dead,' she added miserably. 'I can't believe it. Such a young woman. So healthy looking.' She sat in glum remembrance. 'Mind you, I shouldn't be surprised when I think of her cooking and how she made pastry. You know yourself that bad pastry is no good for the heart. It lays heavy on the chest, and where's the heart if not in the chest? So if you got all that weight pressing on it what can you expect?'

'She certainly wasn't a patch on you as a cook,' said my grandmother appreciatively as she spread chopped liver on a slice of rye bread.

'Which reminds me,' said my mother with an agitated flurry of movement, 'the soup must be boiled away by now.'

During the meal there was the usual small talk and family gossip interspersed with mournful references to Mrs Sox, until my mother said: 'By the way, who's doing the cooking now at the boarding house?'

'Some refugee woman she took on as a cook,' said Mendel. 'But she's no good. He pays her four pounds a week all found and she's still no good. Four pounds! More than they pay at the Savoy Hotel, but she's still rubbish. Like I always say, if it's not your own business you're running, how can you put your heart in it? Also she's got a hand heavy like lead when she makes things. So the customers complain and Moishe Sox is also complaining. From heartburn.'

My mother looked hard at Aunt Zillah. 'Even people who don't cook in boarding houses can give heartburn. Even palpitations.' To Mendel: 'But you're right; a cook you pay money to isn't the same as the real thing.'

'She can't be a patch on you as a cook,' said Granny Abrams.

Ben spoke for the first time since his arrival. 'Trenches. I wouldn't have minded your cooking out there, Minnie. All we got was bully beef, biscuits with weevils in and shrapnel for afters. Bang! Bang! Do you think that's what the woman serves at Moishe Sox?'

'Shut up!' Mendel snarled. 'Weevils! In the middle of the roast veal.'

My mother's 'Where?' was more an agonized howl than a word. Mendel: 'Where what?'

My mother: 'Weevils. You said there was weevils in the middle of the roast veal. So where? Show me. I'll sue that lousy butcher for every penny.'

Aunt Zillah made calming noises. 'Not your veal, Minnie; Moishe Sox's veal.'

'Weevils in Moishe Sox's veal,' my mother echoed, aghast. 'What a terrible thing. Who is this cook of his? Can't she choose meat? Does she let the lousy butcher twist her round his little finger? . . . They're in it together, that's what it is! I bet you anything you like. They're both robbing him left, right and centre . . . And when you add the baker, the grocer, the fishmonger, the greengrocer – my God, the money they must be diddling him out of, the poor devil. He should beat her to death and then chuck her out on her ear.'

Mendel looked at Granny Abrams and raised his eyebrows. She nodded. He turned to his wife who frowned, shook her head and said meaningfully: 'What about the children?'

Granny Abrams: 'The children have got to know.' A passionate believer in hygiene, she removed her upper dentures and began cleaning them with a hairpin. 'Ruthie's a big girl now and Simey's *barmitzvahed*. They can understand.' She replaced her upper plate, removed the bottom one and squinted at it, hairpin poised.

My mother: 'Please, as a personal favour, will someone tell me what's going on here?'

Mendel straightened his tie, twisted his moustache-ends into fine points and cleared his throat. 'Er . . . Minnie . . . About West-cliff. You like it there. The . . . er flowers and things. Good for the arthritis. And Moishe Sox has got a nice house. No mice. No Town Hall.' His voice rose an octave. 'May God strike me dead and then paralyse me for life if I lie, but there's no Town Hall there. No Jew-baiting. No mice. No nothing. And since you like cooking . . . well . . . it stands to reason, don't it?'

'What stands to reason?'

'It's logic, Minnie. Marvellous synagogues so Simey can do his learning to be a rabbi. Ruth can wait at tables, eh Ruthie? Think of the tips. And nice boys. Boys with money. After all, there must be money at Westcliff with all those houses. And so . . .'

'Wait a minute! Wait a minute!' my mother shrilled. 'What are you talking about? What are you saying? You . . . you want I should work for Moishe Sox as his cook?'

Mendel shifted in his chair, picked up a piece of bread and stared at it. In an unnaturally small voice: 'Not work for him, dolly.'

'What then?'

'He . . . er . . . well . . . he . . . um . . . he wants to marry again.'

My mother gave a long exhalation of relief. 'Is that all? So let him marry.'

A long silence, broken only by crumbs crackling between Mendel's fingers, my mother's heavy breathing and the click of my grandmother's dentures as she eased them back into place. Finally Granny Abrams said: 'What's the good pretending? Minnie darling, it's you we're talking about. It's you he wants to marry.'

With Granny Abrams, Mendel, Ben, Zillah and Ruth, I tensed myself for a monumental torrent of hysterical rage. But my mother disconcerted us with a series of slow, knowing nods. 'So that's it,' she said, eyes narrowed, but almost calm. 'So that's her game, eh? You've been listening to that Pearl Weinberg. Is that it? The wicked beast. I wondered what she was on about. And just before you happened to come. I suppose she knows this Fleischmann, some lousy marriage broker, and is trying to get a few pounds commission. The crafty cat! I never did trust her. I always thought there was something funny about her . . . But to think you're all in it together. Mine own mother and brothers plotting behind my back! What a thing to have happen!'

Mendel, with spitting fervour: 'May God break both my legs if I know what you're talking about! May I be struck deaf, dumb and speechless!'

Granny Abrams: 'So sure my grandchildren should marry it's got nothing to do with this Mrs Weinberg. It was something we talked about after Mendel saw Moishe Sox. So sure as I should have a good year.'

Aunt Zillah: 'Weinberg? Is she the same Weinberg who used to have a hairdresser's near Aldgate Pump? . . . No, it can't be: my Mrs Weinberg died three, four years ago. It must be a different one.'

Uncle Ben, hopefully: 'Maybe she's the one putting the weevils in Mr Sox's veal.'

My mother raised her hands and patted the air. 'All right, so not Mrs Weinberg. Forget Mrs Weinberg. But why is everybody so anxious to marry me off all of a sudden? Just tell me. Am I such a burden to everybody? Is that it? Am I such a bother, such a nuisance that you want to get rid of me? Is it my fault I'm a widow with no husband?' Miserably: 'Don't worry. I'll be out of your way soon. I'll be dead and buried and then I won't be no bother to nobody. I'll be under the earth quick enough and then you'll be happy.'

Granny Abrams: 'It's not nice, such talk. Get rid of you! How can you say such a thing? We're thinking of your own good; you and the children.'

'What else?' said Uncle Mendel, 'Westcliff's got hot sea baths, fresh air just the way you like. Healthy for the children. And Moishe Sox has even got his own telephone. How about that? And I'll tell you something else.' His voice dropped to a whisper. 'Moishe Sox has got Cobham Road freehold. Freehold!' he repeated, his voice rising. 'So no landlords. It's got every advantage.'

Ruth said: 'What about when we go to America? Do we leave Moishe Sox behind?'

My mother looked at her gratefully and patted her knee. Mendel rolled his eyes, despairing of his niece's stupidity. 'Leave behind? Did I say such a thing? He'll come with us like everybody else. With his training, his knowledge, he'll make a fortune in America. Have you seen the hotels they got in America? Not boarding houses; real hotels. There was this film at the Empire about a hotel in Miami. The entrance alone was as big as Windsor Castle. With a fountain in it. May I never again see my children alive if I tell you one word of a lie – a fountain. And everyone staying there was a millionaire. Every single one. Mind you, the one played by Paul Muni, the one who lit his cigars with dollar bills – dollar bills! Did you ever hear anything like it? – he turned out to be a crook, but the spitting image of the real millionaire (who was also Paul Muni) who was pretending to be a tramp, a hobo, so as to get this girl who was the sister of the other Paul Muni if you follow me. But anyway, it's the hotel I'm talking about. So with a hotel like that – fountains, fitted carpets, lifts, swimming pools – why should Sox want to stay in Westcliff? Of course he'll come with.'

My grandmother said to me: 'And you, Simey; how do you like the idea?'

'I don't know,' I replied. 'If Mum wants to do it, or doesn't want to do it, I suppose she knows best.' My mother rewarded me with a smile.

My grandmother asked the same question of Ruth who said with some bitterness: 'Much difference it makes what I think' – and squeaked as my mother pinched her arm.

Aunt Zillah said: 'It's good to marry while you got the chance. None of us is getting no younger. How old are you now, Minnie?'

I leaned forward eagerly, for this was a question I often used to put to her until I grew weary of the reply: a string of wild oaths and a beating with whatever weapon was at hand. But my mother merely said tartly: 'If anyone asks you, say you don't know.'

My grandmother giggled. 'I tell people I'm as old as my tongue and a little older than my teeth.'

My mother tapped the table with a spoon. 'As for marrying this Sox, I suppose I got no say in the matter. And while you were talking I was just thinking that with a war coming Westcliff is going to be dangerous. It's on the water so battleships can come as well as bombs. And with the sea in and out all the time, the air-raid shelters must be soaking wet. Worse than the trenches they're going to build here, the pig-dogs . . . And another thing, how can you talk of marrying when I hardly know the man? I only met him for five minutes.'

Granny Abrams wagged a finger at her daughter. 'Only since I been in England I hear this talk. For thousands of years Jews married like I did, without seeing their husbands even once before the engagement. And for thousands of years they was good marriages. Now, all of a sudden, they got to meet them first, talk to them – and you're still no wiser. What matters is that your family finds out whether he's the right sort of man, a good Jew – not take notice of the rubbish he wants to tell you. So do me a favour and don't talk silly.' She thought for a moment then gestured wearily. 'All right, have it your way. See him again first. After all, you're not a baby. I know he's coming to London Friday, so why not have him for supper? Mendel will tell him on this telephone machine and I'll give you a few shillings towards the meal. Can I say fairer?'

'Let him come,' said my mother in a tired voice. 'I haven't got the strength to argue. But remember that just because he has a bite to eat don't mean I'm going to run off with him. Let him come Friday. Just don't nag any more. But a meal is a meal, not a marriage contract. Believe me, if I was to marry every man who comes here and has a bowl of soup and a biscuit I'd have more husbands than the Shah of Persia. So let's change the subject and I'll put the kettle on and make a nice glass of Russian tea.'

Eleven

MY MOTHER was such an obsessive cook that our basement flat was never free from the rich aroma of some sort of food in one or another stage of preparation or consumption. Mingling with it, by way of olfactory *bouquet garni*, the smells of Mansion Polish, Sunlight Soap and carbolic. Our home was damp and dilapidated, and the furnishings old and shabby, but my mother kept everything immaculately clean; scrubbing, sweeping and polishing with evangelic zest as though hoping that by removing the dust and dirt she would also obliterate the decrepitude on which they lay. So there was an empty ring to her solemn Monday morning promise: 'I'm not doing no extra cleaning this week. If Moishe Sox don't like the way we live he can lump it. After all's said and done, who does he think he is: the Chief Rabbi maybe, or the Duke from Gloucester?'

My mother made Ruth and I swear not to repeat a word of the previous day's conversation and did not refer to it herself until Friday morning, and then only to say: 'Don't be late home; we got someone coming for supper.'

If her silence was uncharacteristic it was understandable. Her quandary was cruel in the choices it offered. On the one hand marriage to Moishe Sox meant not only the long prayed for release from Daffodil Square, but also the realization of a seemingly hopeless dream: living in a house at Westcliff-on-Sea. Further, the marriage promised financial security and an opportunity for her children to receive a better start in life. On the other hand marriage meant a terrible and irrevocable betrayal of my father's memory, to which she was as passionately devoted as she had been to the man himself. And although the family were urging her into this union, the very process of going through with it and moving from London held a symbolic as well as an actual significance, as though she would be severing a mystic umbilical cord. For while other members of the family had moved to the outer suburbs and the provinces, and despite my mother's longings for Westcliff, her feeling of insecurity if she was more than a bus ride from Granny Abrams and Uncle Mendel for any appreciable period of time had endured throughout her married life, and was probably stronger in middle age than it had been in childhood.

As she would doubtless have put it had she raised the subject: 'For once I can't even ask Mendel. There's no one to turn to, nobody to advise. How am I to know what to do for the best?' She had asked my grandmother and Mendel to join Moishe Sox at dinner, but they said they had Uncle Dave and Aunt Lilly coming on that day. So my mother brooded and debated in silence, and greeted Friday with a sigh and a shrug.

She made two concessions to our guest: we were to eat in the 'front room' and not the kitchen, and as she lighted the Sabbath candles I saw that she was using the silver cutlery and what remained of our best dinner service.

Moishe Sox arrived all smiles and lavender brilliantine, beautifully dressed in what was clearly a new suit since the price tag was hanging down from inside one sleeve. He carried a large attaché case from which he produced a bottle of *kümmel*, chocolates, a bunch of flowers (roses by happy choice), a basket of fruit and a dozen hard-boiled eggs. 'I happened to have over and didn't want they should get wasted.'

My mother was genuinely moved by the gifts, except for the eggs which she eyed with deep suspicion. 'You boil them yourself?' she asked.

Sox, puzzled: 'What else? Why, is something wrong?'

My mother told him of the curious habits of the women of India. Sox expressed polite astonishment, although it seemed that his eyes held a suggestion of panic.

The rest of the pre-dinner conversation was taken up by Mr Sox's heavy praise of Ruth and myself between sips of *kümmel*. I was a lovely boy, big for my age, certainly top of the class, a devout Jew, as strong as an ox, as brave as a lion, destined for Great Things, with a good head screwed to my shoulders and certain to be a credit to my mother in her old age. Ruth was as pretty as a picture, had a beautiful smile, was obviously brainy, and was bound to make a fine marriage and have a dozen angelic children.

During the meal my mother blocked all attempts to discuss Westcliff, his late wife or the possibilities of marriage by refusing to talk about anything but food.

Sox: 'They're certainly lovely children, Mrs Ashe, but a bit of sea air would bring a touch of colour to their cheeks. It's the ozone.'

My mother: 'We'll talk about it later. First eat. How's the chopped liver?'

'Like a dream, Mrs Ashe. A dream with just the right amount chicken fat. If I served chopped liver like this at my boarding house my rivals would go bankrupt. I'd have queues stretching to Chalkwell Park. Which reminds me why . . .'

'I'm glad you like it. Have another bit. Please – just a mouthful. The real secret with chopped liver . . .' She managed to drag out her recipe until the soup was served. 'And is the lokshen soup all right? Too much salt perhaps, or maybe not enough?'

'Beautiful,' said Moishe Sox. 'That's the only word for it: beautiful. Lokshen soup like this must have been the manna from Heaven God gave the children of Israel in the wilderness. No wonder the Egyptians didn't stand a chance. And the lokshen itself is cut so thin. My poor wife . . .'

'If the soup's so beautiful drink it while it's hot. Talk can come later. Mind you, I'm glad the soup is nice. These days people buy from tins, but I don't hold with such things. You never know what's inside. There was a case in the paper only the other day of a man who bought a packet of ready-made biscuits and inside was a toenail. A toenail! In a packet biscuits! Can you credit it? Then there was a man who made a living from it. He'd go to Lyons, buy a bath bun, take it home, cut it careful and put a mouse or a cigarette-end inside. Then he'd go to the Corner House, order a cup of tea and a bath bun and when the waitress wasn't looking he'd change the buns round. You follow me? Put the real bun in his pocket and change it for the one with the mouse. Then he'd cut it open, scream the place down and send for Mr Lyons and threaten to sue him for every penny. So do they want a scene in the Corner House with thousands of people watching and thinking all the bath buns are filled with mice? So they'd quick give him five, ten pounds to keep quiet and go away. Mind you I'm not saying there is mice at Lyons – they make lovely cream-sponges – but if it did go to court you know what some people are. They'd say no fire without whatever-it-is. So in every Lyons tea shop in England he did it. And not only Lyons; also the ABC. That's how they caught him in the end. He went into a Lyons somewhere or other and did his trick with the bath bun. But the manageress was no fool – I think she was a Yiddisher woman – and recognised that the bun wasn't from Lyons but the ABC.'

'Is that so?' said Mr Sox. 'So he went to prison?'

'I think he got ten, fifteen years hard labour. I forget now, but it was in all the papers.' She had made this story last until it was time to serve the roast chicken. 'So how is it, Mr Sox?'

'Tender like butter. It melts in the mouth. There used to be an old saying in Yiddish that when a poor man eats chicken one of them is ill, but you prove them wrong, Mrs Ashe. The woman I got cooking for me since Dora (may she rest in peace) passed away . . .'

'Have another potato, Mr Sox. I made special.' My mother was nearing exhaustion, but she managed to drag out a lecture on the selection and cooking of chickens until the *strudel* was on the table. As Moishe Sox swallowed the last crumbs from his plate, my mother asked in a voice that was reduced to a hoarse whisper: 'You like it, Mr Sox? Have another piece. Just a small slice. It'll only get wasted.'

'No more, thank you. I'm full to the brim. But it was very nice.'

My mother frowned, detecting in Sox's tone some lack of enthusiasm, some implied criticism. 'You sure it was all right? Speak up. Don't be afraid to say. Be honest. If there's something gone wrong I want to know for next time. So tell me.'

Mr Sox gave a nervous smile. 'It's nothing, Mrs Ashe; nothing at all . . . Only if we're going to see more of each other, as I hope we are . . .' A pause here for a comment that did not come . . . 'then we must be frank with each other. It's no good pretending if we're going to be er . . . good friends. You see, I've got to give credit where it's due. That's only fair.' He licked his lips and gave another uncertain smile. 'Like I told you, the chopped liver was perfect.

Just the right amount of onion and chicken fat. Beautiful. And the *lokshen* soup was also beautiful. Strong and a good colour, and the *lokshen* itself – even the King of England doesn't have better. The chicken I told you: a miracle of cooking. And the vegetables the same.

'But I must be fair to the memory of my wife, no? I'm sure you wouldn't want it otherwise. And so, since you ask, I'll tell you: your *strudel* was very nice, but in all honesty to my poor Dora, for my taste I found I preferred the way she made pastry. It was . . . well, different somehow. I hope you didn't mind me saying, but you did ask, and honesty is after all the best policy between two people in our position.'

Looking back to that moment I cannot think how my mother managed to control herself. But she merely sat for a few seconds, eyes closed, fists clenched, then rose to her feet, hands gripping the edge of the table, and said in a voice that trembled only slightly: 'Of course, you must say what you think. Nobody's perfect. There's room for improvement in all of us. Who would say different?' She swallowed. 'So thank you for coming, and thank you for the presents and I hope we'll have the pleasure of seeing you some other time . . . Simon, get Mr Sox's suitcase. Ruth, go open the door. It was nice of you to come. A real pleasure.'

Mr Sox stood up, knocking his chair over in his agitation. 'B-but, Mrs Ashe,' he said, bewildered, 'I . . . I . . . I mean can I stay and talk for a minute? Perhaps we could have a cup coffee or a glass of Russian tea or something. There's things we must discuss. Talk about.'

'Another time, Mr Sox. I'm tired – it's the *kümmel* and I'm not used to drinking. And we've got to get up early in the morning. So thank you again and goodnight.'

In a daze Sox picked up his case and went to the door which Ruth was holding open for him. 'But Mrs Ashe . . .'

'Yes, very nice. Some other time.'

Nonplussed, Moishe Sox stood on the doorstep as the door closed in his face. It was several minutes before we heard him ascend the area steps. My mother shook her fist after him.

'All right, so if he complained about the chopped liver it wouldn't be so bad. Or the soup or the chicken. Or to say the *strudel* was too cooked or underdone. Or that the filling wasn't right. Like I said, we all make mistakes. None of us is perfect. *But the pastry!* To criticize mine pastry when I remember like yesterday wasting that entire day at Westcliff trying to teach that woman how to make dough and hold a rolling pin proper. Of all things to choose, the pastry! Did you ever hear of such a diabolical liberty in all your born days? The pastry!'

My mother stood with lips compressed recalling that disastrous day by the sea, then rushed from the room. We heard her bedroom door slam and the unnerving sound of frenzied sobbing. But Ruth and I were never able to decide whether she was hysterical with grief or laughter.

Uncle Mendel: 'Did he propose? Did you say yes? What happened? Don't keep me suspended.'

My mother, blankly: 'He came. He had supper. He went.'

Mendel, perplexed: 'He didn't ask you to marry him?'

'No,' said my mother truthfully, 'he didn't.'

Mendel thrust out his lower lip. 'What's his game then? What's he up to? He was supposed to come round special to ask you. I'll get on the phone and find out what he thinks he's doing.'

'Don't you dare,' said my mother quickly. 'Suppose he changed his mind? Suppose he don't want to marry me? And then to ask him! It would be very embarrassing all round. He's a grown man; you can't treat him like a child.'

'I suppose not,' said my uncle. 'But it's logic I should be curious. It stands to reason. On the other hand maybe it's better to say nothing.' He sucked at a tooth, drew himself up and thrust out his chest. 'After all, that we – the Abrams family – should go begging that nobody from nowhere to marry us! We're a family famous throughout the East End. And to go like dogs yet to a . . . a . . . boarding-house keeper! Don't you dare do any such thing, Minnie. I . . . I forbid it.'

★   ★   ★

Matters matrimonial occupied much of my mother's interest during 1938.

In July of that year the Spanish Civil War entered its second year; the King and Queen visited Paris, Esther Cooperman was convinced she had cancer (she had dreamed on three consecutive nights of the turn-ups on men's trousers); an LNER train reached 125 miles an hour between Grantham and Peterborough; Uncle Mendel bought part of a shipment of transit-damaged pails ('You use what they call soldiering. A touch of soldiering and Sexton Blake himself wouldn't know the difference'); the Jews of Vienna were forced to scrub the pavements on their hands and knees while wearing sacred items of religious regalia; despite the heart-burn, Moishe Sox married his cook; Howard Hughes flew round the world in three days, nineteen hours, seventeen minutes; the Japanese continued their advance into China; a number of cousins joined the Territorial Army; Pearl White died; my mother swore to sue the vet when the only mouse ever to be seen in Daffodil Square ran into Itchky's mouth, backed out and disappeared under the front door; Britain urged the Czechs to make concessions to the Germans; and Jacob Abrams married Leah Cohen.

Jakie, Uncle Dave's eldest son, was in his twenties: tall, swarthy, curly-haired and neckless, with tiny blackcurrant eyes, a large, red-veined and aggressive nose and moist, smiling lips. He was employed as a salesman in a Spitalfields furnishing store and was marrying the owner's daughter. My mother submitted Leah Cohen to a humiliatingly intimate cross-examination and re-examination: a verbal third degree that even Mendel marvelled at despite the films he had seen with Edward G. Wassisname and Thingummy Cagney. At the end of it my mother acknowledged that the match was an excellent one, a coup that only an Abrams could have achieved. For although the bride had a cast in one eye and was obese to the point of absurdity, her father had no other children to whom he could leave what was agreed to be a veritable gold mine. 'Anyway,' my mother enthused, 'it's nice to have a wedding in the family – so long as it isn't supposed to be mine.'

The problem of what to wear at the wedding was solved, as usual, by members of the family contributing from their wardrobes. The choice of a present was no easy matter since my mother did not have enough money 'to buy from even a fish knife'. By sheer chance, searching in a cupboard for a pair of satin slippers she hadn't worn for a dozen years but were still as good as new and had to be somewhere since she was certain she had never thrown them away, she came across a brown-paper parcel: an oak biscuit barrel with silver hoops and handle that some cousin had given her for her own wedding. 'I knew it would come in handy for something,' she said as she set about it with Mansion Polish and Silvo.

While some people quoted Yiddish proverbs and others the Talmud, and Iron Foot Yossell could always find an apposite pearl of wisdom in the Commentaries of Rabbi Pinkus, Julius Cohen had his mottoes. For the marriage of his daughter it was 'A bird in the hand is worth doing well', and he spent something of a small fortune proving it. After an elaborate ceremony in a synagogue off Commercial Road, a fleet of hired cars and taxis took the guests to the reception at La Boheme Ballrooms in Mile End Road. There were other establishments specializing in Jewish celebrations – Gold's, Silberstein's, the Queen's Hall, the Cottage Grove Ballroom, the King's Hall – but Julius Cohen insisted upon La Boheme when Uncle Mendel told him that a cousin of Lord Rothschild had celebrated his *barmitzvah* there.

Drinks flowed. The women wept and the men laughed. My mother saw Aunt Sarah and Ada, but she ignored them until they walked across and her sister asked: 'How are you, Minnie? It's been a long time.'

My mother adopted her Queen of Sheba pose. 'And who's to blame for that?' In a clear, strong voice: 'You're not looking well, Sarah. That so-called daughter of yours still feeding you cat's meat and dog biscuits? You could do with some of my pork-fat soup – or is she still trying to starve you to death to get her hands on your engagement ring?'

Sarah and Ada hurried away. Fortunately we were not seated near them at dinner. The meal was long and each course was almost of Daffodil Square proportions: smoked salmon, soup, grilled sole, roast chicken, fruit salad, coffee and sponge cake – with Percy Lipschitz and the Cable Street Seven struggling bravely to make themselves heard above the noisy chattering of the three hundred guests. There was white wine and red wine and brandy, and champagne for the toasts that followed the long and predictably familiar speeches. As the tables were moved away for the dancing there was a general stampede back to the bar.

Herschel came up to me, whispered that he had helped himself to a bottle of cherry brandy and invited me to share it with him behind a screen in the far corner. As I followed him towards it a hand gripped my shoulder. I assumed it was my mother, but it was an elderly, wrinkled little man with auburn hair and a long neck stretching tortoise-like from the top of his oversize tail suit. I thought he was the manager or head waiter who had seen Herschel making off with the cherry brandy, but he said: 'Simey? Simey Ashe? I'm your cousin Morrie. The retired furrier. Morrie Frankel. Come sit down, little man, come tell me the news.' Tightening his grip he steered me towards the chairs lined against the wall. 'Your great-grandmother on your mother's side and my father were fourth cousins by marriage, although today I'm here on the bride's side, her father and me also being cousins by marriage. A small world, isn't it?' To my horror, he lifted his hair and scratched his head. 'I was at your mother's wedding. For that I was also on the bride's side. Your father had no family. But he was a lovely man: tall, handsome, strong – a real man. So good looking. Really lovely.' He peered at me and said briefly: 'You take more after your mother's side.'

Still holding hard to my shoulder he made a wide gesture with his other hand. 'It's nice to see all these people happy. Eating, drinking, laughing, dancing. It's also nice to dress up once in a while, no? Especially for weddings. They say in the Talmud: "The world is a wedding".' He hiccupped. 'But then again there's an old saying: "Dance at every wedding and you'll weep for every death".' His wig slipped to one side. 'Mine own wedding lasted a week. In those days in the Jewish villages in Poland there was no beautiful synagogues. They was wood and falling to pieces. But it didn't matter. It was the word that was important: the heart, not the show.' He belched. 'A good meal today – no? People wonder why the Jews make such a fuss about food. The answer is that to the Jew food is important because always through history it's been scarce. My wedding was in my father's house in Veklev. Four people held the canopy over our heads and we was married. None of this modern synagogue show-off. But the celebrations . . . you should have been there to see, little man. They lasted a week . . . My name's Morrie Frankel, the retired furrier.' His wig fell to the floor from a completely hairless head. He did not seem to notice. He made another sweeping gesture. 'All that laughing. Some rabbi said that of all the animals created by God only man laughs. And for why? Because only man suffers so much he had to invent laughter. He said that where there's real happiness there's no laughter. No need for it. You understand me? They also say that a Jew's joy is not without fright, so that maybe is why Jews laugh so loud . . . I'm a philosopher, no? Actually I'm a retired furrier, but when I was your age I studied with the men in the synagogues and in the rabbi's house. That's how I know such things. These days nobody studies . . . At my wedding . . .' The hold on my shoulder eased as Morrie Frankel fell asleep. I skidded across the dance floor to join Herschel and the cherry brandy.

No Jewish wedding is complete without its drama: food poisoning, a heart attack, the announcement of an engagement, the loss of a diamond ear-ring, a brawl – or a shattering insult to someone's pride.

My mother had seemed happy enough before and during the meal, despite Sarah and Ada. She had drunk a couple of glasses of Benedictine, one glass of wine and perhaps two of champagne, had not criticized the food and had prattled away amiably with the Fogels who shared our table.

I emerged from behind the screen to find her sitting bright-eyed and breathless, fanning her face and neck with a paper doily. 'I just had a dance,' she explained. 'Your Uncle Dave insisted. When he was a young man he could have won silver medals for the waltzing. Mind you, I wasn't so bad myself. Light on my feet like a feather. But it's so long since I last danced, and what with mine arthritis, I'm past it now.'

The bride's mother came up: a bow-legged little woman with frighteningly bulging eyes. 'Mrs Ashe? You enjoy yourself? Everything all right? Enough to eat? Have a drop of something. I'll call one of the waitresses we've hired. You like the meal?'

'Very tasty.' My mother gave a little cry as though reminded of something. 'By the way,' she said, pointing, 'who sat at the table at the end? The one on the right by the door?'

Pearl Cohen turned down the corners of her mouth and spread her arms. 'With three hundred people here how can I remember. Why, is it so important?'

My mother's head rocked up and down. 'Very important. I mean, you know who was at the top table and the other tables at that end of the room, don't you? But this table – I mean, it's not important, is it?'

'If it's so special, Mrs Ashe, why not send your boy to go look at the table plan?'

'It is special,' said my mother, eyes glittering. 'Very special.' Her head was still nodding. 'Certainly very special: I sat there.'

'A-ha!' Mrs Cohen exclaimed. 'Now I can help you. By your table was the Fogels. Phil Fogel does my husband's bookkeeping. A nice man.'

My mother's head had not stopped nodding, but Mrs Cohen did not know her well enough to read the signs. 'So that's what I thought, Mrs Cohen – a common workman. And who else was at the table? Me! Another six inches and I'd have been sitting out in the Mile End Road. Eating on the rotten pavement. Me and mine children was sitting there.'

Mrs Cohen looked around for some escape, but apparently could find none. 'Please,' she said soothingly. 'Someone had to sit at that table. We can't all sit at the top table.'

'And why not?' asked my mother, jabbing a finger into Mrs Cohen's fleshy upper arm. 'Why not? You sat there.'

'Me? B-but I'm the bride's mother.'

'And the bridegroom's side of the family don't count, is that it? Me, his aunt; his own flesh and blood who's known him since he was so-high. So close to him I practically gave birth to him. So I have to sit out in the street with your husband's bookmaker.'

My mother's voice had risen steadily. There was now an interested circle of listeners. Mrs Cohen, acutely embarrassed: 'Please

– we'll talk about it some other time. But now is the middle of my daughter's wedding.' Almost begging: 'Please – no scenes.'

'Am I the one making a scene?' my mother yelled. 'All I'm saying is that you admit it isn't an important table – otherwise why put the bookmaker there, out in the street? – and that you've also admitted to me that you put me there because the Abrams side of the family don't count. Those were your own words in black and white. One end for the rich, one for the poor.'

Mendel loomed up, swaying slightly. "Wassermatter? Wassertrouble?'

My mother clung to his arm. "Mendel, you're a witness.' She gave him a choleric and scarcely coherent version of 'the filthiest insult since Mordecai Kort made those remarks about the bedclothes. So say something to her,' she concluded. 'Do something about the wicked cat.'

My uncle put an arm around her waist. 'So why make a business, Minnie? It's a wedding. Be happy. It's not logic to quarrel at a wedding. Come – we'll have a dance.'

'Dance? Dance! With that . . . that thing insulting us right, left and centre? And how can I dance? From sitting half out of the street in a draught I've got a pain across the small of my back I only wish on her. Dance yet! How can you think of such things? We'd do better to go home.' She raised her voice still higher and screamed: 'Home! Everybody go home! We've been insulted. Home!'

People smiled, moved away or turned their backs and started earnest conversations. Mrs Cohen burst into tears. 'You're ruining everything. You're turning my daughter's wedding into dust and ashes. If you want to go – go, but don't upset everybody else's enjoyment.'

Ruth said: 'I don't want to go. I'm having a nice time.' Emboldened by port and lemon: 'Why not just say sorry, Mummy, and forget it ever happened?'

My mother stood frowning, then looked doubtfully at Mendel. He gave her an encouraging wink. She threw up her hands in a gesture of weary, reluctant resignation. 'All right, all right. I'm the last person to cause trouble. You all know that. Forgive and forget is what I say. So apologize and I won't say another word.'

'I? . . . Me? . . . You mean? . . .' The rest of Mrs Cohen's reply dissolved into a foam-flecked splutter. Her husband, coming from somewhere behind me, pushed his way to her side and massaged her hands between his own. 'Julius!' she managed between spasms.

'Sssh . . . All right, angel . . . Cherub . . . Sweetness . . . I heard. I heard. But turn the other cheek and hope for the best, that's my motter. So do like she says.'

With some effort Pearl Cohen said: 'I apologize.'

My mother shook her head. 'I want from a public apology.'

Mrs Cohen's eyes threatened to fall from her head. 'But I've just said.'

'Public,' my mother insisted. 'For everyone should hear.'

Mrs Cohen, loudly: 'I apologize.'

My mother smiled. 'So now is forgotten. You've apologized, so not another word . . . I'll have the glass *kümmel* you offered me.' She marched off towards the bar.

My mother's scene with Mrs Cohen was not in itself worthy of becoming one of the oft-told tales in the folk lore of family weddings. Quarrels on such occasions were as traditional as the roast chicken, speeches, wedding cake, dancing, noise, indigestion and hangovers. What stayed in the memory to be recalled in moments of nostalgic reminiscence, were such outrages as the man at Mendel's wedding who deliberately had an epileptic fit 'just to annoy everybody'; the bride in a loosely flowing dress who seemed such a nice girl but whose labour pains began during the playing of the National Anthem; the distant cousin who, in an alcoholic frenzy, stabbed an even more remote cousin in the nose with a cocktail stick (it took years to remove all the splinters and heartrending stories were told of the sufferings of the victim when he had a cold); the father who laid on the biggest wedding reception since King Solomon married wassername – and was then exposed as an undischarged bankrupt 'unable to pay even from the menus'. This was the stuff of historic consequence, and there was indeed such an incident at the wedding of Jakie Abrams – although we did not hear of it until we were back at Zanzibar Terrace where, because of the late hour, we were put up for the night: myself sharing with Herschel, Ruth with one of the girls, my mother in Ben's bed and Ben outside on the landing.

As Aunt Zillah explained these arrangements over a cup of tea and a plate of sandwiches it was realized that Ben was missing. It transpired that he had stayed on with another ex-Serviceman to argue the relative horrors of the Western trenches and the Gallipoli campaign, but when he finally arrived home he had a classic tale to tell, one with a specially piquant quality for my mother.

As the Fogels were leaving, Mrs Fogel's bloomers fell down (Ben seemed to think it particularly significant that they were green bloomers) and from them tumbled nine coffee spoons, a salt cellar, two fish forks and a wing of chicken wrapped in a linen serviette. 'Ructions,' said Ben. 'Mrs Fogel said someone put them there. Someone else said who'd want to go anywhere near her bloomers. They was green ones . . .'

My mother: 'Such talk in front of the children!' She attempted to thrash me with a smoked-beef sandwich. 'You shouldn't be listening. You should be in bed. Go to bed this instant!' I stayed where I was and my mother was too enthralled by Ben's story to notice.

'. . . So Mr Cohen, where is he? On his daughter's wedding night? He gave Fogel the sack and went straight back to the shop. He said if they can steal from the wedding, what's Fogel been doing with his books? So he's in the shop checking everything. That's where he is. For my part I'd have kicked in a few ribs. Bang, bang!'

Pandemonium: a head-splitting chorus of strident vociferation as Mendel, Ben, Zillah and my mother shouted at the tops of their voices, the words dissolving into a meaningless jumble from which one could distinguish only tonic attitudes – shock, outrage, anger, disbelief, delight. After two or three minutes of this bedlam my grandmother banged the table. The voices became softer, then silent.

Said Granny Abrams: 'A bad business – but I wish I'd been there to see it. It must have been a comic sight . . . Thank God it's Cohen's worry, not ours . . . Or just think if Jakie had married into the Fogels.'

'What a thought!' Aunt Zillah exclaimed. 'It's a scandal enough without that.' She went on to reveal that she had never liked the look of the Fogels from the first moment she set eyes on them at Julius Cohen's shop. 'I said to Mendel – *didn't* I, Mendel? – there was something funny about them and I'm proved right.' Piously she added: 'I wish I wasn't.'

Uncle Mendel agreed that it was a scandal and said that hanging was too good for them – principally, he implied, because they'd had the audacity to commit their crime at a wedding at which he, Mendel Abrams, had been present. 'The chain gang, like in that picture at the Rivoli. Then exported for life. There's no doubt they're crafty. I mean to say, I was there too, wasn't I? And I saw nothing. They . . .'

'Don't talk rubbish,' said my mother. 'You was sitting at the top table with the nobs. I was the one sitting out in the street with the bookmaker. Bookmaker! Jack the Ripper more like. I'm the one that was diddled. I'm the one that was bamboozled. So how can you . . .'

'What matters,' Mendel growled, 'is that they're professionals. Members of a gang. It stands to reason. With you and the children sitting there how can they stuff things down their drawers without being seen unless they're gangsters? Like with Al Capone.'

Ben said: 'The kitchen. They wasn't stole from the table. The kitchen.'

'What difference where they stole, what they stole, how they stole?' my mother asked crossly. 'What matters is that dirty Cohen woman made me sit at the same table with them. We could all have had our throats cut. And she did it deliberate, because if you ask me they're all in it together, the Cohens and the Fogels.'

'How come?' said Mendel.

'Don't tell me Cohen didn't know about the Fogels. Of course he did. That's why his wife (a black year she should have) made her husband take him on, to diddle the taxes. So now he's turned the tables and done Cohen out of all his money. And serve them right.'

Perhaps recalling the circumstances under which she and her husband came to England, Granny Abrams said: 'Don't judge too quick. Maybe the poor devils are hard-up and need for food. To take a leg chicken . . .'

'In that case it still serves that Mrs Cohen right,' my mother argued. 'If the Fogels are so poor it's because she made her husband underpay him . . . Putting me, a member of the family, out in the street with a common criminal. She'll suffer for it, believe me. She'll pay for the way she's treated me. She'll be sorry for the way she tricked us all. She'll live to regret twisting Jakie into marrying that fat beast – and what's the bargain now Cohen's going to be made bankrupt?' Her mood underwent one of its bewildering changes. She laughed and rubbed her hands. 'But I got an apology from her. A public apology. A real apology, eh, Mother?' Granny Abrams' reply was an open-mouthed, teeth-trembling snore. Dropping her voice to a near-whisper my mother said to the others: 'A public apology. A real public apology like you see in the Sunday papers – which is more than anybody else in the family can say.'

With that morale-boosting thought to end her day, my mother went to bed.

Twelve

FOR THE next weeks the wedding dominated my mother's conversations. Her account of it, told to neighbours, tradesmen and anyone else who would listen, became progressively more lurid. It reached the point when hanging did indeed appear to be too good for people possessed of such a degree of wickedness that compared to them Adolph Hitler was no more than a mischievous cherub. Gradually, however, the Fogel Affair found its properly balanced place in life's marginalia, although there continued to be one frequent, if oblique, reference to it. I first heard it on the next occasion my mother railed against the butcher. 'If that piece of meat weighs an ounce over three pounds may I never leave this room alive. I've a good mind to take it back and get it weighed. You've got to watch that toerag every minute of the day, the stinking liberty-taker.' A few well-known pleasantries followed, including blindness, cancer, constipation and ingrowing toe-nails, and the hope that he would chop his fingers off and bleed to death. 'If I find out that meat weighs less than three and a half pounds I'll sue him for every penny,' she said, adding with venomous satisfaction: 'And then demand a public apology.'

Our butcher, Sam Mendoza, was a fat, red-faced little man with a pencil-line moustache, who wore a tall chef's hat at a jaunty angle and was for ever whistling what he called his operatic gems. It was extraordinary that he continued to allow my mother into his shop, for quite apart from the money she owed him no visit was complete without its ritual of threats and castigations. Much of this was motivated by a sense of pride, for it was 'a well-known fact' that all butchers (even those at Westcliff) were ex-convicts, and if this one had devised some cunning, undetected method of cheating her, my mother wanted him to know that she hadn't really been deceived; she'd realized all along what he was up to. So he had to be denounced as a robber, a liar and a twister whose meat stank the place out, whose chickens came from museums, whose offal was of doubtful origin (although probably from pigs) and whose scales and arithmetic could get him sent back to prison for fraud. He was a menace to the community who should be punished by God and reported to the Chief Rabbi.

Mendoza took it all with a smile and a few bars of the Toreador's Song from *Carmen* or One Fine Day from *Madame Butterfly*. I suppose he must have had a genuine affection for my mother, as well as being a basically kind man; and maybe, like Harry Jaye, there was also the thought at the back of his mind that while only a miracle would see his account settled in full, there was always the possibility of that miracle – as long as my mother remained a customer. And if he did not realize that her antagonism and mistrust extended to all butchers, perhaps Mendoza had some glimmer of awareness that the reason her rages were so excessive in their violence was because they served as an emotional safety-valve; a defensive outlet for her feelings of bitterness, frustration and helplessness in an antagonistic world ruled by an implacable deity who, for some undisclosed reason, had singled her out as the object of his vengeful wrath.

So Mendoza smiled blandly and whistled a gem or two while my mother poured out her abuse, and he never responded more strongly than to ask from time to time: 'So why don't you go somewhere else? So find another butcher. There's plenty in London.'

To which my mother would retort: 'That's what you'd like, isn't it? That's what you're after, because I'm up to your tricks. But I want to keep my eye on you. So there!'

'In that case how about paying off some of the money you owe? I've got a meat bill from the wholesaler that would make your hair white just to look at.'

My mother would reply: 'What a funny man you are, Mr Mendoza. If I can't afford to pay mine own meat bill, how can I be expected to pay yours?'

Mrs Cooperman and Mrs Kemensky obtained their meat and poultry from Mendoza, Mrs Weinberg bought her meat there (poultry came from the family business), but Mrs Lewis went to a butcher in West Hampstead. Her given reason for this 'most peculiar' behaviour was that while Nathan Gritz was no better, no worse, than any other butcher, he was an old friend of her late husband and so charged her a penny or tuppence a pound less on her purchases. 'Mind you,' she added defensively, 'what with the bus fares there's no real saving on my few bits and pieces, but I go for old times' sake.'

Soon after my mother heard this story she had occasion to go to Mendoza for some calf's liver, for which he was asking three shillings a pound. Prepared to use any weapon in her campaign against him, she pointed an accusing finger and said: 'Gritz in West Hampstead is tuppence a pound cheaper. He charges my friend Mrs Lewis only two-and-ten a pound.'

Mendoza shrugged. 'So go to Gritz.'

'I did,' my mother lied, 'but he was sold out.'

Mendoza waved a sharpening steel under her nose. 'When I'm sold out of calf's liver I also charge only two-and-ten a pound.'

My mother paid the price asked, the butcher hummed Your Tiny Hand Is Frozen – and the vendetta continued.

My mother had sporadic quarrels with other tradesmen, memorable among them a row with a greengrocer whom she accused of charging her for tomatoes which had not been delivered. The climax came when my mother called him, at the end of a long list of other things, a common guttersnipe and hinted that if he claimed to have a known father he was an even bigger liar than she'd supposed.

Maintaining his dignity with some effort, Mr Seymour replied that his name had originally been St Maur, that his paternal ancestry could be traced back to the Norman conquest, and while it was regrettable that evil times had forced the family to enter trade, one of his forebears had signed Magna Carta. At my mother's request he explained Magna Carta to her, adding pointedly that as a result of it all sorts of undesirables had been permitted to enter the British Isles.

My mother picked up a banana and shook it at him. 'This Magna-whatever. So one of your ancestors signed it. So what? What's so wonderful? What's so marvellous? Let me tell you this, mister: one of *my* ancestors signed the Ten Commandments. So stick that in your pipe and smoke it.'

The enormous pleasure it gave her to tell of this exchange was destroyed when she was informed by the milkman that Humphrey Seymour was a local councillor. The thought that for years she had given her custom to one of her traditional enemies caused my mother to suffer an attack of palpitations no amount of *lokshen* soup seemed likely to cure. To rob a widow of her tomatoes was crime enough, but that the thief should also be a local councillor . . . To the palpitations were added giddiness and aggravation. And for Seymour to have kept his terrible secret without even a word, a hint . . . And she had bought her fruit and vegetables from him! It was as though she had made lavish donations to Mosley's Fascists. This last thought had its corollary, and it cheered her a little to remember that she owed Seymour a not inconsiderable amount of money. 'Let the lousy councillor take it out of the rates. From what I pay and what I get in return they must be making a profit that could keep me in tomatoes for the rest of my born days. The anti-Semitic swine! Like that Mayor who wants to kill us all in our beds by making the house fall down with his trenches – and on top of that force us to live in them like wild animals. He should be the one to live in them, with his *verstinkener* greengrocer.'

One day in early September I encountered the man in the bowler hat. With his team of workmen he was taking measurements somewhere off Priory Road. I reminded him of Daffodil Square and told him that my mother was concerned about the sort of air-raid shelter that was to be built there.

He backed away, shut his eyes and covered his ears with his hands. 'The sort of shelter? The sort of shelter? Are you barmy? Cor blimey, you can't go around asking questions like that. The sort of shelter? 'Ow am I to know you aren't a German spy?' He lowered his hands, opened his eyes and looked me up and down. 'A midget spy done up with surgery to look innocent. You could end up in the Tower of London asking questions like that.'

'You mean you don't know.'

He raised a great beetroot of a fist. 'Cheeky bleeder! Don't get cocky with me, tosh. Don't know indeed!'

'Course you don't,' I taunted him.

'Course I do! That's my job, ain't it? And how could I do it if I didn't know they was to be made of bricks with concrete roofs? Course I know. But it's all secret, tosh. Comes under DORA.'

'Dora? Dora who?'

'Dora no one, you daft 'aporth. D-O-R-A: Defence of the Realm Act. The sort of shelter! Asking questions like that could get us all in the nick.' He took a pouch from his hip pocket and skilfully rolled a cigarette. When it was lighted:

'Daffodil Square, eh? I've got something down about that.' He replaced his pouch, took a red notebook from his breast pocket and thumbed through its dog-eared pages. 'Here we are . . . I thought so . . . There ain't going to be no shelter in Daffodil Square.'

'No shelter? None at all? Not even a trench with mud and rats and things?'

'Not even a bleedin' tin 'at mate. There's a dirty great main sewer under that square. Can't build the foundations.'

I thanked him, ran home and breathlessly passed the information to my mother. She was so delighted she hugged me, kissed me, announced I wasn't entirely bad after all, and rushed out to tell her cronies. Her delight was due less to the fact that no trenches were to be dug than to what she considered to be a long-awaited and well-deserved victory over the local council. 'You remember, Mrs Weinberg? You was there when that dog-faced Mayor came along. You heard what I told him. You're a witness. I told him off, eh? I gave him what for. You know I'm not exaggerating from one word. I gave him such bunions he was forced to take notice.'

My mother saw me smiling and scowled. 'So why are you standing there like a stupid ox? I know they're putting around the story that there's a sewer under the square, but how does that make sense? All under London they got sewers, electric, gas, telephone and the underground railway. So where can they dig trenches when every inch you walk on has its pipes and roots from trees? Does that mean there isn't going to be no air-raid shelters from London?' She jerked a thumb in my direction. 'This Cossack mother-killer is a baby, the milk still wet on his lips (and the trouble I had!). He believes everything they tell him. But I know different. I told the Mayor off good and proper. That's why there's going to be no trenches dug in this garden, and no other reason. Mrs Weinberg is my sworn witness.' She stamped a heel hard on the toes of my left foot. 'And don't you say otherwise.'

I said nothing. Her friends expressed enthusiastic admiration for my mother's achievement, making her cheeks acquire a startling luminosity, until Mrs Weinberg asked: 'What about the greengrocer? Now maybe you can get him slung off the council.'

'Who? . . . Him! That one! Don't worry, Mrs Weinberg, his turn will come.'

'What will you do?' asked an excited Mrs Cooperman.

'Leave me alone for five minutes!' my mother snapped. 'I'll deal with that dogsbody when I'm good and ready.' She clearly did not like being reminded of Councillor Seymour, resentful that the glory of her triumph over Goliath should be lessened by the recall of a minor humiliation along the way.

She wasted no time before informing Sam Mendoza of her new-found role as the scourge of the Town Hall. He hummed *On With The Motley* as he listened, and broke off only when she advised him: 'So change your ways. I've only got to raise my little finger and they'll all come running.' He looked at her, the suspicion of a smile crinkling the mathematical accuracy of his moustache. 'Tell them not to bother to run; I'll be here all day' – and returned to Monteverdi.

My mother received as little satisfaction from Harry Jaye. Our landlord appeared to be encouragingly impressed until my mother warned: 'One word from me and you'll be in prison for life.' Jaye's hands reached out imploringly. 'I don't know what the word is, Mrs Ashe, but please – as a favour – say it. Do me that favour and I'll forget the rent. I'll give you the flat. Give. Free. A present. Just say that word. There's nothing I'd like to do more than to go to Dartmoor for a little peace and quiet. I'm told they got a prison hospital that's the envy of the world. I'm fed up worrying about mine stomach: let them do the worrying for a change.'

Uncle Mendel was also a disappointment. My mother told her story. Mendel nodded gloomily. 'So what you think?' she asked. 'I done a good day's work, no?' Instead of replying, Mendel told her he was being nagged by Zillah to do something about their daughter Sybil who at the age of eighteen should have been thinking of marriage, but was still afflicted with the acne of her adolescence. Put out of her stride, but feeling she ought to say something, my mother could only manage: 'On her it's very attractive.' Realizing this was not the most helpful comment, she added: 'Stop worrying. All over children have acne. Didn't Noah have it? Remember? They called him Poxy Noah. Now his complexion's clear like snow.'

'On the other hand,' said Uncle Mendel, 'there's Poxy Mike. Fanny Moscow's son. You could throw a handful of beans at his face and not one would fall to the ground. And these boils of mine I've had since I was eleven, twelve. For a boy it's one thing, but who's going to marry a girl with more holes than a cullender?'

My mother tried to cheer her brother by recalling women they both knew who had married despite such apparent setbacks as withered limbs, consumption, curvature of the spine, twitches, baldness, inability to cook, lazy eyes, deafness, humps, hare lips and beards. Mendel reminded her that these women had all been compensated by having large dowries and rich parents – which brought him to the main cause of his preoccupation.

'All my life I've worked hard like a black to building up mine business. I want to expand, to build into what the Americans call a whatsit . . . a typhoon. And why not? Old man Woolworth started with a barrow, selling from collar studs. Goldwyn began with picture postcards, and when you think of it Roosevelt had to make a start with just one vote. They all started small, like me. And it stands to reason don't it, it's logic, that if Woolworth and Goldwyn and the others can do it, so can Mendel Abrams . . . The trouble is they went to America as children, and once you're there it's easy making from millions of dollars. If only Mother had gone there at the same time with Aunt Hannah.'

He sighed sadly at the depressing consequences of this lost opportunity, then tapped his head. 'It's all there, in the brain. The business sense is there – but I need capital. I'm still not too old, and anyway there's the children to think of . . . One big deal and we're made. One big deal and we'll have our private chauffeur-driven train, our holidays in Miami, our Pacific playgrounds. There was this picture at the Rivoli about a boy who came to America with nothing and ended up with millions. Millions! As sure as I'm sitting here – millions. He was an Italian, not a Yiddisher boy, so if an Italian can do it how much easier for a man who's already trained like I am, who's already got a business brain. It stands to reason, no?'

The story, familiar enough in itself, lacked the usual aggressive confidence in the telling. Uncle Mendel sounded defensive, almost apologetic, as though he had suffered a long dark night of spectral revelation. 'Aie, aie, aie . . . Maybe I am too old.' There was a hint of self-pity now. 'Perhaps I've missed my chance. Perhaps it's written that we should never go to America.' He looked at us anxiously, eager to be rebuked for this profanity; to be assured that instead of sitting there we ought to be packing our suitcases for the big deal that tomorrow would certainly bring.

But Granny Abrams said: 'America! From my age who cares? I'll be dead soon, so what's the bargain to be buried in America instead of England?'

Now the cries of protest. My mother said: 'You mustn't make such talk. It brings bad luck.' She spat three times to ward off the Evil Eye. 'You're still a young woman. You've lived a good life, been a wonderful wife and mother, a marvellous Jewish home you've made, so may God spare you to be a hundred and twenty.'

Granny Abrams laughed and said in Yiddish: 'If I'm such a marvel, such a saint, why should God wait until I'm a hundred and twenty if He can have me now?'

Aunt Zillah: 'With war round the corner we could all be dead. In the meantime we got to live.'

My mother: 'If it's capital you need, Mendel, suppose we was all to help? A few shillings here and there from everyone in the family . . .'

Mendel gave her arm a squeeze. 'You're a good girl, Minnie. Always was. It's not shillings I need, but pounds. Hundreds, thousands even.'

'That sort of money nobody's got,' my mother admitted.

'What I need is a partner,' said Mendel with some of his old fire.

'A backer. In America, you go to Edward Arnold or some other rich backer and he makes a snap decision. He asks how much you want. A million dollars? Two million? And there you are. But here, try to borrow a lousy few quid to buy a gold mine in damaged wafers from ice-cream and they laugh at you as though you was potty. That's why this country is going to the dogs – no imagination about the possibilities from damaged ice-cream wafers.'

Granny Abrams said: 'Maybe what you should do is start again, like your poor father used to do. Business after business he had, but when they failed he'd cut his losses and begin from another.'

Mendel's face blotched. 'What d'you mean, failed? I'm short of capital, that's all.'

'So why else do businesses fail?' asked Granny Abrams. 'There's nothing to be ashamed. So long as like your father you never done nothing dishonest. We had hundreds fail: baking, drapery, grocery, fish and chips . . .'

'I peeled a sack of potatoes every morning before breakfast,' said my mother.

'. . . So he'd call in an expert – I forget the special name – and if he advised we'd cut our losses and go bust and start again. Like with a doctor, a specialist; you take from a second opinion.'

'But it don't mean you automatically have to go bankrupt,' said Zillah enthusiastically. 'Like by a doctor, you may need certain treatment.'

Mendel demanded hotly: 'If this expert can run my business better than me why isn't he the millionaire in America? It stands to reason.'

'Because he's not a businessman like you,' said my mother quickly. 'Some people are good at giving advice to others, but for themselves – nothing. You're the doer, the businessman. These others are very clever with words, but they can't put them into deeds . . . And what's the harm asking?'

'That's true enough,' Mendel conceded. 'In America for instance, you press bells and the entire town comes running: bankers, cashiers, income tax, the Governor, secretaries – just at the press of bells. But me? I haven't got one bloody bell to press in the whole lousy house. Not even on the front door.'

Granny Abrams said: 'What about Herman Lefkowitz in Aldgate High Street? A cousin from Mrs Shapiro what sells the carrier bags.'

'The accounter?' Mendel asked.

'That's the word I couldn't remember. That's what Lefkowitz does.'

Mendel brooded. Presently he said: 'Such people cost money' and again sank into a lip-chewing silence. Finally he banged his fists on his knees. 'That's what I'll do. I'm glad I thought of it. After all, maybe I need to reorganize, branch out with agents in other districts. He'll tell me. Mind you,' (glaring at his mother) 'I'm not promising nothing. I'm not saying I'm going to take notice of this Lefkowitz. I'll listen, which is only logic if I'm paying good English money. After all, I'm the businessman, he's only the accounter . . .' He broke off, his face went blank, creased into a slow smile – and suddenly his entire body convulsed with sobbing laughter. 'He . . . he's . . . the acccounter, but I . . . I'm . . . I'm the one that counts! Get it? He's the accounter . . . b-but I'm the one that . . . counts!' Tears rolled down his cheeks. The rest of us joined in the laughter with varying degrees of sincerity. Mendel wiped his eyes with the back of a hand. 'I should have been a comic on the stage, like from Eddie Cantor.'

Granny Abrams, severely: 'Cantors are supposed to sing in synagogues, not be comics. Comics in synagogues I don't hold with.'

'It's not important,' said Mendel. His good humour restored, he insisted upon pouring each of us, including the children, a glass of the *kümmel* he kept for special occasions. As we left Zanzibar Terrace Mendel's voice boomed after us: 'Tell the girls in the square – he's the accounter, but I'm the one that counts.' His laughter followed us round the corner into Commercial Road.

On the bus taking us home my mother complained only perfunctorily about the heartburn caused by Aunt Zillah's macaroons: she was too occupied with Uncle Mendel's troubles and the possibility of helping him solve them. After dinner she took a pencil and after much licking of its point made a list on the back of a paper bag. She added and deleted, re-wrote and corrected, but finally admitted defeat: there was no way in which we could save money.

It was impossible to cut down on the placatory sums paid to

Harry Jaye if he was to receive any money at all; gas, electricity and the water rates had to be paid or those services would be denied us; the general rates could not be ignored beyond the final notice or our few sticks of furniture would be seized before we were thrown into the workhouse; we could not economize on clothes since we never bought any but the basic essentials (and then only when we could be arrested as beggars); pocket-money depended upon the charitable whims of others; and food was such a basic need that to cut down on our meagre menus would be like asking a dying man to breathe less.

Ruth said that while she would not suggest that we ate less, my mother could buy cheaper cuts of meat and less expensive fish, and find substitutes for smoked salmon and chicken livers. This was heresy on a grand scale. My mother purpled, screamed, struck Ruth with a dishcloth and cried: 'The one thing we've never gone short of in this house is good food. I've worked my fingers to the bone to provide you with the best that money can buy. And now you turn on me, you ungrateful cat! That's all the thanks I get; all the appreciation. You're worse than your brother.' With eyes rolled upwards: 'Why have you cursed me with such children? What have I done to deserve it? Just say . . . As for you, you hussy, I'll feed you bread and scrape tomorrow and see how you like it.'

'I'm only thinking of Uncle Mendel,' Ruth shouted.

Instant calm. My mother's face set in an expression of sublime spirituality. 'For Uncle Mendel I'll try.'

The school holidays had not yet ended and the next day I accompanied my mother to the butcher. Mendoza was humming *Nessun Dorma* as my mother walked in and asked in a firm voice for 'the cheapest piece stewing lamb you got. Maybe the neck – but lean. And no fiddling with the scales if you don't mind or I go straight to my friend the Mayor.'

'Have veal,' said Mendoza. 'It's free today.'

'And none of your sauce. It's easy to poke fun at a poor widow because she's got no one to defend her. But don't you worry; there's a God in Heaven who's got it all written down in a gold book. If I want neck of lamb I got my reasons.' From this starting point she worked herself into a classic rage, and although

Mendoza attempted to interrupt her once or twice there was no stopping her until the butcher began to wrap the meat. '. . . And do it up in last Sunday's *News of the World* and *Pictorial*, and I also didn't get a chance to see the local paper if you got it.' Obligingly, Sam Mendoza sorted through the newspapers stacked behind the counter.

'So how much do I owe you?'

'I tried to tell you: it's free today. That's why I told you to have veal. I tried to say, but you're so busy making a scene and screaming the place down and carrying on like a madwoman, I didn't get a word in. So now you got scrag-end instead.'

My mother was stupefied. 'Free? What do you mean, free? How come free?' Her eyes narrowed. 'You trying to get round me? You frightened I'll report you to the Town Hall? A bribe? . . . There's something fishy going on. Who ever heard of a butcher giving free meat?' Eagerly: 'Unless there's something wrong with it. Is that it? The meat's rotten. Why else should a butcher give meat away?'

Sam Mendoza picked up a giant knife, waved it over his head like a cutlass and crashed it down on the chopping block. As he struggled to ease it free: 'You try my patience, Mrs Ashe; you really do. I never understand why more butchers don't commit murder . . . Today is my silver wedding anniversary. So what I could do is offer you a cigar – you want a cigar? – or a glass champagne. Instead, from the goodness of my heart I decide to give certain special customers a treat. Free meat today. Not everyone, just those I think most need – I mean who I think would most appreciate. And what thanks do I get? Insults. You take all the pleasure away.' He was really quite upset.

My mother dropped her eyes, pouted miserably and threw up her hands. 'I . . . I'm sorry. I didn't know. I didn't realize. I . . . I'm sorry. I apologize and wish congratulations. Please God, you'll enjoy your diamond wedding.' She picked up her parcel and weighed it glumly in her hand. 'So thank you. Thank you very much.' She looked longingly at the veal in the window and then at Mendoza. But the butcher had turned away and was boning a shin of beef.

Walking home my mother said: 'Just my luck, eh? Just my rotten

luck. On the day the lousy butcher gives meat away – God knows
the dirty dog can afford it, mind you – I get a few penn'orth of
lousy neck of lamb . . . That idiot sister of yours! It's her I blame.
She's the one. If I hadn't listened to her I'd have ordered veal,
chicken, liver, beef – enough to keep us going for a month. Instead
I got this muck.' A pensive pause. 'But who was to know? Who
was to know?' A longer silence, then: 'Perhaps I was a bit harsh on
him. I know he's a butcher, a thief, but to give free meat . . . Veal
or neck of lamb, it's the thought that counts. It shows he's got a
conscience . . . Maybe I shouldn't have said those things. Not that
they aren't true, aren't justified, but today of all days I should have
been easier on him.'

'But at least you apologized,' I said by way of consolation.

'That's something, I suppose,' said my mother. She stopped and
looked at me. 'There was nobody else in the shop with us, was
there?' I shook my head. 'That's all right then.' She gave a sigh of
relief.

'What's the difference?' I asked.

'Don't you understand anything, you gorilla? If he was alone
in the shop, that was an apology. But if someone else was there it
would have been a public apology. And I don't give no butcher no
public apology for all the meat in London.'

The drama of the day was not yet over. When we arrived
home my mother unwrapped the meat, threw it into the larder,
smoothed the newspapers in which it was wrapped, selected the
local weekly – and gave an absurd little squeak. I looked over her
shoulder at a portrait of our Mayor, resplendent in the robes and
chain of office.

My mother squinted at it. 'Simey – is this the man in the bowler
hat?'

'No,' I replied, 'he was a fat man with a moustache and a huge
double-chin.'

'That's the one. This Mayor is different. How come two
mayors?'

'Who said the man in the bowler hat was the Mayor?' I asked.

A baleful stare. 'Of course it was the Mayor. Who else?'

'So who's this?'

My mother removed a hairpin and scratched her head with it. 'Come – we'll go see the others.'

There was no one in the square, but we found Mrs Weinberg at home drinking coffee with Mrs Cooperman. The latter was as baffled as my mother, but Mrs Weinberg said without hesitation: 'If what you say is right, missus, you done more than you thought you done.'

'How come?'

'Don't you see? These councils don't like to be made fools of. You made a fool of the Mayor. Made him look a fool by stopping him build shelters here. They can't have the Mayor treated like that. So they've give him the push. He's been fired. They got a new Mayor. Now do you see? You got the low-life sacked.'

My mother bit her lip. 'You really think so?'

'Of course I think so,' said Mrs Weinberg impatiently. 'What else is the reason?'

Mrs Cooperman nodded her agreement with a vigour that made her crimson toque fall into her lap. 'You're a heroine, Mrs Ashe, like with Samson and the Moabites. Everyone will want your autograph. You'll need picture postcards printed. When you do, let me know; my Lennie can get done wholesale. Lennie! I can't wait to tell him.'

My mother made a self-deprecatory gesture. 'It was nothing. If only I could solve all mine problems so easy . . . You really think I got him the sack, Mrs Weinberg?'

'I've told you.'

'Will I get into trouble? I mean, can he sue?'

'Sue? Don't be silly.'

'But wait a minute,' my mother exclaimed. 'Wait a minute. I've just had from an idea. You know there's a saying about new brooms sweeping old ground. So what if this new Mayor decides the trenches should be built after all? You mean I got to go through all that rigmarole again? If so, I tell you straight it's somebody else's turn.'

Instead of relishing her success, my mother sat thinking. When she spoke again it was to say: 'Mind you, I didn't want to get the poor devil the sack; just that he shouldn't build his lousy shelters and get us all killed . . . There's so much unemployment around as it is . . . Maybe we ought to arrange a collection, or I'll make him a few cakes.' She rose quickly to her feet. 'That's what I'll do – make him a bowl soup and a few cakes. That'll soon put him right as rain. All pure, all goodness; better than all the trenches.'

And make him soup and bake him cakes she did. A quart of *lokshen* soup was decanted into a milk bottle, *strudel*, cheese and yeast cakes were tenderly wrapped in tissue paper, the finished parcel labelled: *Please forward to THE OLD MAYOR (in the bowler hat) from a WELL WISHER,* and delivered to the Town Hall by a protesting Ruth.

Thirteen

ECONOMIES TO help Uncle Mendel came to an abrupt end with the
neck of lamb. Attempting to devise further ways of assisting her
brother, my mother was granted a moment of divine revelation
which could be summarized as the realization that we were all
confusing cause and effect. Mendel was infallible and indestruc-
tible, a businessman and a genius. Thus it could not be a question
of where Mendel had gone wrong, but of seeking out and anni-
hilating his enemies; the evil, jealous and doubtless anti-Semitic
men who were plotting his downfall. While their plans could not
succeed, they produced certain petty harassments, such as my
uncle's present setback, and my mother expressed surprise that
someone as brilliant as Mendel had not seen this from the very
beginning.

She did not immediately leap on a bus to tell Mendel of her
God-given solution, but first sought confirmation from 'one or two
respectable and clever men who know about such things': Rabbi
Tsimmus, Leonard Cooperman and Iron Foot Yossell Teitelbaum.
(It always gave her comfort and confidence to back an argument
with the assurance: 'And that's not just my opinion; so-and-so also
says I'm right.')

The Tsimmus household was in turmoil when we called. Rachel
Tsimmus had been told that as part of civil defence gas masks
were to be issued: rubber gas masks, and since they would provide
'good protection to keep electric from the face, eh? Hmm? Eh?'
she was continually badgering the postman whom she supposed
would be the person to deliver them. None of this troubled the
rabbi's studies, but he roused himself when his wife decided that
as an orthodox Jewess she ought to shave her head – but instead of
wearing a wig she was going to wear a rubber bathing cap on her
hairless skull: 'That's where lightning strikes, from above, on the
top of the body.' The rabbi told her there was nothing in Talmudic

law which said that a woman had to shave her head. What the
Talmud did say was that a married woman's hair must not be
exposed loosely in the streets. To prevent this happening (it was
grounds for divorce) a wig could be worn over the hair – but so
could a suitable scarf or hat such as she currently used. He added
that if God had intended her to be bald He wouldn't have given
her hair to start with – and concluded with the promise to beat the
demons from her with his leather belt if she so much as looked at
a pair of scissors. Since Rabbi Tsimmus was a man of his word his
wife had taken to her bed, covered herself with a rubber sheet and
had lain there for three days sulking.

As for my mother's problem: 'The Lord giveth, the Lord taketh
away. If He whose name I am not worthy to mention has brought
affliction and sufferings to your brother, He has His reasons. Let
your brother not waste his time with earthly things, but try to
prepare himself for the World to Come. Not question, but try to
be at peace with Almighty God.'

'Be at peace with Him?' said my mother timidly. 'Since when
was my brother at war with Him?'

The rabbi's fingers twitched, as though anxious to tug my
mother's ear. Instead he launched into a twenty-minute lecture,
made up entirely of complicated quotations of which neither my
mother nor myself understood a word.

When he had finished my mother asked politely: 'Maybe there's
something in the Bible? Something we could look up when I get
home?'

'The Bible is a history book. We must be concerned with The
Law. The Rules of Behaviour. The Spirit. Those parts of the Bible
which concern The Law are in the Talmud and its Commentaries,
and the Commentaries on the Commentaries. Even a sentence, a
word, can have a thousand meanings.'

'Of course,' said my mother. 'What else? I agree a hundred per
cent. That's what I'm always telling the children.'

It was another half an hour before we could escape.

As my mother should have known, Leonard Cooperman argued
that if Uncle Mendel was in trouble he should endure his misfortunes with joy. 'Of course, your brother has enemies,' he added,

not without a certain relish. 'All Jews have enemies, dear lady . . . There was the case of Oscar Kretch. Also a businessman. From Leeds. Now his wife died (may it never happen here) and left him a fortune. But she was a good Jew and didn't want a big, vulgar, showy tombstone. Just a small stone to mark where she lay. You understand? You follow me? You comprehend? Well then, Oscar did what she wanted and continued with his business.

'It so happens, knowing that the value of money changes, Oscar Kretch invested some of his wife's money in a diamond ring. I don't know from how many carats – I'm a watchmaker, not a jeweller, as you are aware – but it was big like a walnut. So there were jealousies. Such jealousies! I only hope a nice lady like you should be spared the like. So imagine, visualize, conceive what happened when they put around the story, spread it like wildfire, that his wife said that when she died she'd wanted for Oscar to buy, not a simple stone, but a huge stone. And so he did – a huge precious stone.

'Close your eyes and try to picture! His enemies told everyone the story and he was shunned. An outcast. A leper. A pariah in the wilderness of life. In the end he went bankrupt despite all his wife's money. But ah, dear lady, he was a better Jew for it. So tell your brother to smile, be brave, have joy.'

My mother declined, not without a struggle, Iron Foot Yossell's offer to cut the cards to see what they held for Uncle Mendel. Denied this, Yossell quoted the Talmud between mouthfuls of fried middle cut of plaice: 'Man is born with his hands clenched, he dies with them open. Entering life he desires to grasp everything; leaving it all his possessions have slipped away.' Rabbi Pinkus was kept for the *strudel*: 'In the midst of adversity we must see the bright side, for as Jacob said when he heard of the death of Abraham: "Just as my coat of many colours has a silver lining, so there, but for the grace of God, goes Isaac".' Gulping down his tea he assured my mother: 'Your brother is going to be all right, Mrs Ashe. I got a feeling like I haven't had since the afternoon Max Sontag bit everyone in the barber shop. I said at the time no good would come of it, and was I wrong? Now I got another of my feelings, and I say cheer up, everything's going to be all right.'

When we did go to Zanzibar Terrace my mother's inquiry about the accountant put Uncle Mendel into a black rage. His entire body seemed to tremble, even his moustache-ends quivered, and the boils on his neck were a volcanic range on the point of eruption. 'The lousy accounter!' he snarled. 'The filthy Lithuanian bum-boy! May his kidneys fester and his bowels catch fire! May he turn blue and be buried alive! . . . And may I never live if I pay him one stinking penny!' A growl became a bellow of laughter. 'Don't take any notice, Minnie. It's just that I lose my temper for a minute when I think of that Lefkowitz . . . I'll tell you.

'He comes here and looks at my books. Very thorough, like the Income Tax. Which stands to reason, that's what he's paid for. But he goes further. He wants to know why I bought such-and-such a thing for so much, and why I sold for what I did; and the same with something else . . . and something else. So I keep calm and I tell him, I explain. I feel perhaps he's entitled to know. He goes on to ask the rent I pay, how much I pay Ben, what money the children bring in, what other money there is, how much is the coal, the gas, the electric, how much we pay food, rates – there wasn't from one tiny thing he didn't want to know. And I tell him everything. It's logic that if he's going to help me he needs what the Americans call the whole whatchercallit.

'So he works it all out and does his sums like a real professional: special paper with lines on and uses two sorts of ink, blue and red. So I sit patient and wait until he's finished. And then what does he tell me? Eh? He tells me to pack in the business and for me and Ben to go get a job! He says that according to his figures we shouldn't have no house, no clothes, no food, no nothing. So go get jobs.' A tremor shook Mendel's body. His voice rose. 'I call him in to tell me how best to expand, open branches, start import and export, get agents, make the business bigger so I can get the capital for the big deal that's going to take us to America – and that's what he tells me! I chucked him out the house. Slung him out. And I can tell you that he won't forget so quick what I told him as he went.'

Mendel laughed. 'So we have got a house, we have got clothes, we have got food, and we have got coal, gas, electric. All we haven't got is a poxy Lithuanian accounter.' He clapped his hands.

'And we got more! We got a consignment seaside rock coming in. You know the lettering that goes through seaside rock that says Margate? Well on this, for some reason the lettering's back to front. Like with a mirror. So what difference? How many kids that eat rock can read? I'll sell to Robinson down the Lane as Polish rock. Back to front Margate looks Polish, no? I'll say it's Warsaw or Lodz rock. We won't make a fortune from it, but it's a start, a beginning.'

My mother expressed her admiration, then told Mendel of the enemies who were behind his current misfortunes. My uncle shrugged it off. 'Don't worry, Minnie; don't worry. We'll hear good news soon. It stands to reason. On top of which I got a feeling in my bones that something's going to happen.'

And something did happen. It began at breakfast with footsteps and the rattling of the letter box. 'Esther Cooperman,' my mother groaned. Then came the postman's double knock. She went to the door grumbling: 'What bill is it this time?' and returned ashen and shaking, holding a letter in her shivering hand. It carried a New York postmark with Hannah Feiner's name on the back of the envelope above an address in Brooklyn.

'A . . . a . . . letter. From Aunt Hannah. W . . . what can it be? What can it mean?'

'Open it and see,' I suggested.

'Suppose it's bad news? After all these years why write to me?'

'You won't know if you don't open it,' said Ruth.

My mother put the envelope on the kitchen table, smoothed it, touched it with a forefinger, clutched at the neck of her dress and said to me, 'You open it.'

I did so.

Dear Minnie,

My friend Mrs Adler is writing this because my eyes aren't so good these days. I lost my husband Mark, may he rest in peace, in 1929 when there was the Wall Street crash. The real blame, as everybody knows, was Henderson the stockbroker. Mind you, they were all committing suicide, but for Henderson to take Mark with him was a liberty. But what is to be, will be – as my poor mother used to say. My son Howard, in real estate, can't be bothered with me. And there's no other children because of the operation, and no grandchildren because Howard never married. He's in California and living so much like a Gentile now my friend Mrs Adler says she wonders if he's still circumcised. (She meant it as a joke.) He doesn't want to know me, and in any case I don't even know the name he calls himself these days. But he'll be punished. Like it says in the Talmud, men should be careful not to make a mother weep for God counts her tears. I'm getting old now and I want to spend my last days with my sister, your mother, if she's still alive, if not, with my dear English nephews and nieces. I'm coming September 18th Southampton and maybe you can arrange for somewhere for me to stay. I'm writing to you because I don't know the other addresses. I got them all from Shaindel Goldberg who was previous Shaindel Katz when she and the family came to New York on their way to Canada about five years ago. We met accidental at a wedding. I lost all the other addresses except yours. I know I should have written before but my eyes aren't so good, but that doesn't mean I don't think of you every minute of the day.

Your loving aunt,

Hannah Feiner

My mother screamed, snatched the letter from me, read it herself eight or nine times and collapsed into a chair. Ruth offered to pour her another cup of tea.

'Tea? Tea? At a time like this? My shoes and hat and coat. I've got to go see Mother and Mendel.' She rose to her feet and swayed. 'I've got palpitations . . . My God, Hannah coming! And in only a week's time!'

I said that I had to go to school. Ruth said that she would be late for work.

'School? Work? With Hannah coming any minute? How can you aggravate me like that? Be so selfish? With all this excitement I'm probably going to have a heart attack on the bus and you'll leave me to die . . . So why are we sitting talking? Hurry! Hurry!'

We hurried.

At Zanzibar Terrace tear-drenched chaos was followed by wild and hysterical speculation – until Mendel revealed the true import of Hannah's letter.

'Don't you see?' he bellowed. 'Read it again. Uncle Mark was in Wall Street, like from the stock exchange over here. A stockbroker. A wealthy man. I once saw on the pictures about such people. With Edward Arnold. A house in Long Island. A swimming pool that made the Serpentine a puddle. A ranch in Texas. Private aeroplanes. Cars. And that's not the half of it.

'So Mark, too, was a stockbroker. All right, so the firm went bust. Because of this wassisname – this Henderson – he kills himself (may it never happen here). But what about his private money? Don't tell me a man with Long Islands and a ranch in Texas don't have them in his wife's name. It stands to reason. And even if he didn't, what about the furs and jewels? Diamonds like the Cohenwassername.

'So don't you see? With a no-good son she don't like and whose name she don't even know, and no other children, no grandchildren, for what other reason is she coming if not to leave us her money? It's logic.'

I swear that the noise that followed Mendel's statement made the entire room shake and caused the furnishings to bounce on the floor. Following the familiar pattern, it continued until Granny Abrams signalled for silence.

'You know,' she said, wiping her eyes with the hem of her skirt, 'after all these years with not a word, not a line, I thought Hannah was dead, God forgive me. Poor woman, all alone in the world. A son who doesn't want to know her . . . Funny, only the one; it isn't natural somehow.

'What I'm saying is that she's alive and younger than me. So don't get too excited. If everything in America is like Mendel says, and the doctors such marvels, she could live, please God, to be a hundred and twenty . . . But I suppose it's nice to have something to look forward to. Not for myself – except I could do with some new teeth – but for the children and grandchildren.'

'A house in Westcliff,' said my mother. 'Roses. A new wireless. Fitted carpets. A hot sea bath.'

'I fancy Golders Green,' said Aunt Zillah. 'Very swank. Buy businesses for all the children. The Gowns. The Wireless.'

'Westcliff! Golders Green!' Mendel yelled. 'What you women talking about? New York we're going to. America. All of us. As for jobs, the kids can do what they want. For Herschel the doctoring, eh, dolly? For Ruth the shorthand-typing. Simey can go in for the writing and Sybil . . .'

'So we all go to America,' Granny Abrams interrupted. 'If you're waiting for Hannah to die, I told you, you might have a long wait. And if you go while she's still alive, what do you do? Leave her in London?'

Mendel took this in his stride. 'She'll come with us. It stands to reason that she's more at home there with the penthouses and swimming pools and oil wells and yachts. She's only coming here for the family. We'll be doing her a favour to take her back.'

'In the meantime,' said Ben, 'she's not here yet. And when she comes where's she going to stay?'

'Stay?' Mendel thundered. 'What do you mean, stay? At the Ritz she'll stay, or Claridge's. Park Lane! Mayfair! It's a good job I thought of it: I must book her one or two floors at the Savoy or the Dorchester.' He clapped his hands. 'The banquets we'll have! Every meal will be like a wedding, eh, mother?' To Ben: 'Such a question to ask. Where will she stay? Where d'you think she'll stay after all she's been used to? Zanzibar Terrace? Does it make sense? Does it stand to reason?'

'Of course it stands to reason,' said Granny Abrams crossly. 'What's good enough for me isn't good enough for Hannah? I remember when all us girls had as a bedroom was a corner of the kitchen behind a curtain. On the floor we slept, on straw, near the stove to keep warm. If because she's been in America and has got a few shillings she's suddenly got ideas like Countess Potocki I'll remind her different. In any case she's my sister. I haven't seen her for what – getting on fifty, sixty years? So I'm not going to have her in my own house? Does that stand to reason?'

'Where's she going to sleep?' Zillah demanded.

'She'll have Ben's room,' said Granny Abrams.

'And Ben?' my mother asked.

Mendel said sulkily: 'We'll make up a bed on the landing . . .
I'm worried. I mean to say, I know this is our home, nothing to
be ashamed of, but it's not Buckingham Palace . . . I'll have to get
a few things done.' More cheerfully: 'After all, it's an investment.
We'll give Ben's room new wallpaper. I know where I can get a
few rolls cheap – something about the pattern. A new chain for
the lavatory – a new lock as well, maybe? And what else? . . . In
America they got what they call ice boxes, but there's plenty boxes
in the cellar and I can always get ice from the fishmonger. So what
else? . . . A bottle of that special American whisky and for the rest
we'll find out as we go along. And maybe new clothes.'

He banged his forehead as a new thought occurred. 'Suppose
she expects us to dress for dinner?'

Granny Abrams: 'Already we eat naked?'

'I mean suppose she expects evening dress?'

My grandmother: 'Then she'll have to suppose. I told you, she's
mine sister, not the Queen from England.'

Mendel: 'So the clothes we'll see about, but if she does stay
here we can still go to the Savoy in the evenings, no? Champagne,
caviare, black velvets.'

'What sort of mad talk is this?' asked my mother, appalled. 'I
wear my black velvet for funerals.'

'It's a drink,' said Mendel testily. 'Made from something or
other. In America everyone drinks it in the bath.'

'You mean we got to go to the Savoy, in the bathroom there, to
drink this?' said my mother, startled. Hopefully: 'Are they hot sea
baths?'

Mendel clenched his fists and his teeth and I had the impression
his toes were curling.

'What's caviare?' Herschel asked.

'It's a sort of fish,' said his father. 'Costs a fortune. You got to eat
with silver forks. In America they eat it all the time . . . Aie, aie, but
there's money there. Only last week at the Troxy . . .'

'I can get all the fish I want round at Ruda's,' said Aunt Zillah.
'And haven't we got silver fish knives and forks Minnie gave us for
our wedding which we never used yet? And aren't you forgetting
something else? All this spending you're going to do with money

from God knows where: suppose your Aunt Hannah's close? A miser. Some people got money but don't part with a penny.' Loudly: 'Like that Mrs Koski downstairs.'

Mendel gnawed at a thumbnail. 'So, for the sake of argument, let's suppose we're talking about when she . . . er . . . goes. So all right; no champagne, no caviare, no Savoy. But as I said before, isn't it as plain as the nose on your face from her letter that she's coming here to leave us her money? Who else is she going to leave her houses and black velvets? I mean, why write at all? Why come? Read the letter again for yourself. It stands to reason, don't it? Like they say in Yiddish: "They don't make pockets in shrouds".'

Unexpectedly, Ben spoke. 'Don't count on too much. In the Talmud it says: "The camel wanted horns and his ears were taken from him".'

Mendel turned angrily to his brother. 'Instead of reading the Talmud you'd do better to get on with the hairpins. They're a bit rusty,' he explained to my mother, 'but a soak in paraffin and they'll be as good as new . . . What a brother! What an assistant for a businessman. The things I have to put up with.'

Ben shuffled to the door and quoted rebelliously: 'One does the work and the other does the grunting.'

The coming of my great-aunt overwhelmed Granny Abrams: it was difficult for her to accept that her sister was still alive and that they would be meeting again. She wept and sighed and shook her head, and was really rather frightened at the thought of the physical return of someone who had become part of the sentimental remembrance and legend of a generation and a world remote in place and time.

It did not take long for the news to reach the remotest fourth cousin by marriage, inspiring curiosity and greed and a desperate clutching at the last frayed threads of crumbling hope. As for my mother, thoughts of personal gain came second to the genuine delight she felt for her mother's sake at Hannah's reappearance. And when the last eyes were dried at Daffodil Square she had to endure much heavy banter from her friends – not without its undertones of envy.

And so on September 18th, dressed and behaving as though attending a wedding, and much to the amusement of the railway staff, the family went *en masse* to Waterloo to meet the boat train, Granny Abrams having vetoed Uncle Mendel's suggestion that a couple of Rolls-Royces should be hired to go down to Southampton.

Hannah was greeted with tears, ecstatic shrieks, hugs, kisses and moans of joy. One of my cousins was sick and a group of aunts led by Zillah danced on the platform until restrained by a railway policeman. Hannah wept in return: an old and tiny woman wearing pebble glasses, dressed in a black overcoat and a blue straw hat and clutching a brown-paper carrier bag.

Granny Abrams and her sister clung to one another as Mendel, his face wet with tears, helped them into a taxi. Those of us who were invited to lunch (and Aunt Zillah had none of my mother's qualms about paring down the guest list) made our own way to the East End, while Uncle Ben followed with Great-Aunt Hannah's baggage on his barrow.

We arrived at Zanzibar Terrace to find that the two women were in Granny Abrams' bedroom. We sat fidgeting and spoke in whispers, while Zillah banged about in the kitchen, fuming that the lunch would be ruined. When, after an hour, the sisters emerged, dabbing handkerchiefs to their reddened eyes, Uncle Mendel took his mother to one side. 'Well?' he demanded.

'Well what?'

'Well, what did you find out? About you know what as well as I do.'

'We hardly spoke a word, we was too busy crying. And what we did say was about our parents and brothers and sisters and . . .' The rest of the sentence dissolved into a tearful wail.

Later, as we sat eating roast beef and stuffed neck of chicken, the excitement began to ebb away, replaced by a certain restlessness; an uneasy belch-punctuated silence. Aunt Zillah nudged Mendel and muttered: 'Well . . . ask her.'

Mendel's answering whisper rattled the windows: 'How can I?'

There was a further period of tense impatience, then Great-

Aunt Hannah said: 'You're a good woman, Cissie, to give me a roof over my head. Some would have refused.'

Granny Abrams spread her hands. 'Mine own flesh and blood I should let sleep in the streets?'

Hannah wiped away a tear with a wrinkled forefinger. 'I'm only sorry I've come empty-handed. Not even a present for the children.'

'Don't worry,' said Mendel. 'It's the thought that counts.' Winking at Zillah: 'London may not be New York, but we also have shops.'

'Sure you do,' said Hannah unhappily, 'but I'm talking about money. When I'd paid my fare I didn't have a nickel left to bless myself with.'

An angry rumbling. Mendel frowned. 'Not a nickel to . . .' He took a deep breath. 'What . . . what happened to the mink coats? The aeroplanes? The house in Long Island?' He was plainly worried now. 'But the jewels must be worth a few thousand pounds, eh? It . . . stands . . . to . . . reason . . .'

Hannah stared at him. 'Jewels? Minks? Hairplanes? What talk is this?'

Mendel was sweating. 'But your husband, the stockbroker – may he rest in peace. Stockbrokers don't die beggars.'

'Stockbrokers? Who said anything about stockbrokers?'

'You did, in your letter,' Mendel yelled. 'You said Uncle Mark was a stockbroker from Wall Street and because of the crash he committed suicide with this wassisname . . . Henderson.'

Hannah looked up at the ceiling. 'God in Heaven, what sort of a madhouse have you put me in?' To Granny Abrams: 'Where was all this supposed to be written? By my life I wrote no such letter. Your son's a crazy man. Just show me the letter.'

Granny Abrams said: 'Letter, *schmetter*! Just say: was Mark a stockbroker or wasn't he?'

'Stockbroker! I wish he was. Stockbroker! Huh! He was a pedlar. An honest man, God rest his soul in peace. He sold shoe laces, razor blades, toothbrushes, combs and such things from a tray round his neck. He had a very nice-class trade with people working in Wall Street. So this Henderson shoots himself and stands by the window to do it. Right? And he falls out of the window from twenty floors up. Right? And what happens? I'll tell you. He falls on my Mark and kills him. That's what happens.'

For a full ten seconds there was silence, then it seemed as though Granny Abrams was having some sort of a seizure. But the grunting noises from deep down in her stomach slowly emptied into a great, rolling explosion of laughter. It went on until she choked. Aunt Zillah banged her on the back until her upper dentures fell out.

When the laughter stopped I could hear the grumbling murmur of my uncles, aunts and cousins. I turned to my mother. Tears were rolling down her cheeks. 'Diamonds . . . islands . . . motor-cars. My aggravations I wouldn't wish on my worst enemy.' She sighed. 'I should have known better than to hold out hope.' She quoted in Yiddish: 'With my luck, if I sold candles the sun would never set,' and rose from the table. 'Simey, Ruth – it's time to go home.'

On the way back to Daffodil Square she said: 'What really matters is that she's here and that your grandmother is happy. That's what counts. That's the important part . . . At the same time I'm sorry for Mendel. He had such high hopes . . . And I don't mind telling you that I also thought once or twice that a few pounds would come in handy. Pay a few bills, and you both need new overcoats for the winter . . . It's the Mrs Malik story all over again. And it serves me right. With my luck I should have known better . . . And on top of everything else, heartburn from the rotten beef. Like a red-hot dagger. You'd have thought at her age she'd know how to cook a piece of beef. . . . Just the same I admit I could do with new shoes.'

When I saw Uncle Mendel about a fortnight later he seemed a broken man. His moustache-ends drooped and his shoulders were bent. Even his voice was lower. When in the same room as Hannah he would not look at her, and he did his best to avoid speaking to her. He felt he was the victim of a monumental and unforgivable confidence trick, and his mood was in no way improved by the frenzy of wild dealing into which he had been forced in order to settle the debts that resulted from his preparations for Hannah's arrival. Further, when he had tried to be friendly and asked her about her life in 'Li'll ole Noo York', she had enraged him by describing a Brooklyn of rat-infested tenements, penny-scrimping poverty and slum degeneracy, while he knew from the films he had seen that Brooklyn was really a charming suburb with only muted violins by way of noise, and inhabited solely by philosophic Jewish tailors, Irish tenors and lovable Italian barbers, all of whom enjoyed a standard of living of which Rothschild himself would not be ashamed.

This apart, Great-Aunt Hannah was not a sympathetic personality. Truculent and dyspeptic, she spent her days complaining about the shabby difference between things American and things English, of her failing eyesight and her rheumatism, of the hardness of the mattress on her bed, of the wireless which could not pick up the soap opera she followed, of the absence of Mrs Adler, of her son, of the British climate – and of anything else that came to mind at a given moment.

My mother tried to like her since she was, after all, her aunt, but she admitted that she was glad she didn't have Hannah Feiner as a neighbour (although my mother was nearly won round when Hannah complained of the lack of central heating and added: 'I've certainly got my own with the heartburn I get from the cooking in this house').

Nor did Granny Abrams really take to Hannah. This woman with her curiously accented English and Yiddish, and her eternal disparagements, was not the person with whom she had shared secrets on a straw bed, had visited the ritual bath, had held hands as the Sabbath candles were lighted and with whom she flirted with the shoemaker's sons. The girl with whom she had taken turns at milking the cow, had hidden in the woods at rumours of a Cossack raid, and whom she remembered as the vivacious player of practical jokes who had to be defended with fierce protectiveness. That Hannah was indeed dead, as dead as youth itself; this Hannah was a sour old woman with a vague, tantalizing quality of evoking memories of a life of which she herself could never have been a part. Granny Abrams confided to my mother: 'She's mine sister, mine own flesh and blood; but do you know – and may God forgive me for saying it – if someone said she wasn't it wouldn't upset me too hard.'

Hannah never came to be loved or even respected, but since it was acknowledged that she would be at Zanzibar Terrace for the rest of her days the family accepted her with that pessimistic fatalism inbuilt into the Jewish character.

By preferring to think that Great-Aunt Hannah did not exist, Uncle Mendel soon recovered his optimistic good humour. When my mother asked him how he was managing with an extra mouth to feed, he replied: 'No trouble at all.' His moustache-ends were like bayonets, his back was erect and his voice echoed from the walls. 'Don't worry. I got a load of butter coming tomorrow. From the fire in Liverpool Street. It melted from the heat, but it's hard now and just needs cutting into lumps. We'll have money to spare. Maybe even enough to join Aunt Han . . . Well, anyway, just wait and see. Half-price butter. The demand will be enormous. It stands to reason, don't it, Ben?'

Ben shrugged and reached out delicately towards one of the tulips on the dining-room wallpaper.

Fourteen

THERE WAS a certain ambivalence in the family's attitude towards the coming war. There were the natural reactions of fear and revulsion, and the fervent hopes that somehow it could be avoided; but confused with these emotions was an impatience to see it started, for war would mean the end of Hitler and Nazi persecution.

Only Uncle Ben looked forward to the war without the slightest reservation. He owned *The British Jewry Book of Honour*, a thick blue volume titled in gold which listed every Jew who had served in the Great War, with photographs of those who had achieved senior rank or had won high awards for gallantry. If Ben's copy was placed on its spine, usage made it fall open at the same page: where there was entered the name and official number of Private Benjamin Abrams of the Middlesex Regiment, holder of the Military Medal. Ben would spend hours just staring at it, recalling his years of service and how they had provided the only worthwhile moments in an otherwise futile existence: when the brigadier pinned the medal to his chest, and when cheering neighbours crowded the pavements and waved Union Jacks on the day of his homecoming. For Ben the next war could offer only further glory: perhaps promotion to sergeant; even another decoration.

And so, one morning in the spring of 1939, he pinned on his medals, put his discharge papers in his pocket, presented himself at the local recruiting office, saluted smartly and announced that he was reporting for duty, being anxious to serve King and Country and kill a few Germans – bang, bang! He felt that while with his experience he ought to start off as a lance-corporal, if they couldn't see their way clear to do this he'd begin again as a private. So God Save the King and Hang the Kaiser.

That much of the story was more or less as Ben told it. What followed came from Granny Abrams and Uncle Mendel who heard it from Sergeant Lucas of Leman Street Police Station.

Because of Ben's age, hernia and shell shock, he was turned down. Ben said they were idiots. He was the sort of person they needed when war came: an old soldier, a trained man whose marksmanship couldn't be sworn to (from the trenches who's to know whose bullet hit what?), but who had killed his share of the King's enemies with bayonet and rifle butt. He could offer even more: if officers were short he had experience at saving them. The recruiting sergeant said he appreciated Uncle Ben's good intentions, that Ben was a very brave man, but he had done his share and was no longer fit enough for the Army. Ben lost his temper. 'You try pushing that bloody barrow! We'll see who's fit!' he shouted, and went on to call the recruiting sergeant a Blackshirt, an anti-Semitic bum-boy and a traitor to the country who should be shot down like a dog and then sent to the front line. The sergeant laughed, whereupon Ben knocked him cold. Two other soldiers appeared. Uncle Ben dealt with them in like manner. He was halfway through wrecking the office, shouting: 'Who's fit now, eh? I'll kick in a few ribs, bang, bang!' when the police arrived and took him to the police station. Fortunately, Sergeant Lucas had had experience of my uncle's outbursts and persuaded the recruiting officer not to press charges, arguing that Ben's motive – an excess of patriotic zeal – was really to be commended. So Ben was brought home and urged by Sergeant Lucas: 'Be a good boy and don't do it again.' To which my uncle cried: 'Hang the Kaiser!' and squared up to the sergeant like an old bare-knuckle fighter. Mendel dragged him indoors.

'A disgrace!' his brother roared. 'We'll be the laughing stock of the neighbourhood. May God strike me deaf, dumb and covered in scabies if I don't have him put away. Behaving like a hooligan. And hitting soldiers yet! You could be field-marshalled and sent to the warehouse.'

'Glasshouse,' said Ben, polishing his medals with his jacket sleeve.

'Warehouse! Glasshouse! Craphouse! What difference? They'll find somewhere to put you, you madman . . . And suppose, for the sake of argument, the Army was so hard-up they took you. Who helps me run the business? Who should push the barrow?

Your mother? . . . And suppose you got killed this time? You selfish pig-dog, always thinking of your own pleasures . . . Fighting in the streets! It's the last straw. The straw that broke the camel's whatsit. God blind me for life if I don't have you locked up.'

'Throw him out of the house,' said Aunt Zillah. 'I swear on my poor father's memory I won't cook so much as another potato for him.'

'That's a punishment?' asked Great-Aunt Hannah. 'But I agree: throw him out.'

'Quiet a minute,' said Granny Abrams. 'Don't be in such a hurry to throw out. I know Ben's a dummy. Like they say in Yiddish, if he fell on his back he'd break his nose. I know what he is better than anyone. And I know it's his own fault. It serves him right, going in the Army when no one asked, and then saving the life from a *scheisspot* officer. I know all that.' She looked sharply at her sister and daughter-in-law. 'But in this house me, and no one else, says who gets the chuck out. All right?'

Mendel began to bellow, but Ben did not wait to hear. He shuffled from the room and the house and went to the nearest civil-defence office and asked to join 'from Air Raid Precautions'. They were delighted to enrol him, were not certain in what capacity he could best be used, but did not think they would take up his offer of removing dead bodies on his barrow. Ben's joy at being accepted was marred by there being no immediate issue of any uniform. He returned to Zanzibar Terrace, rummaged in the basement and unearthed two souvenirs of the Somme: a rusty German bayonet and a battered German helmet with a spike on the top. He tied the bayonet to his left hip with a piece of string, inexpertly painted ARP on his helmet and thereafter was never to be seen without them except at synagogue, and then only after protests by the minister. After a while the police took the bayonet away, but Ben continued to regard the scabbard as essential to his outdoor dress.

Uncle Ben did not seem altogether certain what ARP involved, and his first action was to see how best 23 Zanzibar Terrace could be fortified against a German attack. He succeeded in annoying everyone as he measured rooms and calculated the strength of walls, worked out angles of fire from the windows, and nearly fell

from the roof while testing the slates with a hammer to determine
their resistance to shrapnel. He concluded that the house was
unlikely to protect its occupants from even a burst of machine-gun
fire, and was deeply upset when Mendel refused to have it sand-
bagged, or to stock-up with bully beef, tinned stew and jam, arrow-
root biscuits and other iron rations. Ben abandoned his scheme for
turning number 23 into a blockhouse when he realized that to do
the job properly meant knocking down the houses on either side
– a project he was prepared to admit was beyond his scope or influ-
ence. (Nor did it help when he tried to take the measurements of
Madam Koski's Superior Corset Salon and walked into the fitting
room when the Reverend Luppatutnik's wife was trying on her
new stays. That good woman promptly fainted and Ben was driven
from the shop by Madam Koski who cried: 'Now look what you've
done – killed the only customer I got who pays cash.') Ben then
took to teaching the rudiments of arms drill, marching and coun-
termarching to his 'reservists' – a group of neighbourhood urchins
armed with broomsticks, curtain rails and metal rods.

'I don't know what to do with him,' Mendel lamented when
next he came to tea. 'He gets madder every day. I'll end up with his
blood on my hands, just you wait and see.'

'Don't upset yourself,' said my mother. 'He's not so bad really.
He means well.'

'Means well! If you was a German you'd say Hitler also means
well. Fighting soldiers. Brought home by the police. Smashing up
the roof. Raping Mrs Luppatutnik.'

'Language!' said my mother severely.

'With my aggravations you'd also use language.'

'Have another bowl soup. It's marvellous for aggravations.' As
she served it: 'So what else is new?'

'That's not enough already? . . . So what else?' Halfway through
the soup he remembered. 'Ah yes; Max's boy still wants to marry
the Bernard girl.'

The Bernard girl was a bold-eyed seventeen-year-old with a
provocative wriggle and aggressive breasts that threatened to burst
through whatever she was wearing. My mother had submitted her
to the customary probing examination and had found her a most

unsuitable candidate for family status. Now she said: 'Let him get on with it. If he won't listen to reason it's his own funeral. I've said what I have to say. It's not my business; he can do what he likes. But mark my words, that marriage won't last a year.'

'I should have such a year,' said Mendel.

'That's what Ben needs.'

'What? A year with the Bernard girl?'

'Don't be ridiculous,' my mother snapped. 'A wife. It's never too late. And it's not right, not healthy, that Ben should be at home with you and mother.'

'Ben marry!' Mendel's laugh was a mocking bray. 'Who'd have him? That bargain!'

'There must be girls on the shelf, widows, who'd be glad of him,' said my mother.

'So how could he keep a wife and a home?'

'He'd still go on working for you.'

Mendel threw out his hands in a gesture of appeal. 'You think I pay him that sort of money? He gets his food, his keep, a few bob spending-money. More I can't afford. With things as they are it stands to reason.'

'Find him someone with money.'

'You're joking,' said Mendel.

'You'd be surprised the people who get married these days,' said my mother. 'I read in the paper only the other week of a rich woman paralysed from head to toe who married a very nice man. In the paper, in black and white. Poor woman was in what they call an iron lung. Couldn't move from an inch.'

'If she'd been married to Ben he'd have thought the iron wasser-name was a cannon and fired her across London.'

'Try,' my mother urged. 'There's still a few marriage brokers left in the East End. Try. Inquire. There's no harm asking. What can you lose?'

Mendel asked. But there was no rich spinster or wealthy widow sufficiently desperate about her situation to exchange it for Uncle Ben.

Why hadn't he married when he was younger? The question worried me. I put it to my mother and was answered with a kick on my shin followed by a warning that there were plenty more where that came from if I didn't stop my mad talk and mind my own stinking business.

One afternoon, while helping Ben to trundle a barrow-load of suspect bicycle inner tubes to Mile End, we stopped at the kerbside in Whitechapel Road and I asked him why he was still a bachelor. With a forefinger he drew a pattern in the dust of the gutter, then lifted his hand and showed me the scar on its back. 'From the fight outside your house. Gave him what for, eh? Bang! Bang!' He gave a secretive little giggle. 'Mendel thinks I got it from a tin can. Still got the teeth in a drawer somewhere.'

As he returned to his design in the grey dust: 'Nearly married . . . Twice . . . Once to Cousin Annie with the twitch. The one married to Hymie who works for the undertaker. Nice girl. She knew about my funny ways,' (looking at me now from the corner of his eye) 'but wasn't worried . . . Nice girl . . . My cousin, but it's all right to marry if the rabbi says. She was a beauty in them days. Thinner. No babies . . . But her parents was also cousins, and also from inside the family. The rabbi – his name was something like Grobber. Dead now – looks up his books and says see the doctor. So we saw. He says not to marry. Frightened the life out of us with talk of babies with two heads. So we didn't.'

Ben sighed, smoothed the dust and started on a new design. 'After that, nobody was right. I don't mean for me. Mother . . . Something wrong with every one. Every one . . . Too tall, too fat, too this, too the other. Not a good family, no money . . .' He lighted a cigarette. 'Where was I up to? . . . Yes, everyone she found wrong with. If she couldn't find nothing then she'd tell them about my funny turns . . .

'I like you, Simey. Good boy . . . My funny turns . . . Forty-eight hours I was in no-man's land. Long time . . . Guns. All the time, guns. But I got this officer back. So I got my funny turns.' He held out his Military Medal towards me. 'But I also got this. Who else you know got one?'

Ben threw his cigarette away. 'Rifka . . . Nice girl. Pretty. . . . Good Jewish home. Her father was a waiter from Schwartz's in Stepney Way. I brought her home . . . She also knew about my funny turns. I remember like yesterday. We had *lokshen* soup and tongue with red cabbage . . . Mother thought she was marvellous. Just the right girl. Not a fault she could find . . .' Ben climbed to his feet, dusted the seat of his trousers and adjusted his helmet.

'But Uncle Ben, if Granny Abrams thought she was so wonderful why didn't you marry her?'

'My father couldn't stand the sight of her.'

He took up the handles of his barrow, said: 'I didn't bother no more after that,' and refused to speak another word for the rest of the day.

One thought led to another, and when I judged the mood to be right I asked my mother how she came to meet my father – ready to rush from the kitchen if I had misread the signs. But she gave a sad shake of her head, dabbed at the tears the question immediately brought, and said: 'It was a romance. Like what you read from the newspapers. I could have got thousands from *The People* for mine story. Now I suppose it's too late. But a real fairy story . . .'

On his return to tailoring my grandfather took over a lock-up shop off Whitechapel High Street, the window of which carried in English and Yiddish one of Mendel's earlier touches of brilliance: ISAAC ABRAMS, TAILOR TO THE TITLED. ('If anyone asks, say you made suits back home for Count Wassisname. Let them prove different.') My mother would sit in the light afforded by this window, working on whatever needed to be sewn by hand 'with stitches small in those days even people with microscopes couldn't see'.

One morning, sewing the lapels of a blue serge overcoat (she was positive on this detail), a sudden brightness temporarily dazzled her. A moment or so later it was repeated. And then again. At first she could not detect the source of this irritation, then saw that it was sunlight reflected from a pair of opera glasses through which a man across the street was watching her. The shock was so great 'I screamed the place down'. Her father and sister Leah came running from the workroom at the back thinking Jack the Ripper had emerged from retirement. One hand to her throat, the other pointing (this pose was powerfully re-enacted), my mother gave a stammering account of what had happened.

'A-ha,' said my grandfather, 'so he's one of those, is he?' A powerful man, he flexed his muscles, took a sinister pair of cutting shears in one hand and a goose iron in the other and rushed across the road followed by my mother and Aunt Leah.

They entered the building opposite, ran up to the second floor and burst into the room at the front where stood a frightened man holding a pair of opera glasses. 'And what a man,' my mother recalled, the tears running down her cheeks. 'Tall, strong, handsome like the film stars you see in the papers. He took after that one whose picture was in *The Evening News* the other day; Robert Taylor, only a bit more Jewish.' My grandfather brandished his weapons, asked the man how he dared to violate his daughter, and went on to tell him that he proposed cutting him into little pieces with the scissors before beating him to death with the iron. As his daughters clung to my grandfather's arms, the man pleaded for his life, pointing out that if Mr Abrams killed him he'd be sure to lose his job.

'How do you know my name?'

'It's on the window.'

'Spy! Snooper!' my grandfather roared in Yiddish. 'It's not enough already that you try to look up my daughter's skirts, you also read my name on the window, is that it?'

The man drew himself up and said with some dignity: 'Listen mister, my name is Nathan Ashe, the son of Reb Baruch Ashkenazi. I am a respectable man. A tailor's presser from Mr Ginsburg upstairs. When I came to work for him three months ago I saw your daughter from the window here and fell madly in love with her. That's why I bought these glasses – to see her better.'

At this point in her narrative my mother wiped her eyes and blew her nose. 'What do you think of that, eh? Isn't it a fairy story? A story like from the papers that someone made up? But that's not the end of it . . .'

My grandfather was convinced that he was dealing with a madman. 'But if you're not a lunatic, where in Poland do you come from? Who are your parents? How much do you earn? What you got in the bank?'

Nathan Ashe was taken aback by so sudden and peremptory a

demand for such intimate information, but he gave it. My grand-father tugged at his beard and took a pinch of snuff. 'No good. You're wasting your time. No money, no prospects, no nothing. It won't do.' He ushered his daughters from the room, warning Nathan Ashe against further 'monkey tricks with opera glasses'. As they descended the stairs my grandfather muttered: 'Spying with glasses yet. Reading names on windows. He should be ashamed of himself.'

They were halfway across the street when he came pounding after them. 'Please Mr Abrams, at least let me take your daughter out one afternoon. Sunday perhaps?'

My grandfather considered this. 'A walk in the air is healthy. Helps digestion. And in broad daylight you can't get up to any monkey tricks. So a walk – all right. But Leah goes with . . . And no opera glasses.'

My mother was weeping again. 'To think I was the one he wanted . . . Mind you, I was the family beauty in those days.' She blinked away her tears. 'Just the same a man like that, so hand-some, could have chosen any girl at the drop of a little finger. Rich girls from Golders Green, even Finchley . . . So anyway, a lovely walk we took. We went right along Commercial Road to Canning Town then back by Brunswick Road and Bow Road. Your Aunt Leah was never much of a walker and went to tea with someone or other, then met us at Gardener's Corner . . . The next Sunday a bus ride, then during the week the Yiddish Theatre, the theatre in the West End, lovely salt beef by Bloom's in Berwick Street, picnics in Clissold's Park, listening to the band in Hyde Park . . .' She sighed at the memories of a lost happiness.

Although it was a long walk from his lodgings in Burdett Road, Nathan Ashe took to attending the synagogue at the corner of Zanzibar Terrace, impressing my grandmother with the fervour of his devotions. Regularly at the end of the Sabbath morning service he would ask the old man for my mother's hand and just as regularly was refused it. He bought flowers for my grandmother and was told not to waste his money. He bought an engagement ring (later to be pawned by his widow and never redeemed) and my grandfather said he hoped he'd find a nice girl to give it to.

He bought the old man snuff and tobacco, but Isaac Abrams was obdurate.

Then one afternoon my mother looked up from her sewing, hoping to see Nathan at his window. But he was out of the window, sitting on the ledge, feet dangling. He waved to her and shouted something. She shrieked, and again her father and sister came hurrying from the workroom. When they reached the street Nathan Ashe called down in Yiddish: 'I been waiting to see you, Mr Abrams.'

'What do you want, spy?' my grandfather shouted back. 'And what you doing sitting out there like a monkey on a stick?'

'I can't live any more without your daughter. If you don't let me marry her I'm going to jump off and kill myself.'

My grandfather yelled: 'So go jump.' My mother held out her hands to catch him. People who had gathered in the street screamed, and Aunt Leah said to her father: 'What about Minnie? Maybe she don't want him to jump.'

My mother was smiling as she told me this. 'So my father looked at me and said: "You want to marry this lunatic?" And do you know, it was the first time he'd asked of mine opinion. Mine feelings. He believed in the old ways; that these things are better left to the parents to arrange. I could see he didn't like asking me, but with Nathan on the ledge and all the people looking at us very nasty, what could he do? So anyway, I said: "Of course I want to marry him", so my father calls up: "All right, so don't jump. Instead come down and marry my daughter." And Nathan says: "You swear?" and your grandfather says: "I give you my word as a Jew." So the people clapped their hands and your father comes down and I fainted in his arms from all the goings-on.'

My mother rocked in her chair. 'It was a big wedding. No expense was spared. Your grandfather was a good man underneath it all. He always meant well . . . We had our honeymoon at Westcliff by Mrs Goldberg in Palmerston Road. Then we come to live here. I didn't like leaving the East End and the family, but your father got a good job by a tailor in Willesden Lane . . . Ruth was born, you came, and nobody in the whole world – not nobody – was as happy as we was . . .

'We had five years. Only five years. The kidneys and also a cancer. He neglected himself, working and working to make things nice for us . . . There's people who'll tell you five years of happiness is better than none, but you know something? – I sometimes think I should have never married him. With my luck I should have known it couldn't last. There are times I think that if I hadn't married him he'd be alive today . . .' She rose to her feet. 'But what's the good of talking? Put on the kettle and I'll make a cup of tea.'

In bed that night I wept for my mother and for the dead father I had never really known. I thought of Uncle Ben and his Rifka: what if he had stood on the roof and threatened to jump unless they could marry? But even as I asked the question I knew somehow that Ben's story could never have had a happy ending. And I wept a little for him, too.

Soon after I learned of the tragic romances of Uncle Ben, and of the wooing and winning of Minnie Abrams, my sister celebrated her sixteenth birthday by falling hopelessly in love. Ruth, now a trainee manicurist, was still plump and plain; as my mother put it to Mrs Kemensky: 'A good-natured girl, but I can't pretend she's any oil painting.' Charles Westbourne was twenty-three years old, tall, blond and strikingly handsome – and was as besotted with her as she with him.

There were two drawbacks to this Kilburn idyll.

Firstly, Charles Westbourne was a butcher.

In itself this was no special problem: although Charles could not understand why the mere mention of his trade was likely to take ten years from my mother's life expectancy, he was prepared to work as a dustman, labourer, road sweeper, tinker – nothing would stand in their way.

Except the second drawback: Charles Westbourne was not a Jew.

Walking hand in hand with Ruth across Hampstead Heath towards the Vale of Health, he urged her to elope with him to Gretna Green. She refused for two reasons: it would give her mother terrible aggravations, and in any case, much as she adored him, she could not possibly marry a Gentile.

Heartbreak. A grand passion was doomed . . . until Charles had his inspiration: he would become a Jew.

The more he thought about it the more sense it made. He was an orphan, so there were no family problems. He wasn't much of a Christian (nominally Church of England, he sometimes went to church at Christmas), so he would suffer no agonies of conscience.

Ruth was enraptured. This was indeed sacrifice; the sort of proof of true love she'd imagined existed only in films and in such publications as *Red Letter* and *The Oracle*. She chose a name for him that retained his initials – Chaim Wiseman – and cleverly created a background that would avoid questions about middle European origins or associations and would explain his Aryan beauty: he was a Norwegian Jew whose mother brought him from Stockholm (or was it Oslo?) as a baby. She died and he was cared for by cousins (also Norwegian immigrants) who had now gone to Australia, leaving Chaim alone in the world. An added refinement: Norwegian Jews did not speak Yiddish, and Chaim had had no occasion to learn Norwegian (not that there was a great danger of encountering anyone in the family circle who spoke that language). Ruth was sufficiently intelligent to realize that the Norwegian background had yet another advantage: it would account for her loved one's lack of Jewishness; that distinctive composite of religious and social attitudes which had evolved during the hundreds of years of apartness in the ghettoes and villages of middle and eastern Europe.

The Jews do not seek or encourage converts. Indeed, the purists claim that it is impossible to become a Jew by conversion: the Jews are the people chosen by God and you cannot elect to be one of the chosen; either you are a Jew or you aren't. This extreme attitude has no historic support: in the Talmud Rabbi Eleazar ben Pedat argues that the Divine purpose for the dispersal of the Jews was to send them into the world to spread The Word; to seek converts – although this attitude was modified when proselytes proved to be enemy spies, and a rigorous screening system developed to determine whether an applicant's religious attitudes were truly sincere. Then there was the added fear that when a man sought conversion he might not be inspired by faith but by a plum dowry. Since this certainly could not apply in the case of Ruth, Chaim was able to demonstrate that he had no venal motives, and his intensity moved a young minister in Shepherds Bush to accept him for instruction.

Chaim had taken up a formidable challenge. Becoming a Jew is not only a matter of accepting a new religious creed, or of learning Hebrew with its distinct alphabetic form. As Rabbi Tsimmus had tried to explain to my mother (who had failed to understand him because he was telling her of something so instinctively inbuilt into her way of life it was as baffling as if she had suddenly been told that she must wear clothes and cook food) Judaism is not only The Word, but its interpretation into The Law: the lengthy and rigorous code of six hundred and thirteen rules which – in theory – a good Jew must obey and which cover every conceivable aspect of religion, diet, hygiene, judicial, social and moral behaviour – a vast exercise in self-discipline which extends even to the correct order in which you should put on your shoes.

Chaim certainly devoted himself to his studies with commendable diligence – and became progressively more absorbed in them. What began as an expedience developed into a sincere love of the Jewish religion and way of life. It is said that just as there is no woman as respectable as the reformed whore, no fanatic is as extreme as the true convert, but for Chaim his experience was less a matter of conversion than the finding of a first faith.

He applied himself with a fierce single-mindedness of purpose. He grew a beard, took to attending synagogue every evening as well as on the Sabbath, wore the ritual fringes under his shirt, and on the basis that 'you never know where you might bump into people', underwent that most uncomfortable operation for an adult male: circumcision. Ruth was delighted; she would be marrying a real Jew; not one in name only – although, as he concentrated on his studies in order to prepare himself for full Jewish status and marriage, she did not see as much of him as she would have wished.

I learned all this much later. The first I knew of the existence of Chaim Wiseman was when my sister mentioned to my mother with elaborate casualness that she'd met a nice Jewish boy at a local Lyons tea shop and was 'very interested' in him.

My mother evinced no great pleasure at the news. 'Already you're chasing boys? You should be ashamed of yourself. Hanging around boys at your age. I was more than twice as old as you before I went out with a man, and then it was your father, may his soul rest in peace.'

'Granny Abrams married when she was sixteen.'

My mother gestured impatiently. 'That was different – and in any case how can you dare compare yourself with your grandmother, a saint among women?'

'I'm just as serious as you were. I . . . I . . . I love him.'

'Love! What can you know about love?' said my mother angrily. Eyes glittering: 'And how can you talk of being serious. Before I haven't even met him yet? Serious! And I don't even know his name. Who is he? What does he do? Where did you meet him? What does he earn? What proof you got he isn't already married?' Without pausing for breath: 'Why don't you answer? Eh? I suppose it's because you can't. You don't know. I suppose you . . . you picked him up in some dirty place and now you want to marry him because of God knows what disgrace you're going to bring on us all. You wicked girl! As if I didn't have enough trouble without this. My own daughter! How will I live it down? . . . And what the family will say I can't imagine. To think I've done my best to bring you up respectable . . . now this! I do believe you did it on purpose just to aggravate me. I wouldn't be surprised if . . .'

'Mummy!' Ruth howled. 'What are you talking about? Nothing's happened. I met a boy. I'm trying to tell you about it, but you won't let me say a word. So all right, if you don't want to hear, you don't.' She made as though to leave the room.

My mother's expression of rage dissolved into pained martyrdom. 'How can you be like that? I haven't said a word. Of course I want to hear. I'm your mother, dolly. I want to do for the best. So sit down and tell me.'

Ruth sat and told us of Chaim Wiseman, the orphaned Jewish fishmonger she met over a cup of tea and a bath bun at Lyons. My mother listened attentively, nodding her head sympathetically, until my sister mentioned Norway.

'Norway? What you mean Norway? How come Norway? That's

up past the North Pole. I read in the *Empire News* only the other day. They live in the ice and eat raw fish. What do they call them? It sounds Jewish; that's what caught my eye. Only they're not Jewish . . . I know: Eskimoses. How can you marry such a man? Mind you, with the draughts and damp in this sewer during the winter you'll probably be better off in the ice. But to live on raw fish?'

Ruth simplified the geographic position of Norway as 'just north of Poland'.

'North Pole, north Poland,' said my mother. 'So anyway, who ever heard of Norway Jews?'

'Why not?' asked Ruth. 'There's Jews all over the world.'

I remembered a school joke: 'There's even Jewish Red Indians – the Ikey Mohicans', and was punched by my mother and kicked by my sister.

'So why not Norwegian Jews?' Ruth continued. 'He's a Jew like any other. The . . . er . . . the only thing is he's blond.'

My mother's hand went to her mouth. 'God in Heaven! You mean he's peroxided?'

'Of course not,' said Ruth crossly. 'It's natural.'

'Now I'm sure you're mad. Blond Jews from north Poland. Who heard such rubbish? . . . But if you're not telling me lies, this I got to see: a blond, Jewish Eskimoses. So bring him home for Sunday dinner so I can ask a few questions, give an opinion . . . Poor devil, living in the ice eating raw fish. He's probably blond from cold. A nice bowl of *lokshen* soup will soon put the colour back in his hair. Better than all the medicines, all the peroxides.'

Fifteen

As CHAIM WISEMAN came through the front door he took off his trilby hat, put on a little black skull cap and said: 'How do you do, Mrs Ashe?' My mother replied: 'God above, you really are a blond Eskimoses! If you're cold, just say; I'll get a blanket.' Chaim assured my mother that he was not cold, that the weather was, in fact, warm for the time of year – and so to the self-conscious banalities of pre-lunch small talk.

When we sat down to eat Chaim asked Ruth to bring him a jug of water, a bowl and a towel. She did so, and as my mother looked on, eyebrows raised, he rinsed his hands and said the appropriate prayer. Her eyebrows snapped down in a scowl as he continued with the grace before meals.

During lunch Chaim outlined a number of theories he had evolved about the authorship of certain of the more obscure Talmudic tractates, and sought my mother's opinions on the correct interpretation of some of the finer points of Jewish law and ritual. Ruth smiled encouragingly; my mother, flattered to be asked but unable to answer, showed signs of restless irritation. In any case, Chaim was at Daffodil Square to answer questions, not to pose them. She tried to fob him off with 'Eat up before it gets spoiled', and 'I really don't know, I'm sure', but when he pressed her about the correct way to blow one's nose (his clinically detailed alternatives in no way furthering our appreciation of the roast chicken), my mother fell back with some desperation on: 'To be truthful I don't care one way or the other – so long it's good for the Jews.' Chaim regarded this as a philosophic profundity and gave a fair imitation of Rabbi Tsimmus in the process of explaining why.

Chaim finished lunch with the longest grace after meals I have ever endured, again rinsed his hands, then told mother how much he had enjoyed her cooking. On familiar ground now, she

mentioned his job, said in a voice that did not allow for argument that all fishmongers were thieves, nearly as bad as butchers,
but conceded that since Chaim was an employee, not the boss,
there might be a small streak of decency in him somewhere. She
discussed with him costs, cuts and the relative virtues of various
fish; impressed upon him that only her expert knowledge of fish
saved her from being bamboozled left, right and centre; and was
delighted when he confirmed her view that the only sure way of
judging quality and freshness was from the condition of the eyes.
She went on to ask him a few pertinent questions about himself,
his background, his salary, prospects and moral behaviour. His
answers seemed frank enough (there were perhaps certain hesita-
tions when talking of his past), but my mother appeared satisfied
– although she kept looking at his hair and beard with perplexed
head-shaking, and astonished references to 'blond Eskimoses', to
the irritation of Ruth and the puzzlement of Chaim.

'There's something from which I'd like your opinion,' said my
mother. 'I got some beautiful hake which was just fresh fried this
morning. I'll put the kettle on for tea and I want you should have
a little slice. Just a taste. A mouthful.' Chaim said he could not
stay: he might be late at the synagogue for evening service. 'Say a
few prayers here,' my mother urged. 'Cheer us all up a bit. Prayer
books we got, and water for washing we also got – and while you're
at it you could put in a word for the money to pay the water rates.'

Chaim was sympathetic but adamant: if he failed to attend they
might be short of the necessary quorum.

When he had gone Ruth spun round on her heels and said
breathlessly: 'Oh Mummy! Isn't he wonderful? Isn't he marvellous?
Isn't he handsome? Isn't he different from any man in the world?'

'He's certainly different,' my mother agreed. 'Very peculiar.'

'Why peculiar?' Ruth demanded hotly. 'Just because he's blond?'

'Blond Jews from the North Pole is peculiar enough,' said my
mother as she started to cut and butter bread.

Ruth, eagerly: 'But he's a good Jew, isn't he?'

My mother: 'That's just it. All the time prayers, the Bible, the
Talmud, more prayers. That also isn't peculiar?'

Ruth brought the fish from the larder and banged it down on

the table. 'What's peculiar about being a good Jew? . . . Anyway, I want to marry him.'

My mother, incredulous: 'Marry?'

Ruth, defiant: 'Marry!'

'It's out of the question. Impossible. I never heard such a thing in all my life.'

'But why not?'

My mother pushed away the bread and butter and took her daughter's hand. 'You know, dolly, there's nothing I want more than you should marry. Not that there's any rush. But to find a nice Yiddisher boy and settle down . . . But Chaim? You've not been brought up for such a life. I know I've tried to make a good Jewish home, but prayers all the time? Rules and regulations? For the daughters of the Rabbi Tsimmus it's one thing; they're used to it. But do you want such a life? You really know what it means? With prayers and the synagogue and all the rest of it? Go ask from Becky Tsimmus. Go ask from Uncle Mendel or your grandmother . . . On the other hand, for once in my life I don't need from their advice. This I know . . . It's a life you've got to be special cut out for.

'There was a time when every Jew was like Chaim. But that was in Poland. This is from England. Things have changed . . . On the one hand you wouldn't marry a Gentile (God forgive the thought), but a religious maniac isn't just as bad? Believe me, your mother knows best. A Jew is a Jew – but that one? Much too orthodox. It's out of the question.'

We suffered a full week of shouts, screams, tears, threats of suicide, sulking, even loss of appetite. Then Ruth tried a different tactic: assuring Chaim that he was as much of a Jew as was necessary, and warning him that unless he could present her mother with a suitably modified image their romance would be threatened with unthinkable disasters.

Chaim replied that Ruth was the one who should change her ways: she ought to be preparing herself for marriage by trying to become a better Jewess. By this he meant not only prayer and study, but the abandonment of such satanic abominations as colourful clothes, cosmetics, cinemas, novels and newspapers, and an end to working as a manicurist – an evil occupation that involved holding men's hands and was therefore no better than prostitution.

The outcome was inevitable. My mother was right when she said that Ruth possessed neither the background nor the temperament for the life to which Chaim was now so obsessively committed. As his religiosity increased, her ardour cooled.

My sister sighed when she told us she had formally ended their unofficial engagement – but it was a sigh of relief.

Regrettably, Chaim's passion burned on with the dedicated, unswerving single-mindedness that was elemental in the man. I saw him a few times in and around Kilburn High Road – muttering to himself, shaking his head and making sudden little gestures as though wrestling with some rabbinic riddle – then he moved from the district. But for all I know he is still alive somewhere in London: a tall, handsome, ultra-orthodox blond Jew, tragically nursing a broken heart – and the memories of Charles Westbourne who went to Lyons for a cup of tea and a bath bun.

I left school in the early summer of 1939, on the same day as Herbert Levinson and Sholto Popplewell, and was the only one of the trio who had no positive plan for a job or career.

Herbie was anxious to join the family business, and while this delighted his father, Jack Levinson felt that the lad should first broaden his horizons by studying the methods of rival manufacturers, and so found Herbie a post as an office boy at the Carreras tobacco factory in Camden Town.

Despite parental opposition, Sholto Popplewell had his heart set on becoming a master criminal, and within a month of confiding this to me he was put on probation for attempting to steal twenty-four bakelite ashtrays from Woolworth's. (He was later sent to Borstal when found by a policeman near the broken window of a draper's, unable to account for his possession of two corsets, five hairnets, six pairs of stockings and a liberty bodice.)

Apart from a vague desire to write I was still lacking any vestige of ambition. I knew I would have to find work, but I did not view the prospect with any enthusiasm. I walked through the school gates for the last time on a Friday afternoon, and my mother, aware that she could no longer delay a decision about my future, reviled me for not having a job to rush out to that same evening. Who did I think I was: the Emperor of China? Did I expect to be waited on hand and foot for the rest of my life? Was she a million-aire to keep me in luxury, working her arthritis-crippled fingers to the bone while I lay in bed all day eating her out of house and home? Why was I such an ungrateful pig-dog after all she'd done for me? Wasn't she my mother who had fed and clothed me while other children lay starving in gutters?

After about ten minutes of this she wept, appealed to the Almighty, and looked hopefully towards the east for some Mosaic pronouncement to thunder across the heavens from the general direction of Zanzibar Terrace. When none came she delivered a powerful kick which I felt certain had shattered my shin bone, and said that on Sunday we would go to see Mendel: 'To settle this once and for all, you dirty layabout'.

Mendel was clearly displeased when my mother raised the subject of my unemployment. He was the businessman, the maker of instant and seismic finger-snapping decisions; it was not his task to deal with the trivia and minutiae of their execution. And as far as I was concerned the fingers had snapped and the decision made: I should become a rabbi. 'What do you want of my life?' he grumbled. 'You want I should take his hand and lead him to the synagogue?'

'He don't want to be a rabbi,' said my mother. Reaching for a handkerchief: 'If my husband was here would I need to bother you? But the boy's got no father, so I come to you, you being the businessman, the brainy one . . . But of course, if you'd rather I asked elsewhere, I will . . .'

Mendel puffed out his chest and grasped his jacket lapels. 'Of course you come to me. Quite right. Who else? It stands to reason.' He frowned at me. 'So you don't want to be a rabbi?'

I shook my head.

Aunt Zillah said: 'My Herschel could have been a rabbi. He was always top of the class at school. But he's going to be a doctor instead.'

'In the meantime,' said my mother, 'he's a baker's boy.'

'A good thing,' said Granny Abrams. 'A man should always have a trade to fall back on. Like your poor father could always go back to the tailoring. With a doctor, if he doesn't do good at it he can always go back to baking bread.'

Mendel banged the table: 'So doctoring isn't a trade?'

'Not everyone needs a doctor,' said Granny Abrams placidly. 'Think – how many years since I seen one, God be thanked? But everyone eats bread. Believe me, Simey must have a trade . . . Listen to me. Years ago in Lublin – or maybe Lodz, I forget now, it was so far back – there was Anna Pfefferkorn. She was the widow from a cabinet-maker. A nice woman, but a poor woman. She had four sons. Three of them was clever boys. One wanted from to play the violin, one wanted to make pictures with pencils and paints and things, and the third wanted to learn Polish and God knows what else and get mixed-up from the politics. The fourth one was like his father, in the cabinet-making. He wasn't clever like the others. A nice boy – Zalman Pfefferkorn, Not stupid, mind you, but not clever. So anyway, Anna was so proud of the three brainy ones. Oi, but she couldn't do enough for them! So the one studied the painting, the other the violin, and the other the Polish. Such brains! Such cleverness! Such marvels! But you know something?' My grandmother wagged a finger. 'If it wasn't for Zalman they'd all have starved to death . . . So take my advice: learn a trade.'

'But what trade?' my mother asked.

'Try the labour exchange,' said Mendel, weary of the subject.

'The labour exchange?' My mother frowned. 'The labour exchange? A bit common, no? . . . Wait a minute, though! Hang on. The labour exchange! Of course the labour exchange! Why not? I pay my rates. All I get for it is misery and aggravation. So why not the labour exchange? Let the lousy council worry about a job. Let them have the responsibility. Mendel, you're a marvel. Like I always said, a genius.'

Mendel flicked at his moustache-ends. 'It's nothing. After all, like you say, I'm a businessman. I got to know such things.'

Early next morning I presented myself at the labour exchange, went after the first job they offered, was accepted at the interview and started the following Monday as a fourteen-shilling-a-week assistant at the local underground-station bookstall. The work suited me admirably: once the rush hour was over I could sit reading for most of the day.

My mother was appalled. 'Selling newspapers? What sort of trade is this?'

I shrugged. 'That's where they sent me from the labour exchange.'

Enlightenment came slowly. 'That dirty, filthy council! That's who's behind it. They've never forgotten with the trenches. Never forgiven. Now they're getting their own back. I've half a mind to report them to someone or other. They should be ashamed of themselves, the swines; taking advantage of widows and orphans. They should be orphans themselves – every one. That would teach them a lesson . . . Selling newspapers yet! Making mock of us all.'

'If you feel so badly about it,' I said, 'I'll give a week's notice.'

'Don't be so quick noticing. Fourteen shillings a week is fourteen shillings. Look for something better, I agree; in the meantime fourteen shillings is better than a broken leg.' Later she added: 'And perhaps you can bring home a few papers. Old ones they don't need no more. Save me having to go on my bended knees to that lousy butcher.'

When he was told of the job I had taken, Iron Foot Yossell chuckled with pleasure. 'Didn't I tell you, Mrs Ashe? Didn't the three spades say he'd be something to do with writing? And what's newspapers if not writing?'

My mother waved a fist at him. 'Would it have been such a terrible thing, such a hardship, to have chosen from the three from something else? All the hundreds of cards in the pack and you have to choose selling newspapers.'

'It wasn't my choosing,' Yossell protested. 'It was Fate.'

'Fate I got plenty without your help. All my life I've had Fate. More I can do without. For a change I'd like a bit of good luck.'

'You shouldn't talk like that, Mrs Ashe. The Rabbi Pinkus says in his Commentaries; "Fate moves mountains".'

'It's easy for Pinkus to give advice. He don't have to deal with no swine of a landlord, no anti-Semitic Town Hall.'

Yossell rumbled his disapproval and quoted: 'If God Himself was living on earth, people would break His windows.'

'Stop talking and have another piece apple pie,' said my mother. 'God will manage without your help for five minutes.'

My mother's cronies tried to soothe her with assurances that even the humblest job could lead to nobility and greatness – an opinion confirmed by Uncle Mendel when next he came to see us. 'It's a beginning for the boy. Some Yiddisher fellows have done very nice in the newspapers. Like Lord Rothmeyer from the *Mail*. Also sells papers. Sure, he sells by the million, but he had to start small like everyone else. People all need newspapers; for reading, wrapping, the lavatory, cleaning windows.'

'But is it a trade?' asked my mother.

'When you got his money who cares what it is? In any case, please God when we get to America . . .'

'America!' my mother shouted. 'That reminds me. You was the one who told me that with newspapers they was always drinking and killing women.'

I said: 'That was writing for them, not selling them.'

'Buying! Selling! What difference, you drunken murderer?'

'Please Minnie,' said Uncle Mendel, 'no quarrels. I've already had one today and that's enough.'

'A quarrel,' said my mother, paling. 'Who with?'

'Who do you think with? With that *dumkopf*, Ben. Who else?'

'Poor Ben. He means well.'

'That's what you always say. But listen. I send him to this sailors' hostel down Surrey Docks. They was closing down and there was these sheets at the auction. So what does that remind you of?' My mother shook her head. 'Don't it remind you of the shortage of bandages during the last war? So with this new war they'll also need bandages, no? So I thought I'd buy these sheets cheap, get the girls to cut them into strips, roll them nice in greaseproof paper, paint on a red cross, and when the war comes – a fortune! It would be like the elastic all over again.

'But what happens? I can't get to the auction because there's a consignment of false teeth arriving (among other things I thought I might find a nice set for Mother). So what can I do but send Ben?

I tell him clear as day how much to bid, how to arrange the credit for paying – everything. And what does he do? He admits to me, bold as brass, that he's had one of his daydreams. You know what he's like – eyes staring, mouth grinning like a stuffed dummy – and when he decides to wake up it's too late: the sheets have gone to Fleischmann (may his children have knotted guts). And then what does Ben do? My clever brother? Because the sheets have gone he bids for blankets. Blankets! God strike me dead and then give me a black year if I lie – two hundred khaki blankets I'm stuck with. If you can tell me how I'm going to pay for them, or what I'm going to do with them, I'll give you ten thousand pounds. Blankets! I should wrap that crackpot brother of mine in them and sling the whole bloody lot in the river . . . Blankets! So tell me: what do I do with them?'

'Don't look at me,' said my mother. 'I don't want no blankets from sailors. Sailors come from all over: China, Africa, America, India. And God alone knows what diseases they got. Terrible things you can catch. I read in the paper only the other day, in black and white, that you get shocking diseases from blankets. Worse than towels. Make sure you wear gloves when you touch them and disinfect with Keating's. It gives me the itch just to think about it.'

Mendel grimaced and wriggled. I said: 'Uncle, would you really pay ten thousand pounds to know what to do with them?'

His look was bellicose. 'You got an idea for them? You know better than me, a trained man? If me, the businessman, don't know, you do? All day long I been beating my brains out, and no answer. But you got one, eh? You think that's logic? Does it stand to reason?'

'That's right; tell him off,' said my mother approvingly. To me: 'How dare you contradict your uncle after all he's done for you? After he's been such a good man you got the sauce to answer back, you Cossack?' She threw a slice of bread at me. It missed and landed on Uncle Mendel's waistcoat.

Mendel bellowed a protest. My mother howled: 'Now look what you've made me do, you . . . you Fascist,' and rubbed the butter deep into her brother's waistcoat with vigorous and well-intentioned strokes of a teacloth.

I felt it prudent to leave the room, but as I reached the door Mendel said: 'Well, what is this marvellous solution?'

'Black-out curtains.'

Mendel gaped. 'What do you mean?'

'Everyone's got to black-out their windows for the war, haven't they? Ordinary curtains are no good because the light will show through. They've got to be thick – and big so no light shows round the edges. So why not blankets?' Audaciously I added: 'It's logic; it stands to reason.'

Uncertain how to react, my mother looked at me then at Uncle Mendel. She saw him gazing at me with astonished admiration. 'The boy's right,' he roared. 'Simey – I'm sorry. I take it back. I apologize. And since your mother's here that makes it what she'd call a public apology. Can I say fairer?'

'A public apology?' my mother asked sourly. 'For him? After all you've done for him, he's the one who should go on his bended knees, the ungrateful drunkard.'

'Now, now,' said Mendel. 'Give credit where it's due. Even a boy can have a flash, an idea. There was that film a few months ago about a kid in New York working for this boot factory. So the firm was going bankrupt. Half the staff had to be fired. Given the boot . . . Get it? Given the boot!' Mendel's laughter deafened the ears and sent the cat scurrying under the gas stove. 'So like I was saying, what do you do with half a staff? No one knows, not even William Powell. Until Mickey Rooney, a wassername . . . a messenger, a nobody, says to him one night in the Diamond Horse-shoe, what's like from the Corner House over here, that he's got the answer; with half a staff make half-pairs of shoes. Because this Mickey's sister's got only one leg and there's millions people with one leg who don't want a whole pair shoes. You know, I don't mind admitting I wish I'd thought of it myself. So anyway, they make a fortune; William Powell marries the sister, the band plays *The Star-Spangled Banner* and Mickey gets a new bike for his messages . . . So here's another clever boy. Only for you I haven't got no bike. But take this.'

Uncle Mendel handed me half-a-crown. I thanked him and hurried away, suffering mild pangs of conscience: had my mother read the newspapers as thoroughly as she claimed, she would have seen in the previous day's *Evening Standard*, in black and white, a story suggesting the use of old blankets for black-out curtains . . .

As the summer wore on Daffodil Square prepared for war. Mrs Lewis bought more amulets from Yossell Teitelbaum, and as an added insurance arranged to join a niece in Sheffield in the event of London being bombed. A charity organization offered to evacuate Mrs Kemensky to a billet in the Home Counties, but she refused to move: 'I've done enough running. As a girl I run from mine parents, the pogroms, the police – in the end even from Poland. I can't run no more. My father, may he rest happy in Paradise, used to say that each anti-Semite needs his given portion of Jewish blood. I'm an old woman now; I've lived my life, for what it was worth. So if what mine father said is true, then maybe if I'm killed someone younger will be spared. Not that I believe in all this superstitious rubbish,' she hastened to assure us, 'but I'm still not going nowhere.'

Leonard Cooperman regarded the war as just another of the trials the Jews must suffer in order to prepare themselves for the Messiah, and his one hope was that God would give him the strength to endure the ordeal with joy and laughter. His wife's fatalism was of a different order. She had recently experienced a series of dreams of which men's legs were the mildest feature. There were also buttonhooks, saxophones, pig's trotters, armpits, elastic-sided boots, Dutch cucumbers, and a manifestation of a male nipple – a cumulation so horrible that Rabbi Klothboltz wrote its meaning as a Cabbalistic cryptogram which Leonard Cooperman refused to decipher. But his wife had no doubts: 'Bombed to pieces in cold blood.'

My mother said: 'What you mean, cold blood? You want they should warm it up for you? . . . Sit down a minute and have a smoked haddock. Very good for the cold blood.'

Mrs Weinberg was waiting to return to the East End to take over the shop when her son went into the Army. Meanwhile she bullied the other women into knitting balaclava helmets and mittens for the armed services. My mother could not afford to buy khaki or blue wool, so enthusiastically unravelled old garments found in cupboards and drawers. The results were beautifully-knitted night-mares: crazy explosions of colour that only a blind sailor isolated on a remote iceberg, could possibly have considered wearing.

With nowhere to move to, my mother prepared her defences: strips of sticky brown paper on the windows to protect them against blast, black-out curtains from well-laundered and disin-fected blankets supplied by Uncle Mendel, iodine and bandages, senna pods and towels, changes of underwear. A veritable cauldron of life-giving *lokshen* soup was kept in fresh supply, either bubbling away on the stove or ready for instant reheating. She dusted our huge and crumbling American trunk and rehearsed filling it with the family treasures: the biscuit tin containing her gramophone records; photographs; our silver candlesticks and knives and forks; Mrs Malik's teapot; birth, death and marriage certificates; prayer books and items of religious clothing; her best corset and a plait of Ruth's hair.

Unfortunately, the photographs alone filled the trunk. It was some hours before she could bring herself to admit that about half of them would have to be left out. But which?

'I know I've forgotten who this one is, but suppose she's someone important? You can't just throw people away. It's very unlucky. It's bad enough having to hide them in the dark. Very bad . . . And here's your cousin Ada. A swine, a dirty cat. But she's still our own flesh and blood, isn't she? . . . Seven pictures of Mendel. If only I could make up my mind which are the three best. It's a wicked business, having to make such terrible decisions . . . I can see as well as you that this one's black and fuzzy and you can't tell what it is. But how can I ignore the only picture of what might be your Uncle Mordisch? . . .' Eventually the choice was made of those who would be protected from aerial devastation in the trunk, and those who would have to take their chances of survival on shelves, mantelpieces and walls.

Further tests showed that the trunk could be filled in ten minutes if the three of us worked flat-out. Then came the ques-tion of the safest place to keep it. I suggested burying it in the square – and was struck over the head with a framed portrait of Herschel taken at the time of his *barmitzvah*. 'Burying! Making graves! You wicked swine. You want everything should be crushed by the roots and eaten by the rats, is that it? You want that your poor father should fall into the sewer that's down there? If only he was alive he'd give you sewers. Right in the face and the stomach he'd give you, you Cossack filth.' She threw out her arms in appeal and raised her head. 'Why have you cursed me with such a son? Just say. Just advise.' She stood listening, then lowered her head and let her arms fall against her side. 'It's like talking to a brick wall,' she muttered. 'You'd think that just once in a lifetime he'd answer a simple question' – and aimed a wild kick at my knee.

In the end it was agreed that the trunk would share with us the protection afforded by the space beneath the kitchen table, although my mother urged Ruth and I not to mention this to the neighbours.

'Why not?' my sister asked. 'You think they might be spies?'

'It's not that,' said my mother uncomfortably. 'It's just that . . . Well, it would be embarrassing, not nice, we'd look such fools if we've been through all this paranaphalia for nothing. We'd be the laughing stock of London. We'd look so silly.' She sighed. 'Not that it's easy to know what to do for the best. If you take precautions, there may be no war; if you don't the pig-dogs can catch you unaware . . . If your father was here things would be different.' (Her voice implied that if my father had lived no one would have dared start a war.) 'But he's not here, so that's that.' Angrily: 'So long these dirty Germans aren't just taking us for fools.'

Her doubts on this point were resolved only when she heard Neville Chamberlain's doleful Sunday morning broadcast. 'So that's it,' she said flatly. 'War. A shocking thing. Bombing. Killing. Crippling . . . But they'll be sorry, you mark my words. They'll regret this as long as they live – not that they should live long, the Hitler *scheisspots*. In the earth they should be, with the rats and the cancer and the butchers . . .' Anxiously: 'I hope Mother's all right. She's got Mendel there, of course, and Ben's a soldier; he knows what to do. Just the same . . .' She shook her head helplessly.

'I remember when the First War started. Everyone shouting, singing, waving. Today's like any other Sunday. It don't seem real . . . But he said on the wireless in black and white that we're at war, so I suppose we must be . . . So what to do? See how the others are? Go to the East End?' She spread her hands in bewilderment and suddenly looked old and tired.

'Shall we pack the trunk?' I asked.

She gasped. 'Of course! The trunk! Ruth, put a light under the soup. Simey, go fetch the gas masks from the hall. I'll start the packing.'

We hurried about the flat. Everything went as rehearsed – until that historic first air-raid warning. Ruth squeaked. I gulped. My mother screamed – and dropped the Huntley and Palmer biscuit tin. It hit the corner of the trunk, bounced off and fell to the floor with a flat crash followed by an almost mocking tinkle.

My mother fell to her knees, wrenched off the lid and tore at the prayer shawl. The gramophone records were jagged fragments.

Ruth and I stood motionless as my mother gave a choking moan and rocked backwards and forwards on her heels. There was a silence so complete, so absolute, I could hear my sister's breathing, the rustle of my mother's clothes as she moved, the purring of Itchky, the hissing of the gas under the *lokshen* soup and the footsteps of someone passing in the street at the front of the house.

After perhaps two minutes my mother sighed and whispered to herself: 'Sophie Tucker smashed. Al Jolson in ruins. My luck, eh? My rotten luck. As if I didn't have enough to put up with; didn't have enough aggravations in my life . . . The dirty, stinking Germans . . . They should be reported. Sued for every penny.' And the tears rolled down her cheeks, staining the white silk of my father's prayer shawl.

ALSO AVAILABLE FROM VALANCOURT BOOKS

Lightning Source UK Ltd.
Milton Keynes UK
UKHW011446040820
367682UK00004B/1180